Klock / Dennis Webster

This book is a work of fiction. Names, characters, places, and incidents are purely fiction and entirely the work of the author's imagination. Any resemblance to persons, living or dead, business establishments, events, or locales, is entirely coincidental.

Copyright © 2013 by Dennis Webster
All rights reserved

Dedication: This book is dedicated to my cousin and first reader, Evelyn Webster.

Without limiting the rights under copyright reserved above, no part of this publication may be reproduced, stored in or introduced into a retrieval system, or transmitted, in any form, or by any means (electronic, mechanical, photocopying, recording or otherwise), without the prior written permission of both the copyright owner and the above publisher of this book.

Cover Design: Bill Anderson

Cover Photo: Courtesy of Freedom Guide Dogs

Cover Photo Yellow Lab: Vegas the Guide Dog

Klock

You can do anything you put your mind to!!

Dennis Webster

Chapter 1

Rachel Klockowski was blind. She had no clue what the color was on the walls of her new apartment, yet she didn't care, for this was the first step of her independence. She sat next to the stack of cardboard boxes that held her meager belongings from her eighteen years of living, but it was her newly awarded private investigator badge that made her the most excited. She'd always wanted to be a cop but losing her vision made others tell her it was impossible. This was the closest she could get, for now. Her full name was Rachel Esther Klockowski but everyone called her Klock.

"I don't understand why you want to live here," declared Klock's mother, Kasha Klockowski, as she set another box next to the rest. "This place is full of degenerates."

"This is all I can afford on my disability check, Mom," said Klock. "Besides, Castlewood Courts are only a few blocks from the police station, seeing as I'm going to be working on cases." Klock held up her new badge towards her mother and smiled.

"Subsidized housing? This is an embarrassment, Stosh," said Kasha to Klock's father who was silently moving things, and trying to fly under the radar from her mother's wrath. "She's going to live in this dilapidated high rise with drug addicts, scumbags, and criminals."

"My kind of people," replied Klock as she stood up and put her badge in the back pocket of her jeans.

"That's not funny, Rachel Esther Klockowski," said Kasha.

"Call me Klock, Mom."

"Help me here, Stosh," said Kasha. "She's a child and she's not going to be safe."

Klock knew her father would never oppose her mother, but knew she could get whatever she wanted from her father, the old Polish softie. Her father stammered, then came back with, "Well, it's got the furniture, and it's near the bus stop, so that makes it easy for her."

"Really, Stosh?" said Klock's mother grumbling at her father. He had gone back to moving boxes for her, although she really only had her clothes, television, laptop, and her kitchen and bathroom implements. "She's only a teenager and she has this pipe dream that she's going to be a police officer. You need to move back home, Rachel."

"I'll stop taking disability checks and move into a better place when I start making money on cases, Mom. I'm eighteen and I'm an adult," replied Klock looking in the direction of her mother, crossing her arms, and standing her ground. She knew she was too much like her mother to be moved. She had her resolve ingrained from the time she could walk, right through her slow vision loss, to her complete blindness. "You two can go now. I'll unpack everything on my own."

"You're too stubborn, just like your father. Fine, young lady. Be sure to call when you need help. Your old bedroom is open whenever you're ready to come home."

"I hear what you're saying," replied Klock, not wanting to further aggravate her mother. Klock knew her mother had always spoiled her and tried to do everything for her, protecting her, especially when the retinitis pigmentosa accelerated causing her complete vision loss. She was sixteen when the world faded to black. Her mother had to learn to let her go. She had gone totally blind a few years earlier so she had spent her sweet sixteen birthday learning to read Braille and use JAWS, her talking software, on the computer.

She listened to her mother grumble, walking away to Klock's bathroom, where she shut the door, and was running the water. Her father grabbed her by the hand, got close enough, and whispered in his soft voice, as he placed crumpled paper in her hand that she assumed was money. "Here's a hundred dollars, Sweetie. All twenty dollar bills." He took his hand away and left the money clasped in her fist.

"You know I can't take this, Pop. I need to make it on my own. Independence is my motto."

"Please, humor your old man."

"Fine. But you know I'll pay you back." Klock shoved the money as fast as she could into her front pocket before her mother came back out from the bathroom. She'd go ballistic on her father for slipping her some cash. He worked hard as a mechanic in a garage, and Klock knew he must've squirreled away tips to give her this generous gift. She reached out, felt her father's side, then hugged him. "Thanks, Pop."

"I think you need to move, Rachel," said her mother. "I saw a cockroach in the bathroom. So gross."

"If I don't see it, then it doesn't exist," she said smiling at her mother, pointing at her dead eyes.

"Really?" replied her mother.

"Don't worry, Mom. I'll call the building manager and have them send over an exterminator. Nothing you say is going to make me come back home. I've had enough of the pampering."

"Fine," replied Kasha. "C'mon, Stosh. We've got errands to run."

"Kick those law breakers asses, Klock," said Stosh with cheer in his voice.

"Don't feed into her delusions, Stosh," snapped Kasha as they gathered their belongings, headed for the door, talking to Klock's father as if she were not even present.

Klock said nothing but waved them goodbye. She listened to them scamper and leave, clicking the door shut. She was more excited than nervous, that she was finally ready to go out into the world and do something with her life. First, she had to unpack everything and get oriented to her apartment, which shouldn't be too difficult since it had one bathroom, one bedroom, a cozy living room, and a small kitchen. She pulled out the twenty dollar bills and folded them in the way she always does. All paper money was the same size so she had to fold the dollars, fives, tens, and twenties in a unique way as to differentiate them. She took out her private investigator badge and rubbed it a few more times before she placed it on her kitchen table.

* * *

 Klock spent the rest of the day unpacking and placing things around the apartment, bumping her shins and head a few times as she got used to the layout. She left her cane on the coffee table since she only used it when she had too. She took out the dog harness and sat on the couch thinking about her deceased guide dog Vinny. He'd been with her since she was thirteen when she still had usable vision. He'd died months ago and she was waiting for another dog, but she knew none would ever take her heart like her loyal black lab. "Love you, Vin." She held the harness for a few more minutes before she packed it away to be used on the next guide dog. She pressed her talking watch and it said in its electronic voice that it was three thirty PM. She fumbled around for her flip cell phone. She wished she could have one of the fancy smart phones as they now had voice commands and speech apps that she could use, but they were too darn expensive. She had to make do with the old flip cell phone with Braille bumps added to the numbers. She had called the number so many times she knew it by heart. She felt the bumps on the number pad and pressed away. After a few rings a nice, live operator said, "Mohawk Valley Guide Dogs."

 "Frederick Schmidt, please," said Klock.

 "Just a moment."

 Klock had to listen to the guide dog propaganda used to solicit donors as she waited for the president of the agency to pick up.

 "Fred Schmidt."

 "Hey, Fred, got a dog for me yet?"

 "I told you yesterday, Klock, that I think we might have one for you."

 "Vinny died months ago and I'm tired of using my cane."

 "This isn't fast food. I might have a dog for you within the next week or so. We're done training the "B" litter. Give me a few more days and I'll get back in touch with you."

"Tomorrow would be even better don't you think?"
"Fine. I'll call you tomorrow."
"Great. Thanks, Frederick," she snickered as she hung up.

Klock had enough grief about Vinny. She was ashamed to use her cane in public but it was all she could do until she got the new dog. The infernal long white cane screamed out "disabled" to everyone in the city and was a symbol of shame. She hated people seeing the little blind girl with her cane clacking. She tended to slap into people with her cane. She was not good at using it. Klock decided to head to the Ft. Schuyler Police Station and see what business she could drum up. It was January, so she put on all of her winter gear, for walking through the icy Mohawk Valley winds. She'd never gotten used to the deep freeze after almost twenty years of living in it. Before she left her apartment, she found her small handheld digital recorder, and placed it in her pocket along with her badge.

Klock took out her cane, unfolded it, and moved forward. She lived on the 4th floor so she decided to take the elevator in case she encountered someone in the stairwell. She waved her cane back and forth as she moved forward with it hitting the right side of the wall, which let her know she was in the middle of the hallway. She knew she was near the elevator when she came to the end of the wall. She took off her gloves and felt for the buttons, until she found them, and read the Braille for the down button. It took a while for the elevator to get there. She could hear it groan on its wires that she imagined were rusty and not greased. "The poor have loud elevators." She laughed to herself. The doors opened and she went in, feeling for the button for the ground floor ignoring the stink of what she could only guess was rotten orange peels and pee. She wouldn't let that snuff out the excitement of being on her own. She was out from under her mother's constant badgering. Free to be herself. Free. She needed to become an adult and not have her blindness hold her back. Freedom to mess up would give her that.

She got out of the elevator and immediately ran into a nosy resident of the complex, who said in a slurred, drunken voice, "You new?"

"Yes, I'm new," she replied as she put her winter gloves on. "Have a nice day," she said, as she went out into the January afternoon. She remembered that at this time of year it would be dark by four in the afternoon but she was in permanent darkness so the night couldn't frighten her. Klock took her first steps towards her exciting career.

She had used her laptop to get the directions to the Ft. Schuyler Police Station. She had no appointment, but she thought she'd just barge in there and see what they could throw her way. She knew that was kind of a bad move, yet she was never shy about doing whatever it was she wanted, unlike many people, who can see where they're going. Her lack of sight couldn't stop her vision.

The wind was whipping into her face and she wished she had a scarf as the icebox wind felt close to zero. The end of the block was a lot longer than she thought but she was determined to get there. She knew she had to go one block down, turn left, and go three blocks. It was as if Castlewood Courts were built to be conveniently located near the police station. The cops would have a hive of criminals in close reach.

The cane was working fine but she found crossing the one main intersection to be a challenge. Normally, she'd have an orientation and mobility instructor teach her to get where she had to go but she didn't have the patience for them. The crossing light was of no use to her. Ft. Schuyler was an older city that had no talking crosswalks so she had to basically stand and listen to the flow of the traffic as it went by her, and had to take the chance that she was moving with the right flow, so she wouldn't get plowed over. The cars stopped moving, so she went forward into the snowy intersection, knowing the cars would slide right into her if she misjudged it. The first step with her cane made her nervous as she went for it, and found she did it right. She took twenty steps and still hadn't been run over. She could hardly wait to get another guide dog as this would never happen again. The pup would be her eyes. Vinny was the best at getting her around. She'd cried too many times when he passed and now she looked back fondly on his dedicated and loyal service.

    Klock got to the other side and stumbled slightly on the curb when she was stepping up. No heroes jumped forward to assist her, not that she wanted any help from any sighted person. "Who cares about them and their good eyes!" she shouted as she pumped her fist into the winter air. She continued onward and soon figured she was in front of the police station, but had to stand out front to wait for a person to come by.

    "Excuse me, is this the police station?"

    She got a passing yes so she turned with her cane and proceeded up the steps. She smiled and nodded. She knew her life would never be the same.

Chapter 2

Klock walked up to the front desk of the police station and leaned on her cane until a man behind the desk asked her, "May I help you?"

"I need to speak with one of your criminal investigators."

"Is there a crime you want to report?"

"Not exactly," said Klock trying not to smile. She knew this was real, and not a game, so she had to have steel willpower.

"Have a seat over there, Ma'am and someone will be with you when they can."

"Blind. I can't see where you're pointing."

"Oh, I'm sorry. It's about fifteen feet to your left. There's a bench there. Do you need help getting over there?" asked the desk cop in a nicer voice.

"Nope. I'm good."

Klock went over to the bench and just listened to all the commotion in the station. People were talking all over the place and others were coming and going. She folded up her walking cane, put it in her jacket pocket, took off her gloves. She held her cold bare hands up to her lips and breathed hot air into them. It warmed them up. The Mohawk Valley winters had always been bitter and the wind seemed to always speed up downtown between the buildings. She sat for a good fifteen minutes until someone finally came forward.

"Can I help you?" asked a man standing in front of Klock.

Klock stood up. "Are you an investigator on the force?"

"Yes. I'm Detective Mulvi. I'm a criminal investigator."

The pause told Klock that he was probably holding his hand out to shake her hand so she did the shameful move that made blind people shake in fear, she held out her hand in dead air, in a token of friendship.

"I'm Rachel Klockowski but you can call me Klock." Detective Mulvi took her hand with a strong grip and shook it firmly.

"Nice to meet you, Klock. What can I do for you?"

"I'm looking for work."

"What do you mean?"

"I have my private investigator license and I'm wondering if I can have your overflow? Maybe I can assist you on some cases per diem?"

"Is this some kind of a joke?"

"Absolutely not," she declared as she fumbled into her pocket and took out her badge, holding it out for Detective Mulvi to see. "Here's my badge."

"Ok. I'd rather you come in to my office and talk rather than in the hallway. Follow me please."

Klock stood up and said with one finger in the air, "Just a moment, Detective Mulvi. I need your elbow."

"My elbow?"

"I'm blind and I need to hang onto it so I can be walked to your desk."

"Alright, where's the camera?!" barked Detective Mulvi in a tone that told Klock he was confused and mad.

"What do you mean?" she asked, putting her arm down, and hiding her badge with both hands.

"You doing this, Wilson? I don't like practical jokes!"

"This is no joke, Detective Mulvi," she said giving him her best mad look while crossing her arms.

"I'm so sorry, Klock. It's just I'm a rookie investigator and they've been hazing me. Especially Detective Wilson."

"Not a problem. Are we going to talk business or what?"

"Ahhh. . . what elbow do you want?"

She reached out her right hand and replied, "Your left will do just fine." She clasped on and pulled herself next to the detective. Klock felt small since she was barely five foot, and by the location of his elbow, she guessed he was well over six foot tall. She liked the sound of his voice. It was deep just like the tough cops on television. Detective Mulvi clumsily slalomed her through the building until he halted.

"Don't be stiff with me. Just relax and walk normal," she said with a smile. Every time she had to do this, and it was a person's first time, they'd walk on eggshells, yet she was tough. Klock was no delicate white orchid.

"Here's a chair for you," he said.

"Thanks," said Klock. She let go of his elbow and reached until she located the arm of the chair. She guided herself into the seat. She went through her jacket and pulled out her small handheld digital recording device and held it up. "I hope you don't mind. I can't take notes with pen and paper like you sighted people."

"No, I don't mind. Now, let me get this straight. You're a private investigator and you're looking for work."

"Yes."

"And... you're blind."

"Yes." Klock raised her eyebrow.

"Sorry to be rude but you're looking right at me. I'm no doctor but it looks like you're faking it."

"I haven't been totally blind my entire life. I've lost it completely just a few years ago. The reason I look at your face is because I had the gift of sight. People who are blind from birth will never look another person in the eyes. They'll look at the floor or up in the air. They don't know what it is to look in another person's eyes. And just because my brown eyes look undamaged doesn't mean they're functional. You can say my eyes are like a spoiled Hollywood actress, pretty on the outside and useless on the inside."

Detective Mulvi cracked up. Klock could hear the creak of his chair, as she guessed that he must've been leaning forward, and perhaps waving his hand in front of her face. She wondered if people did that move as they might not believe she was totally blind.

"Whose badge is that, Klock? I mean you have to be eighteen years old in New York State to take the exam to be a private investigator.

What are you thirteen?"

"I'm eighteen. I'll show you my drivers license if you like."

"How can you be blind and drive a car?"

"Sorry, it's the non-drivers driving license. I need it for identification."

"Ok," said Detective Mulvi. "Listen, I'm new in this department and I'm not sure how all of this works."

"I know. You're a rookie. What are you twelve or something?" she asked trying her best to frown.

"You're funny. I'm twenty four. I'm a rookie to this department. I worked the beat and patrol for a few years and proved myself capable so I'm getting a shot at criminal investigations."

"Do you still wear your uniform?"

"Only to ceremonies, funerals and such. Listen, Klock, I have my hands full right now so I have to cut this short. If we ever get anybody looking to hire a private detective, I can recommend you. I'll need your contact information."

Klock spent the next few minutes giving her cell phone number, her e-mail, her physical address and telling Detective Mulvi not to text her as she can't read it. She'd prefer a voice mail if she didn't pick up the phone. He walked her back out of the station, and halfway through the office, a loud and crude voice rang out, "Hey, I love your new girlfriend there, Mulvi! She come with her own pencil cup!"

"Sorry about that," whispered Detective Mulvi. "Detective Wilson can be a real, well, you know what I mean."

"My father always told me if you ignore a bee it'll go away, but you swat at it, and you'll get stung," replied Klock, trying not to look rattled by the nastiness. She'd confront Detective Wilson in due time. Now was not the place or instance to do it. She needed the work. Hate speech from an overbearing jerk would not deter her iron resolve. Detective Mulvi continued to walk her until she halted when he said they were at the front door. She stuck out her hand. "Thank you for your time, Detective Mulvi."

He took her hand and shook it with strength. His mitt of a hand enveloped hers but he didn't crush her. She knew he could if he wanted. "My name is Dominick but my friends and family call me Dom."

"I look forward to hearing from you, Dom."

"Here's my business card in case you need to contact me."

Klock took the card and felt no Braille on it. She looked up to where he was talking, smirked, waved it front of her face, and said with a chuckle, "Blind."

"Oh, I'm so sorry, Klock. Get your digital recorder out and I'll give you my cell and e-mail. I'm so embarrassed."

"You should be," she said with a snicker, not giving back the card. She couldn't read it but she wanted to keep her first piece of police paraphernalia.

* * *

The ghost hunter Cora Masters lay dead upon the crushed stone that surrounded the large Overlook Mansion up on the highest point of the hill. Her head was flattened on one side where the gravel and gravity converged in one life-ending fall from the top turret of the legendary haunted 19th century estate. The hand held digital recorder that she had used numerous times to record voices from the spiritual paranormal plane lay broken and scattered, yet part of the device still remained frozen within her dead right hand. Her arm was broken and bent at an inhuman angle. Her otherworldly investigative team, the Ghost Chasers, all stood back behind the yellow police tape in complete disbelief and utter shock. Photographs were being taken and interviews were being conducted by the investigator, Detective Wilson, and his partner Detective Hilley, from the Ft. Schuyler Police Department. The Ghost Chasers would be allowed to leave after they gave their statements, and packed up some of their gear, except the digital video cameras, hand held digital cameras, and digital recorders that would be held by the detectives and gleaned for possible evidence.

Some of the team members were mumbling that Cora had finally gone too far in her zealous attempt to communicate with the dead and accidentally fell out of the open window of the top turret of the hulking haunted mansion. They walked away from the scene, as if they, themselves, were the ghosts. Shocked at the tragic death of their spiritual leader. They were stunned so much they barely noticed the pack of neighbors standing on the fringe of the gated property pointing and chatting while dressed in their pajamas. Camera flashes were going off everywhere and the local television crew was on-sight with a news reporter talking in a fake placid voice about the death of a ghost hunter.

* * *

Klock was standing at the stove in her apartment stirring her latest batch of poor man's pot luck tomato sauce, listening to her latest mystery audio book. She had just downloaded the book on her digital reader. That, along with her laptop, were the only pieces of charity that she had accepted. Her pride was smaller than her love of reading mysteries. She loved to solve the whodunits before the big reveal, as she felt it was the best way to keep her investigative skills sharp before her first case came her way. Fictional mysteries and true crime digital books were her passion. She was in a great mood, for the Mohawk Valley Guide Dogs had called and said they were bringing a new working dog over for her. She had been so excited she forgot to ask the name or even if it was a boy or girl pup. She knew she'd not forgotten how to work with a guide dog. It was like riding a bike, although she doubted she'd ever be able to ride one again. Klock was half tempted to try since she heard Helen Keller always rode a bicycle and she was blind and deaf.

She almost didn't hear the knock on her apartment door. She yelled out, "just a minute!" as she took out her earphones, shut off her digital book, and clicked off the heat to her sauce. It smelled yummy but she'd have to wait to boil the pasta and eat. She had yet to bake in her new apartment and could hardly wait to try out the oven with her pie and muffin recipes. That could wait. She needed to meet her new partner. She never used her cane in her apartment as she could move around really well. She never moved her stuff. When she lived at home, her mother would always rearrange the furniture on a monthly basis. Klock figured it was her mother's way of proving her superiority and being there to assist her.

She opened the door and said, "Hello?"

"Hey there, Klock," replied Fred Schmidt. "I have your new guide dog here with me."

"Come on in," she said, as she stepped back and held the door open. She loved the sound of the metal and leather harness as the dog walked by. She shut the door. "Let's go into the living room."

As soon as Klock sat she knew the love was coming for she could hear the noise of the harness being removed. Fred confirmed it by saying, "Be ready, I'm taking Bo's leash off."

"His name is Bo?" she said with a smile. "I'm pleased he's from the "B" litter. I read on your Facebook page about them. They're supposed to be the best litter you guys ever had."

"You're correct, Klock. We wanted you to have the best of the best and Bodacious is the best. He's the best guide dog I've ever seen. Trust me, he was worth the wait. You're going to love him."

"His name is Bodacious? That's awesome!" she said as she got pushed back by a hundred pounds of Labrador. "Is he Chocolate?"

"I know you requested that but he's a Yellow Lab, Klock. Please don't hold that against him."

"Oh, I would never. I'm blind to all colors, as you're well aware." She leaned down and Bo licked her face. For the first time in her life, she knew what love at first sight meant, but it was more love at first lick.

"Hardy, har har. I forgot how hilarious you are, Klock. Listen, I'm going to leave him here with you so you can test drive him. Let me know in a few days if you want me to come and take him back. I can find another person for him. I'll be shocked if you do call me. It looks like he's the perfect match for you."

Klock stood up and reached out to Fred. "I can't thank you enough, Frederick." She shook his hand and pulled him in and hugged him.

"You're welcome," he replied. "Do you still have Vinny's leash? I need this one for other dogs I have to train."

"Yes, I do," she replied.

* * *

Klock spent the next couple days getting dog food, a watering bowl, a dog bed, knotted ropes to chew, and walking the winter neighborhood with Bo. They were getting used to each other. Fred wasn't kidding as Bo took to her routine much quicker than Vinny had. She was a little sad but she knew Vinny would be happy that another dog was using his harness and leash. Castlewood Courts would not allow any pet yet she was covered as she knew that the Americans with Disabilities Act (ADA) prohibited landlords from banning service dogs. She could take Bo into restaurants and any public place without discrimination or persecution.

Klock had returned from a long stroll down the snow covered city sidewalks. She was mad for the Ft. Schuyler city workers did a horrible job of clearing the sidewalks making it difficult to get around. It was far too dangerous for her to walk in the streets. She didn't understand why it was so hard for people to make "reasonable accommodations" for the blind. That didn't help her in that situation but she put it behind her. She attempted to get into a better mood by giving Bo a pig ear to gnaw on while she brewed herself a cup of green tea. She had thrown in a spoonful of honey that her mother had given to her from the Amish farmer's market. In the past, her mother would take her there to troll for fresh fruits and vegetables that was way out of the city in the upper hills of Kuyahoora. She knew, already, the city bus didn't run up into the Adirondack foothills, so she would have to rely on her mother or somebody to get her up there, especially, if she was going to bake pies with fresh blueberries, strawberries and apples. She took a sip of her tea and exhaled a long breath. She was finally relaxed when there was a knock at the door. She hoped it wasn't the religious people again trying to save her soul with literature she couldn't see or read. She thought at least they'd have their recruitment materials in Braille for the feeble minded like her to peruse. Her mother lectured her to ask who it was before she answered the door as one of the resident drug addicts might waltz in and take advantage of her disability. She had Bo and she wasn't afraid of anybody or anything so she opened the door wide and said, "Yes?"

"Are you, Rachel Klockowski the private detective?" came a woman's voice she thought sounded quite high even for a woman.

"Yes," she replied. "Call me, Klock."

"Might I come in and speak to you?"

"Why of course." She grabbed Bo by the collar. "Don't worry, he doesn't bite."

Klock waited for the woman to come in. She shut the door and said to Bo, "Go lie on your bed. Good boy." She walked over to the table and reached for the chair hitting the woman on the shoulder. "Excuse me," she said as she found the empty chair, sat down, and looked best she could towards the strange woman. "How may I assist you?"

"My mother was murdered and I'd like to hire you to find the killer."

"Sure. And you are?"

"Julia Masters. My mother is. . . was. . . Cora Masters."

"The famous ghost hunter?"

"Yes. The police said her fall was an accident or suicide but I know she was murdered. Can you help me?"

"I'd be honored to assist you," said Klock, gritting her teeth to keep her professionalism in check. She didn't want to look giddy. "Let me get my recording device and we can begin." Klock got up and walked over to the kitchen counter feeling around for the device while keeping her head elevated.

"Wait a second," said Julia. "Are you blind?"
"No worries. I'm the best blind detective in the world."

Chapter 3

"A detective from the Ft. Schuyler Police told me they couldn't help me anymore. Their investigation had closed so he gave me your contact information. I hope you don't mind that I came right over without calling first. I just don't know where else to turn. The detective didn't tell me you were blind. You must be good or why else would he recommend you?"

"Listen, I'm a certified private investigator with New York State. Here's my badge to prove it. I might not be able to see, Julia, but I'm dedicated, hard-working, and I like to consider myself reasonably intelligent regardless of my young age."

"You look like a teenager to me. How many cases have you worked on?"

"This would be my first. But before you respond, I ask you to give me a chance. If at the end you're unhappy you don't have to pay me. As a matter of fact, you decide the payment if you feel I deserve it. How can you go wrong with that offer?"

"I see what you mean."

"Blind," said Klock.

"Excuse me?"

"Sorry, just a little disabled humor." Klock turned serious, clicked on her recording device, clasped her hands together and said, "Now, let's start from the beginning, Julia."

"Well, my mother was the lead investigator for a group called the Ghost Chasers. They were conducting a paranormal investigation at the Overlook Mansion. Ever hear of it?"

"Yes, I have. I know it's over on the north side of the city where all the rich people live. I remember reading once in the history of Ft.

Schuyler that the Overlook was one of the oldest mansions in New York State. It's large and prestigious. I watched your mother's television show, "Paranormal Happenings" or listened, as we blind people do, and she was talking about the upcoming investigation. Apparently, it's super haunted, yet nobody had ever investigated in there. On the television show, your mother referred to it as "virgin ghost hunting territory.""

"I'm pleased you were a fan of my mother's work. She spent her entire life looking for proof of the afterlife and now she's amongst it," said Julia, in a slow sad tone.

"I heard on the news that she fell or jumped to her death but that was at least a month ago. Have the police finished their investigation?"

"They didn't conduct much of anything," said Julia. "I felt they just went through the motions and declared she took a swan dive. I know my mother. She loved life too much and was way too strong a person to ever kill herself. I refuse to believe it. Besides, I have a feeling she was murdered."

"Who do you think would have motive to kill your mother?"

"Have you read any social media or online postings about my mother?"

"No. Did somebody confess on one?"

"Not exactly, Klock," said Julia. "My mother could be rather harsh with people, and that's putting it nicely. Especially on the Ft. Schuyler Topix website."

"Just because someone is nasty doesn't mean people want to kill them," replied Klock, bending over to pet Bo on his ribs. He'd snuck over to get a little love and she was okay with that. He was going to be immersed in the private investigative life so extra love time will have to wait. She didn't hear the dog's smacking jowls so she assumed he had finished his pig ear snack.

"Read them later and you'll see what I'm talking about."

"That makes it difficult. Anybody else, specifically, that might have a huge ax to grind?" asked Klock.

"I hate to say it but my older brother Don had big time motivation."

"Your brother?"

"He had been a huge disappointment to my mother with his drinking, drugs, gambling and especially the insurance scams."

"Why would that make him a suspect?"

"Well, the insurance scams for one, and the fact my mother left her entire estate to him."

"I see," said Klock. "I would like to question Donald."

"Don. Don't ever call him Donald. It'll get him really mad, Klock. I can see if I can arrange him being interviewed."

"Don't bring him here. Let's try to arrange a neutral place where I can casually talk with him and feel him out. Another question, Julia. Were you there the night your mother fell to her death?"

"Yes, I was. I'm sometimes an official member of the Ghost Chasers. It was hot and cold with my mother. I jumped at the chance to investigate the Overlook Mansion. This was the Holy Grail of ghost investigations. I tell you there are other teams that were insanely jealous of my mother getting in there," said Julia.

"Other ghost hunting groups?"

"Oh, yeah. Especially RIP."

"RIP?" asked Klock. She knew to keep the questions coming and Julia would keep yakking with some potential clue goodies.

"That's the Rest in Peace Ghost Hunters," said Julia. "RIP is what they like to be called. There are dozens of ghost hunting teams in the city of Ft. Schuyler but RIP is the most aggressive and hateful towards my mother. Their leader, Tad Davis, is as nasty as they come. I heard they had been after the Overlook for years."

"Why couldn't RIP get in there?" asked Klock. She sipped the last of her green tea. She held up her hand before Julia could answer and asked, "Would you like a cup of green tea? I want to have another one. I don't drink coffee."

"I'd like a glass of water, please. You need me to get that for you?"

"I'm blind but I know this apartment better than Bo there knows the scent of his mommy's undercarriage," she said snickering. "Give me a second and we'll get back to the Q&A."

Klock had become really quick at maneuvering in her cramped kitchen. It had one small countertop with a small microwave, a smallish electric stove, and a refrigerator. She only had a few cupboards overhead and below. She was alone with Bo so she didn't need massive space, which was great since the area in the room wouldn't hold anyone of a super size. It was small but it was hers. She was very happy with her little nook. She got the water, not knowing if anything were floating in it, and made her next cup of tea, microwaving the water, dropping in the teabag, and dripping in another spoonful of honey. She didn't offer food as her cupboards were pretty much empty since her next disability check hadn't arrived. It was bare bones so it was noodles and sauce or peanut butter sandwiches until she got the next payment. She wasn't proud to be on public assistance. Klock was determined to get paying private investigation gigs to pull in the cash to make it on her own. She certainly wasn't going to borrow any money from her mother or, forbid, move back home.

Klock was walking back to the table when she bumped her leg causing the water to spill over onto her hand and onto her pants. "No problem. I got it." She was humiliated. She set the cup on the table as close as she could guess to where Julia was sitting, put her own cup down, and said, "Where were we, RIP?"

"Yes," answered Julia. "They were really enraged for not getting into the Overlook to conduct a paranormal investigation and they blasted my mother on Topix."

"Was RIP there that night? This Tad Davis?"

"No, but they had the motivation, and I wouldn't put anything past him, especially due to the heated exchanges he had with my mother on that horrible message board."

"How many ghost groups are we talking about in Ft. Schuyler?"

"Dozens, at least. Ghost hunting is really hot right now."

"I hear you. Like I said earlier, I watched your mother's television show all the time along with Ghost Adventures and Ghost Hunters. I've also listened to a bunch of ghost books."

"My mother's fame made her a big target of ridicule and jealousy, but then again, she fueled the flames. You'll see on the message boards. She couldn't resist shooting arrows at anonymous cowards hiding with their beer muscles behind their keyboards. When it came to getting into the Overlook mansion, it was easy for my mother. The Van Dreasons were new to the area and new owners of the Overlook Mansion. My mother got there first and the other groups were more than upset. The Ghost Chasers are always a step ahead of all the other groups."

Klock nodded and sipped her tea. She set down the cup and replied, "Okay, Julia. Give me your number so I can get back to you. I need to do some basic research. That is if you still want to hire me."

"I'd like to give you a chance. Besides, the optional pay at the end is a great incentive."

"You won't regret it," said Klock, holding out her hand that was met by Julia's warm soft hand. It told Klock that Julia had never done a day of manual labor, unlike Dom's hand that felt like a worn leather glove.

* * *

Once Julia was gone, Klock fed Bo, finished her tea, then decided to call Dom and thank him for the detective referral. She got her cell phone out and had to play the number from her handheld digital recorder. It only took a couple rings before the call was picked up.

"Detective Mulvi."

"Hey, Dom. This is Klock."

"I'm assuming you met with Julia Masters."

"Yes, thank you for referring her to me."

"Don't make me look like a fool, Klock. I have enough heat on my shoulders in this place."

"I'm not even charging her for my services. If I don't do a great job, she doesn't pay, and if she likes it, she pays me what she can afford, or what she thinks I earned."

"Great idea, but people are dirt bags. She won't pay you and neither will anybody else. Especially to a, no offense, a defenseless blind woman."

"First off. Thanks for calling me a woman and not a girl. Second, I won't be taken advantage of, you can be assured of that, Detective Mulvi, and lastly, I'm anything but defenseless. You hear what I'm sayin'?"

"OK. I hear what you're saying there, Klock. Boy, I fired you up."

"Sorry, it's my Polish temper. It flares up once in a moon phase."

"Well, I have to get back to my duties."

"Wait a second," said Klock. "Do you really think Masters committed suicide?"

"I wouldn't know. It wasn't my case."

"What investigator worked on it?"

"Detective Wilson and his partner."

"Crap."

"That's the correct word all right. Hey, gotta motor. Call me if you need any assistance."

"You know I will, Dom. I'd like to meet with you tomorrow. I just want to go over some basics of the case. I promise it'll take less than a half an hour. I'm a taxpayer and I pay your salary after all."

"I hate when citizens say that. OK, but not here. I don't need anymore wisecracks from Detective Wilson. I can meet you at Moe's Place. Know where it is?"

"Is that the coffee shop over on Second Street?"

"Yes, been there?"

"I walked by it with Bo and he wanted to go in there but I kept going forward."

"Bo?"

"He's my new guide dog. You're not allergic are you?"

"No. Does high noon work for you, Klock?"

"That's perfect. I have some research I have to conduct. Thanks again." She snapped her cell phone shut and smiled at her testy exchange. That was the one part of her mother she was glad she had, the tinge of attitude and personality; a fire that simmered then exploded when necessary. She'd noticed that it had gotten worse since she went into the permanent blackness. At least that's what her therapist told her. Forgetting her bad muse mood, she felt excited to have a case. She decided to skip her dinner of sauce and pasta as she didn't want to waste time boiling water and cooking the noodles. Instead, it was peanut butter toast. It was quicker so she could delve right into the research. Her desk was in her bedroom where she had her laptop hooked up to into the Internet. The monthly payment was pricey for her but surfing and watching television were the only hobbies she had after listening to digital books. She liked baking and comic conventions, although a superhero costume in a closet hardly counted.

Before she got going however, Bo was nudging her and that meant only one thing, he needed to be curbed. "Okay, Bo. I got your message." She put her jacket, hat and gloves on first, as once she put that harness on him, he'd yank her to the door. Although that was a bad habit for a guide dog, she'd let it slide. She liked a little stubbornness in boys, especially the hairy, yellow, four-legged ones. She got the small plastic bag to pick up his doggie doody. Leaving the package on the sidewalk was downright rude, gross, and possibly a way for her to get a ticket. She grabbed his harness and had him to her right side and said, "Forward." He took her straight to the front door. She could feel her confidence boost as they moved together as a team. "Forget Sherlock Holmes and Watson. Here comes Klock and Bo. Well, not until we finish Mother Nature business," she said, smirking at nobody as they walked out her apartment door, and into the cold winter night for the poop run.

Chapter 4

Klock sat at her laptop, reading the Ft. Schuyler Topix internet message board for hours, marveling at the language people used on the public forum. It included some of the nastiest and most shocking crapola imaginable. "Cowards," she said aloud to nobody. It seemed that Cora Masters was the only person with the guts to reveal who she really was and it caused a massive wave of vile rhetoric. Klock was no believer in ghosts even though she loved the television shows and audio books. It wasn't that she was skeptical; it was that she'd never had anything happen to her to lead her to believe ghosts were real. She had once listened about Harry Houdini, and how he had tested the world for psychic ability and proof of the afterlife, and it all came up blank.

Klock listened through her JAWS program, that read the Topix postings, and knew what Julia meant about her mother, for Cora Masters had not hundreds, but thousands of posts, under the topic "Ghost Chasers Are Shysters" where she lambasted everyone who dared disagree or doubt the validity of her spiritual plane interactions. Klock couldn't understand what would compel someone to engage in the exchanges, some being posted by obvious instigators, or ghost hunters from rival groups. The ones about Cora's appearance were rather harsh, especially ripping on her age, her makeup, her hairstyle, right down to the inflection in her voice from the TV show.

Klock clicked off the blog site and grabbed her digital handheld recorder and talked at length about some of the screen names of the most vicious attackers, which narrowed her suspect list down to a few hundred. It was daunting to think about it, so she went back online, to read up on ghost hunting and what it entailed. She went on the Ghost

Chasers website and was surprised that it was still up and active featuring a video message from Cora herself asking for people to contact her if they had a place to investigate. She had clips from her television show but not the footage from the Overlook. Klock wondered what happened to all the video and audio taken that night. She assumed the police seized it and scanned it for anything that might make Cora Masters's suicide look like an accident or even a murder. The dismissal of the case by Detective Wilson told her that even if they had looked over the footage from the Ghost Chasers, it probably didn't have squat, otherwise Julia wouldn't be hiring a blind girl to investigate.

Klock searched around and was amazed at the thousands of ghost hunting groups that existed in Ft. Schuyler, the Mohawk Valley and New York State, and she didn't even search for the ones that existed in New York City. She knew the genre was popular but the number of websites and audio books available told her it was red hot to be a ghost hunter. From what she had been listening to on the Internet, all you needed was a hand held digital recorder, much like the one she used, and a K2, which is a small handheld device that reads electromagnetic frequencies. She read the theory of the K2 device which was that ghosts can cause a spike in the electromagnetic field, that makes the K2 spike, unless you have the device near an electrical appliance, like a refrigerator or television. On top off these devices, you need an empty building to walk around in at midnight. The sheer amount of information was a blur but she spent a while going over one website that listed the protocols and decorum when you were on a ghost hunt. She found it amusing that a ghost hunter should ask the spirits for permission to photograph them or digitally record their otherworldly words. She wondered if there were a permission slip for such a maneuver. She understood the rules on not being angry while conducting a ghost investigation, for the negative energy can attract malicious, or dark energy, and spirits, as well as rules concerning conducting paranormal searches in accordance to the lunar cycles. She'd heard the theory before that people tended to act crazy during full moons and Klock was a big believer in Karma, so she fully understood the negative energy thing. Actually, if she really believed ghosts existed, why would they be any different than walking talking stalks of carbon? Mortals and spirits want to hang with fun positive people and not negative types.

Klock knew why the genre of ghost hunting was exploding. Beyond the negativism on the blogs, and the team rivalries, it looked like fun, and she figured people want to try to connect with those no longer in our spiritual plane. She read that Cora Masters used a psychic in her investigations, and Klock didn't believe in them. Then again, she'd never sat down and met with a psychic, so she couldn't completely dismiss their validity.

* * *

Klock wished winter would be over as she bundled up for her noon trip to Moe's Place. It was the end of February and the weatherman was calling for a major snowstorm, making her wonder why her Polish ancestors came to upstate New York in the first place. They could've done their research and immigrated to Miami. She wondered what it would be like to do her private investigative work in a bikini on the beach; then again, it wasn't like she could look at her physical flaws in a mirror. Blind people had freedom from that horror. "Perhaps being blind has some benefits after all," she said to Bo, making him stand up. He nudged against her. Bo loved the snow. "Silly hound."

She didn't bother with her digital recorder as she was going to have a casual chat about the case and seek advice from Dom. She knew he'd talk more openly if he knew he wasn't being recorded. Klock and Bo head out the door and as she shut it she was greeted by a person in the hallway.

"Hey there, pretty girl," said a man whose voice she didn't recognize.

"Do I know you?"

"Not really. People round here call me Bookcase."

"Bookcase? Really? That's what your mother named you? What is she, a librarian?"

"You funny, girl."

"I'm sorry but I have to get to an appointment. Forward, Bo," said Klock, getting a little nervous, as she and Bo went ahead, but the man must've grabbed the harness, for Bo halted and she almost fell. "Don't touch that!"

"Easy, girl," said Bookcase not letting go of the harness. "I just wanted to know if you need anything. Ya know?"

"I'm sorry, Bookshelf. I don't need anything. Now if you don't mind, let go of my dog."

"It's Bookcase, little girl. You live all alone in that apartment? I can come visit you sometime."

"No, thanks," she said in her sternest voice, while looking at the man, while trying to yank Bo free. She couldn't help but gag a little for he had doused himself in cheap cologne that he must've bought at the dollar store.

He let go, making Bo go forward in an awkward movement that almost made Klock fall on her face. He was screaming a bunch of swear words at her. She sallied forth with intense purpose, yet was so afraid on the inside, that she almost thought her mother correct. She had to be a strong blind woman and not a vulnerable teenager, especially if she was going to become a police officer. That was her secret desire, and she knew officers of the law had to be firm, steady, strong, and fearless, not reckless or foolish. She got to the elevator. Thank goodness Bookcase didn't follow her in. For the first time in her life, her blindness made her feel inferior and weak. She hated the feeling but wouldn't let the creep have the satisfaction of drawing a tear. That part of her eyes still worked just fine, unfortunately.

The longer she walked the more her blood boiled but she kept under control as she had to remember the exact place of Moe's. She had heard of it from other tenants in Castlewood Courts as a place for cheap food and it was halfway between her apartment and the police station. Bo halted their progress for a moment so he could introduce his pee scent to some random stationary object. Klock had to stop one person on the sidewalk who seemed annoyed that she was stopping their forward progress. They were kind enough to grumble the location by saying, "Its right there," then moved on. She figured they didn't realize she couldn't see where they were pointing. The cowbell on the door clanged as she walked in. She immediately was greeted by whom she assumed was Moe, or somebody of authority, who yelled out, "No dogs allowed!"

"I'm blind and he's my guide dog," she said back in the direction of the yelling.

"Fine," grumbled the man as she came a couple steps in and halted. She pressed the button on her digital watch that said it was eleven fifty five so she was pleased she was a little early, and she figured if he was in there, he'd shout out or come and get her. She didn't hear anything so she waited until a waitress came up to her.

"May I help you?" asked a person who Klock assumed was the waitress.

"I need a table. In the corner if you have one," said Klock.

"Follow me," replied the waitress.

"Blind."

"Excuse me?"

"It's quicker if I take your elbow and you walk me to the table."

The waitress grabbed her tight by her left elbow and pulled her forward making Klock and Bo shimmy a little bit. She knocked her knee against a chair that someone had left pushed out from their table. She winced as it stung but she kept going until the waitress said, "Here you go."

"I'll wait to order until my friend gets here." Klock felt the chair and sat down. She pulled on Bo's harness and led him under the table so people wouldn't step on him. "Down. Good boy," she said sweetly. Whatever it was they were cooking in there smelled really great. Her stomach grumbled. She'd not had anything good since moving out on her own.

"Hello, Klock," said Dom, as Klock could hear the chair across from her slide out. "You order yet?"

"No. I was waiting until you got here."

"The coffee here is burnt but hot. The rhubarb strawberry pie is to die for."

"I drink tea but a large slice of that pie sounds fantastic," said Klock.

"I'm on duty but I stepped away for a quick lunch. At least the storm hasn't hit yet. They're calling for a big one."

"My father always says that the weather around here is enough to gag a maggot," said Klock.

"Hello, sir. What can I get you?" asked the waitress.

"I'll have a cup of coffee, cream and no sugar," replied Dom.

"What would the lady like?" asked the waitress.

"I think you better ask her yourself," replied Dom.

Klock knew it was coming; all she had to do was wait for it.

"What! Would! You Like?!" said the waitress in a loud saccharine tone, pausing after each word.

"Why are you talking to me like I'm an idiot?" replied Klock."

"I'm sorry, Ma'am. I didn't mean anything by it. . . really, I'm sorry."

"Tea with honey," replied Klock to the flustered waitress. "And a slice of the rhubarb strawberry pie. Make that a slice for each of us."

"I'll bring that right out," replied the waitress who she could hear walking away.

"What did you do that for?" asked Dom. "That was uncalled for."

"I'm sorry. I have a little chip on my shoulder when people in public places treat me that way. It's hurtful and rude to think because someone is blind that they lack intelligence."

"Well, you certainly have the gumption to be a private detective. I always wondered how Helen Keller did it."

"Did what?" asked Klock.

"Communicate."
"You never watched the Miracle Worker?"
"No."
"You know what sign language is."
"Sure, I know what it is. Don't know how to do it."
"Anne Sullivan would sign language and Helen would hold her hands over Anne's and read the words."
"That's incredible all right."
"I'm sorry if I'm a little stressed, Dom. I'm a little edgy from some scumbag approaching me at my apartment complex."
"What happened?"
"I think he was a drug addict, a drug dealer, or some kind of pimp. It was really disturbing. Him and his swagger. I was a little rattled to be honest with you. I know I have to be distrustful of people in this business. Not only that his cologne was the worst on the planet."
"Oh yeah. What do you think of my cologne?" asked Dom, in a joking way that Klock figured was a way to calm her down.
"You don't wear any. Just Ivory soap."
"How did you know that?"
"It was a guess, Dom. If I don't smell perfume or cologne, I tend to guess that a person uses the unscented kind of soap. It's not like I have heightened senses because I'm blind. That always bugs me. That's not authentic. When you see people who are blind in movies and on television, they make them saintly. We're not superheroes that have enhanced hearing, smelling, and taste. They're the same before and after."
"Did this dirtbag give you a name? Ever meet him before?" asked Dom.
"Here you go," said the waitress, interrupting their conversation, and setting everything down as Klock tried to pinpoint the exact location of the tea and pie.
"I want to apologize for the way I spoke to you," said Klock, not looking at the waitress but trying to get her before she zoomed away

to another customer. "It's just that I'm totally blind but I'm actually kind of smart. I know you meant well. I'm sorry for the outburst."

"That's okay, Ma'am. I understand. I love your dog. I love labs. Can I pet him?"

"I'm sorry, but no. If I had his harness off then it would be okay but he's working right now. That would be like your boyfriend brushing your hair while you're trying to wait on tables." Klock looked up to her and smiled.

"You're funny," answered the waitress with a chuckle. "If you need anything else, please let me know."

"Thank you," replied Klock.

"I didn't even see your dog under the table," said Dom all excited. "He's a handsome lab. Look at those eyes of his. What's his name?"

"Well, his official name is Bodacious but you can call him Bo."

"Well, I would love to pet him sometime when he's not working. Now, where were we?"

"The dirtbag," said Klock. "I don't know the guy. I've lived there for over a month and never had anything happen to me."

"Castlewood Courts has a lot of nasty people but a lot of nice people. Not unlike any other subsidized housing building in Ft. Schuyler. You have personal protection?"

"You mean a handgun? No. I mean I'd love to have one but. . ."

"Don't tell me you're going to use the excuse that you're blind."

"I wouldn't be able to see what I'm shooting at."

"Most of the cops I know shoot with their eyes closed anyway. In close quarters, you can be deadly. Besides, being a certified private investigator, you could get a carry and conceal pistol permit."

"What's that? I mean if I decide to get a permit," said Klock. She was curious.

"Well, if a regular citizen were to apply for a permit they would get it as a targeting and hunting license. That's how it is in this county. You can only carry it on your way to the targeting range or hunting area. With carry and conceal you can legally have it on your body everywhere in the state except New York City."

"Why is that?"

"Judge's decisions, Klock. I can certainly understand it since there're enough criminals with guns down there. I can't even carry into the city. I'd have to let the police department in New York City know I'm coming down then I would need special permission. I think you should take the pistol safety course at our gun club then all you have to do is apply at the police station. You'd get it pretty fast being you're already certified to conduct investigations."

"I'll need your help with the handguns. I mean, I don't know how to shoot, or even what handgun would work best for me," said Klock. "I don't know. I don't think I need a gun."

"We have a nice indoor range so I'll take you tomorrow if you like. It's my day off."

"That'll be fine," said Klock. She'd always wanted to try shooting a handgun but she was afraid of them. She knew if she ever wanted to make it to her dream job as a police officer, and maybe a detective like Dom, she had to do it."

Klock heard the door open and footsteps getting closer and wondered why Dom swore under his breath.

"Hey, Mulvi. Who's the gimp? Your girlfriend?"

Klock recognized the voice. It was Detective Wilson.

Chapter 5

Klock couldn't believe that the deputized stalker, Detective Wilson, showed up in Moe's Place. She didn't even dig into her pie yet. She wasn't going to eat it in front of a nasty discriminatory sighted person. It was worse that he was a cop, a person sworn to protect the innocent. She'd love to sick Bo on him. She heard another snicker and knew Wilson had a person with him.

"Very funny, Guys," said Dom. "If you don't mind, I'm on my lunch."

"No offense," said Detective Wilson. "I'm just kidding around."

Klock didn't say anything as they were walking away. She had been offended too many times to recall but the sting never got any gentler.

"Sorry about that, Klock. As you probably know, that was Detective Wilson, and the other one was his silent partner Detective Hilley. I have to work with those idiots."

"You have my sympathies."

"Don't let them see you're upset. Being a detective means you'll be interacting with people like him and much worse. You have to be bulletproof, Klock."

"I hear you. I deal with that nonsense more than you would believe. Can we get to the Cora Masters case before my tea gets cold?"

"Sure. What do you have?" said Dom, clanking his fork on the porcelain plate that held their pie slices.

"I wonder if you could give me some information on her supposed suicide."

"Well, I wasn't the investigator on that case, as it was Detective Wilson with the help of Detective Hilley. I doubt they'd sit down with you. If you prove that Masters was murdered, it would be a mar on their record and could be a major embarrassment."

"Can you get me a copy of the file? Maybe I can borrow it and have it put into Braille?"

"That's a request I can't help you with. Even if you file a FOIL, I don't think I can share that with you. Besides, how would I get it into Braille?"

"If you drop off the file to the Ft. Schuyler Braille Transcribers they'd probable take a few days and convert it for me. C'mon it's worth the risk, Dom," she said, smiling really big. "I'll let you pet Bo."

"Let me think on it for a minute. Have you found anything out yet on your ghost hunter?"

Klock took a sip of her tea. It was bitter compared to her home brew but good enough. "Cora Masters was a universally hated person. Except for, possibly, her children and team members on her ghost chasers. That might change once I interview them. Her son Don was the sole heir and Masters left her daughter completely out of the will."

"Oh boy," said Dom.

"I know," declared Klock. "Can it be that easy? I mean, if Don Masters knew he was the sole heir he could've killed her. The daughter could get everything if he is charged and found guilty of murder."

"Unjust enrichment, no doubt," replied Dom. "However, in my experience these cases are never so cut and dried. They tend to have fuzzy gray edges all over them."

"Then again, sometimes a loaf of bread is just a loaf of bread. I read these online blogs and these people were just roasting Cora Masters and her group on there. It was worse because she'd go on there, identify herself, and just rip people apart. That made the blog mob worse. I think part of it was jealousy for her fame and television show and envy for getting into places nobody else could investigate. Especially the Overlook Mansion. I read that it's the most desired of locations for a paranormal investigation in not only Ft. Schuyler but the Mohawk Valley and the state."

"I hear what you're sayin'," said Dom.

Klock nodded while finding her fork and feeling gently for her plate, getting the edge, then slowly raising her hand until she touched the edge of the slice, then taking a chunk with her fork and raising it up to her mouth. The taste was everything advertised. The rhubarb and strawberries lit up her taste buds, making her wish she could have an entire pie, yet she would not eat any more. She knew that the simple task of eating was something people with sight took for granted. For her and others she had spoken to, a person who is blind eating in public is the most difficult and scary task, since it was easy to be embarrassed and easily mocked by mortified onlookers. She remembered when her sight was still slight and she'd seen a person who was totally blind eating and the sight of this young man eating with his hands and having food smeared across his cheeks was sad and vile. She'd rather get the slice to go and make her dining mistakes with nobody but Bo to see.
"This rhubarb strawberry pie is delicious."

"This place is a dump but people know the pies are the best in the city. The coffee not so much but at least it's cheap and hot. Listen, I have to get to running some investigative errands but I'm going to give you my private cell phone number. I want you to call me if that dirtball gives you any more grief. You never did give me his name," said Dom.

"Bookcase."

"Seriously?"

"So stupid. I shouldn't be afraid of anybody with such a goofy name," said Klock laughing.

"All the more to be careful. I never heard of this person but he has that dumb name for some reason. Call me tomorrow and I'll come over to Castlewood Courts and pick you up. I have a few different handguns you can try at the range. Sound good?"

"You bet. That's if I survive dinner with my parents tonight. I'm their blind helpless daughter. Their only child living alone in the dangerous city."

"I doubt you're helpless. Here let me get this," said Dom as Klock could hear him fumbling around for his wallet.

"I got it," said Klock as she grabbed her small wallet out of her jacket that held her money and identification. "Don't argue with me, Dom. Next time you buy." She felt the way the paper money was folded and took out a twenty and handed it to the waitress. When she came back with the change Klock had to ask Dom to tell her what denominations each bill was and she immediately folded them into their identifiable configurations before nestling them in her wallet with the rest of their like kind. It was all she had but she was no beggar.

"I got the tip," said Dom. "Thanks for the slice and Joe. You need a ride back home?"

"I'm good. Bo needs the exercise. Talk to you tomorrow."

Dom got up. It took Klock a few moments to secure all of her items and put on her jacket, hat, and gloves. The waitress had brought her slice in a little Styrofoam container and she got up from the table, thanked her, and said, "forward" to Bo. She was fumbling with the door when she heard a loud obnoxious comment from Detective Wilson.

"Nice seeing you!" yelled Detective Wilson across the entire diner.

She turned slowly in the general direction of the comment and flipped Detective Wilson her middle finger.

* * *

Klock had to take the leash off Bo so her father could sit on the floor and play with the big softie doggy. She sat on her parent's couch and chuckled as her father blabbered in baby talk at Bo. She could tell by the rattling of his collar that he was eating the positive attention up. Vinny had loved her father as well, the Dr. Doolittle. Her mother was putting the finishing touches on dinner, the smell of Polish sausage and sauerkraut was making her stomach grumble and her mouth water. The food was one thing she missed as her mother made many traditional Polish dishes, but it wasn't enough to keep her under that roof.

"Dinners done," said Kasha, from the dining room.

"You have a chair for Bo?" asked Stosh.

Klock cracked up as she could picture in her mind the grimace her mother was now making at her father and the twinkle in his tomfoolery eye. She made Bo lie down and gave him a rawhide bone that she had brought along to make him happy. It felt weird to place him in the spot where Vinny had spent years sleeping and snoring. That was one thing she was glad Bo didn't do. She'd never heard of any other dog that snored. She didn't need to have her father escort her to the table. Her mother hadn't changed the location of the furniture since she had moved out.

She sat down, and didn't even have her napkin on her lap, when her mother jumped right in with, "How's the roach motel?"

"Great, Mom. I trained them for the traveling circus I'm putting together. Making the tutu for the roach ballerina was a bitch."

"Watch your language, young lady," replied her mother. "I'm just concerned for your safety. I looked up on the Internet and that place has several registered sex offenders, Rachel. It's a veritable rat hole."

"Please don't worry about me. I've been there for months and nothing has happened. Pass the potatoes, please."

"Working on any cases yet?" asked Stosh.

"I have my first case right now, Pop," she said, beaming with pride.

"Someone hired you?" asked Kasha. "Who would do such a thing? I mean, good for you, Rachel. That's nice. . . I guess."

"I can't tell you too much but it's the case of a woman who was thought to have killed herself. Her daughter hired me to investigate and see if she was murdered."

"How much does something like that pay?" asked Kasha.

"Nothing yet," replied Klock.

"Oy vay," replied Stosh. Klock didn't need the warning from her father, for she knew exactly how her mother was going to react. She knew precisely how predictable her mother was. Her mother was as accurate as an atomic clock.

"For crying out loud, Rachel," said Kasha. "Seriously? Nothing?

You'll never get off public assistance. I'm so ashamed."

Klock didn't acknowledge the outburst as she cut into her sausage and put a piece in her watering mouth. It was peppery, salty and as delicious as anything she'd ever tasted. After months of eating peanut butter toast it was better than filet mignon. "Sausage is great, Mom."

"You can go to the agency and work if you want, Rachel," said Kasha. "They have a lot of blind people there. It might do you good to work with your own kind."

"I don't want to work in a factory with other blind people, Mom."

"Can't you at least go down there and meet with them?"

"Sure. I'll call them," replied Klock. She hadn't seen her counselor for a while and it was on the rehabilitation side of the Ft. Schuyler Association for the Blind. She'd been recently asked by the employees of the agency if she was interested in employment in their workshop. She said no. At least stopping in would shut her mother up. At least for a little bit. She'd make an appointment to see the counselor and meet with the workshop manager.

"That's wonderful, Rachel. Isn't that wonderful, Stosh?"

"Good for you, sweetie," her father said.

Klock spent the rest of the night not saying too much. She hated being forced and manipulated by her mother. She did need a little more money. Perhaps they could offer her a part time job. She hated to admit her mother was right. She didn't want to settle for a sure thing when she had a dream to work towards. Everyone thought it was a joke and talked all sweet but not serious to her. She was serious. She wanted to be a cop.

Klock's belly was full from the meal. She sat in the living room chatting with her parents about everything from the weather to relatives she hadn't seen in years. She loved her mother but she drove her nuts. She guessed it was her mother's job to harass. She felt warm, safe, and happy in her parent's house but she knew deep in her heart she had to stay the path. She never asked to be born with a degenerative eye disease, yet she felt that perhaps it was a blessing, for nothing in life was going to be easy, and she wasn't going to have anything handed to her.

She didn't want the evening to end but she was also excited about getting home and going to sleep. Who knows? She might dream. She wondered if someone totally blind at birth ever dreamed. And if so, in what dimension were their blinded visions? At least she could be fully sighted in her dreams and looking at the sky blue as a robin's egg but it was the ceilings she missed most. She'd heard from peers who were born totally blind, as little children, that had no concept of what a ceiling was, until someone would put them on a ladder, have them climb up, and touch them. Her eyes moistened a little bit but she dare not cry. She never cried for she knew nobody in this world cared to see it, nor felt sympathy, especially her strong-willed mother. She'd see it as ample opportunity to swoop in and protect Klock. She didn't need that, not when Dom and the target range waited the next day. On top of that, she needed to set up meetings with Don Masters and most certainly the surviving members of the Ghost Chasers. She had a lot to do and look forward to.

"You okay, Klock?" asked Stosh. "You look so sad, honey."

"I'm fine, Pop. Can you please bring me home now?"

Chapter 6

Klock left Bo home so she didn't have to worry about his reaction to the gunfire. She was too nervous herself and didn't want to be distracted if he was upset. Dom had picked her up in his regular car. He said he didn't drive a regular patrol car now that he was a detective.

They walked in with her holding Dom's elbow and he was a natural at guiding her, which boosted her confidence. She could smell the gunpowder even before they got into the room where all the shooting was taking place. The gun club was a private building in the eastern section of Ft. Schuyler, where all the crumbling factory buildings were that her father had told her once employed thousands of immigrant workers in great paying union jobs that had long ago fled south, or to Asia or wherever labor was cheaper. She rarely went to that part of the city. It was no place that she really needed to be, for all her shopping, and other needs, were close to downtown where Castlewood Courts were located.

When they walked into the shooting room she was thrilled at the loud booms coming from down a line where she imagined people standing at tables firing down the range at paper targets much like the cop shows she used to watch before she lost her sight. All she could do now was listen to cop shows and she'd giggle at some of the stiff dialogue that she never noticed when she was visual. Dom stopped and she let go of his elbow.

"If you reach out right in front of you, you'll feel a table," said Dom.

"Okay," she replied, as she felt the wooden table. It was no more than rough plywood but came up to her waist, which was good for her since being only five foot would've made it difficult if it were higher.

"I have a pair of earmuffs for you and a pair of shooting glasses. You'll need to wear these when either one of us is shooting."

"Why would I need glasses, Dom?"

"Even though you're blind you don't want a hot discharged shell or a flash of gunpowder hitting your eyes. It'll hurt really bad and I don't need your first shooting experience to land you in the hospital. Capisce?"

"Capisce? You're hilarious."

"That's what I've been told. I gave up a lucrative career as a stand up comedian so I can protect and serve."

"Well, what are we shooting today?"

"I have my service weapon I'd like you to try. It's a .45 Colt Semi-automatic. It's powerful but the kick isn't so bad. I also have a .22 Ruger Semi I'd like you to try. I'll have you use the .22 first and see how it goes."

"I thought the Ft. Schuyler Police carried 9mm handguns? I read that 9mm is the best weapon for police use. I do my research."

"You can't believe everything you read, Klock. Eggheads who never wear a badge try to tell us what's best. Real life experiences are much different than letters on a page."

"Or bumps on paper," said Klock referring to Braille.

"As far as using the 9mm's, we used to. We swapped them out because the stopping power is not there. One of the guys on the force shot a man hopped up on methamphetamine with his 9mm and the bullet bounced off his skull. You only need one bullet with a .45," said Dom.

"Stopping power, right?"

"You got it. The bullet hits like a mule kick. Give me a second to set up the paper target. I have to reel it in like a clothesline then clip it on. I'll only put it out there twenty yards so the .22 should be easy for you to hit it."

Dom took his time and taught Klock how to load the .22 clip that held ten bullets. They seemed really small in her hand and she wondered how such a projectile could kill anyone unless the kill shot was in the precise place. He then had her hold the handgun and showed her where the safety was, the trigger, and all the other parts before he let her slap the clip into it. The gun was hefty despite its small caliber. Dom instructed her how to hold it safely with the barrel pointed down, hand off the trigger, and safety on. They spent a while on this before Dom would let her pull back the slide to load the first round. She was scared but she wouldn't show it. She'd seen, when she had sight, millions of cop movies on television yet the real experience was different. She didn't know if she could kill anyone, and her hesitation showed, for Dom jumped in with a statement of purpose.

"This is not a game. These are dangerous weapons that can kill and maim. We treat them with respect. If you don't have the guts to shoot to kill then don't get a permit, don't carry a handgun and certainly never pull one on a criminal. You don't do it unless you're prepared to shoot. Otherwise, the criminal will take the weapon right away from you then take you out with it."

"Got it," said Klock. "You ever shoot anyone?"

"With a gun, no. I had to tazer someone though. They were dangerous and it was a much less lethal way to take them down and protect myself."

"Ok. I think I'm ready to shoot," said Klock. Her hands felt a little shaky and a little clammy. If she wanted to be in this business she had to stop reading about it and jump in and do it.

Dom had her set the gun down, put on the earmuffs, and shooting safety glasses before having her pick the handgun back up, keeping the barrel pointed down. He stood behind her having to talk louder so she could hear his instructions. He showed her how to slide the chamber of the semiautomatic to place the first round in. "It's hot now." He then instructed her to take off the safety, bring it up and aim it forward with him holding her elbows to guide them to the proper location. He let go and said, "Disengage the safety and let it rip."

Klock clicked off the safety, put her right pointer finger on the trigger and squeezed slowly and straight back just like she had read and as reiterated by Dom. The sound wasn't too loud. There was no kick so she pulled back one after the other until there were no more rounds. A few shells had bounced off her shoulder. She knew it was empty by counting off the rounds. She couldn't see the slide stuck back and open as it does with semi's but she felt it. She set the handgun on the table and took off her earmuffs. "How did I do?"

"Let me bring the target in and you can feel for yourself."

She set the earmuffs down and took off the shooting safety glasses while Dom brought in the paper target and laid it down on the table. "Here," he said as he took her hands and set them on the paper. She could feel the holes and the paper sticking up where the bullets had gone through. It frightened her to think what these projectiles could do to soft human flesh.

"See how all of your hits are in close proximity?"

"Yes."

"That's great shooting. You don't want them spread out all over. That would show your hands are not steady and there's nothing worse that shaky shooting. The only thing is you are little low and to the left but considering you cannot see the sights on the handgun to line up the bulls eye, you did fantastic."

"Really?"

"Sure. And you didn't even blink which is amazing. That's a skill you cannot learn. The best marksmen in the world have that trait. It's too bad you're blind or you'd be a top shot."

"Tell me about it," she replied smiling.

"I'm sorry, Klock. I meant no offense."

"None taken. Innocent comments are much different than mean slams. So, you think I'm a deadeye? I mean with the shooting."

"Absolutely. I'd like you to do a few more clips with the .22 before we move onto the .45. You'll find that handgun a little heavier and it kicks more plus even with the .22 you have to be careful with hand position. The slide moves back and forth really quick and if your hands are positioned too high, you'll get caught in the action, and you'll get cut. Alright, take your time and reload and get ready. I'll only step in when it's hot and ready to fire so I can be sure you're aiming in a safe place."

Klock nodded and repeated what she had been taught and found with each series the scared part of her was replaced with an almost liberated feeling. After about ten clips Dom decided to have her switch to the .45. He was right as the bullets were bigger and the handgun beefier. She let her overconfidence get the best of her as she shot the .45 and it kicked much harder and sent her back into Dom who encouraged her to hold the gun tight but steady. The results were not as good as with the .22 as she had a hard time holding the heavier weapon steady. On the second clip she felt a sharp pain in her right hand in the webbing between her thumb and pointer finger. She didn't have to be told she let her hand slide too far up and it got pinched in the slide. It hurt enough that she set the handgun down and held it for she was sure it was bleeding.

"It happens to us all, Klock. I think we've done enough for one day. Let me pick up our stuff then we can talk about what happened. We have people waiting to get in here."

She was afraid to let her hand go and was a little ashamed that it had happened but she seemed more confident. She wasn't sure a blind girl having a handgun would be a good thing. She held Dom's elbow as they left the firing area with all the sounds of gunfire to the quiet of the shooter's lounge.

"What do you think, Klock?"

"I loved it, Dom but I think it's too dangerous for me to carry a handgun. What if I shoot an innocent person?"

"Let's get you in the safety course and apply for your permit. You certainly would get your pistol permit and be able to carry conceal with your private investigator's license but you have to be ready and confident."

"Thank you. I don't think I'm going to have to shoot any ghosts on this investigation so I won't be needing one."

"Think about your personal protection as well," said Dom. "You know where you live is not the safest."

"I'm not worried about Bookcase or anybody else. I can throw a mean right hook if I have to. I'm planning on moving to an apartment in the better part of Ft. Schuyler when I start pulling in the big bucks from my investigations."

"I don't doubt that for a minute. I'll set up your pistol safety course and get you the pistol permit application packet. Ok?"

"Sounds great," she said.

* * *

Klock waited for the bus and she and Bo were freezing as the Plexiglas shelter was not enough to keep the howling winter winds at bay. He didn't complain and she didn't care about the miscreants either at the bus stop or when they were on the bus. Sighted passengers usually took the up front seats meant for the disabled, not that she really wanted to admit her handicap and sit in those seats. She felt there were more deserving people, especially the elderly riders. Not having a driver's license was the one huge thing she wished she could see to have. That and the independence to go anywhere at anytime instead of relying on public transportation or others to get her there especially since she had liked to head north out of the city and visit the Adirondack Mountains. She'd remembered a few times as a child taking the trip with her parents out there to climb Bald Mountain. She could picture in her mind the wonderful view of the chain of lakes from the old rusty fire tower she had climbed.

She almost missed the bus as she was so busy daydreaming. Bo had adapted very well to getting on and off yet she could tell he didn't like the mothball and cheese smell of the vehicle anymore than she did. She had no choice for she was heading to the Jonesville Mall to interview Don Masters as she had instructed Julia not to give out her physical address. She'd rather interview Don in a public place that might keep him from getting riled. The location could possibly make him more comfortable, besides they had the best tea and coffee at the Beanery Express, although the price was enough to make her fill out loan papers, she'd treat herself since she just received her disability check in the mail. She'd be able to splurge just the one time until next month or if she solved this case with Julia Masters making a satisfactory payment.

As the bus jostled, Klock prayed the bus driver would announce the mall stop and not keep going, which happened to her once before, causing her to get off and wait an hour as another bus had to take her back. She was concerned about talking to Don with Julia present since she wanted an independent interview. She'd decided she would ask Julia to take a stroll so they could have privacy.

She didn't mind the mall in the winter since it was a way for her and Bo to stretch their legs out of the elements. It was a Tuesday morning so she was sure there'd be nobody there but bright white sneaker fast senior mall walkers, hopeless mall janitors/security guards and indifferent store employees. Julia had told her they'd meet in the center food court so she figured she'd stroll around, and if Julia didn't call out or approach her, she'd sit at a table and call her cell phone. Julia had warned her about how slick her brother could be.

Klock heard Julia so she went towards the voice and like the Ft. Schuyler Guide Dogs had promised, Bo was the best at moving her between tables and around obstacles. The dog was a human service machine. She got to the table and waited to sit until Julia would introduce her to her older brother. She had an image in her mind of Julia's brother having full sleeve tattoos, wooden discs in stretched earlobes and little metal hoops all over his face and body. She knew she shouldn't prejudge but Don had drug, alcohol and insurance scam issues that would make Klock skeptical of whatever it was he was going to say with the hard part her not being able to look him in the face as she questioned him. She'd read the telltale signs of liars including touching the face, the lack of eye contact and being fidgety but her condition kept her from utilizing these techniques.

"This is my brother Don," said Julia.

"Nice to meet you," said Klock, holding out her hand as he took it. He had a weak and clammy handshake and it made her want to whip out some hand sanitizer but she resisted and put on her best plastic smile. He didn't say anything so she felt for the metal chair that was bolted to the ground and swung Bo around to get under the table. "Julia?"

"Yes?"

"Can you please leave us alone for a while? I'd like to talk to your brother just the two of us."

Julia agreed, and walked away with the mall being so lacking in shoppers that Klock could hear her moving away, making her wait a few more seconds until she could begin her questioning.

"So, my sister says you want to talk to me. What exactly can I help you with?" asked Don in what Klock would consider a deep voice even for a man making her wonder if he were tall in size.

"She didn't tell you what we're here to talk about?"

"No, she didn't," he said in a cheerful pleasant tone.

"Great," said Klock. She knew this was going to get ugly. If she was going to be a successful detective, she was going to have to learn how to question the nastiest people and no better time than the present to cannonball into the deep end of the investigative pool. She clicked her digital recorder on but left it in her jacket pocket hoping it would pick up the conversation. She knew if she put out on the table he'd walk.

Chapter 7

"I wanted to talk to you about the death of your mother."

"That's what this is about?"

"Yes."

"Who are you?"

"My name is Rachel Klockowski and I'm a private investigator. Your sister hired me to look into the death of your mother."

"You can't be serious? What are you blind?"

"Sure, I am. That should have no bearing on my work or this case," said Klock in a mild mannered voice.

"Well, she jumped to her death. Suicide is what the cops determined. I don't understand what it is you have to investigate."

"Your sister feels your mother would never have done such a thing. She said she was a strong willed woman who loved life and her work too much. She was at the peak of her career. Fame, fortune, a television show and a ghost hunting book from what I've found in my research. She was just hitting her stride in life so why would she have committed suicide? Or, perhaps, she might've been murdered."

"You really can't think I would murder my own mother," said Don in a tone that told Klock he was either a great actor or truly of hurt feelings.

"I never made the accusation to anybody about anything. I'm just looking into the circumstances of her death. Both you and your sister were there that night yet she's a member of the Ghost Chasers and you're not."

"I had a darn good reason to be there that night and it wasn't to kill my mother. And you're right, I don't believe in ghosts and all that nonsense. I thought it was really stupid with all their carrying on and crap.

Such garbage."

"Well, Julia wants me to talk to everyone that was there."

"She thinks I did this because my mother left her out of the will. I had no clue and neither did she what our mother's wishes were. Just because I've had past issues with drugs and alcohol doesn't make me a murderer. I loved my mother and I never knew my father. She saved my life numerous times so why would I do such a thing?"

Klock took it in. She paused before speaking again. "Listen, Donald. . ."

Don interrupted before she could finish with, "Don is my name. Donald is a duck. Please don't call me anything but Don."

"Sorry about that, Don. Listen, you're sister doesn't think you murdered your mother." Klock placated Don for Julia did feel that he might've. "For all we know it was a tragic accident."

"It was awful and on the worst night possible. Don't you know why I was there? Didn't my sister tell you?"

"No, she didn't say anything about that whatsoever. I had a feeling there was a possible nugget of information missing."

"Before I go any further, how do I know you're not a cop?"

Klock took out her badge and held it up. "No need for a lawyer, Don. I'm a private investigator not a police officer. Nothing you're saying will be used against you," she said smiling.

"Good, because I'm not guilty of a damned thing. I was there that night because my mother asked me to be there for moral support."

"Moral support for what?"

"It's the reason, I'm guessing why my mother left Julia out of the will."

"Are you going to tell me or keep this game going?" asked Klock. "I'm starting to grow weary from this verbal shell game."

"The death of Joey," said Don. "Our little brother. The night my mother died was the anniversary of his death. I wasn't happy to be on a ghost investigation on that night but she hounded me and begged me to be there."

"Why would Cora want you there? What did the Overlook have to do with his death?"

"Nothing, Klock. My mother was told by Velvet Blue that there was a portal located up in the top of the place. My mother thought she could channel my little brother and get his spirit to come out of the portal and talk with her. Velvet felt it was possible," Don said with heightened emotion and with a little more volume. If only Klock could see his face, look into his eyes to see if he was a pathological liar or if he was truthful.

"Who is Velvet Blue?" asked Klock.

"She's the psychic my mother has used for years on certain investigations."

This caught Klock off guard. She wondered if Cora Masters was truly suicidal since it was the anniversary of the death of her child. She nodded her head and held her tongue for dramatic pause. "What does this have to do with Julia being left out of the will?"

"Because it's her fault Joey died," said Don. "She was supposed to be watching him when our mother was out to a candle party and he got out and was run over by an eighteen wheeler. He was mashed so badly they had a closed casket. He was only four years old."

Klock didn't know what to say other than, "I'm sorry."

"I drank and did drugs to ease the pain but everyone thinks I'm a useless scumbag including my heartless sister. She's colder than my mother ever was and way nastier. Go ahead and ask the other Ghost Chasers. She and my mother fought like you wouldn't believe. Put it all together and it's no surprise she got nothing."

"I think I've asked enough questions. I have to go now, Don," said Klock, getting Bo by the leash and standing up. "Tell Julia to call me later."

"Good luck with your investigation," said Don. Klock moved along not wanting to run into Julia. She stopped briefly to shut off the digital recorder then headed back towards the mall exit where the bus stop was, not caring how long she'd have to stand in the snow and cold, she just wanted out of there. Julia never told her the tragic reason why her mother probably killed herself. She felt rattled and wasn't going to go back to get her tea, she just wanted to get back to her apartment.

"Klock!" yelled Julia from behind her.

Klock was stuck. She knew she'd have to keep her cool. She stopped and turned in the direction of the shout not knowing if there were mall patrons all around. "Julia, I'm done with Don so I was heading back to the bus stop."

"Can we give you a ride back home?" asked Julia.

"No, thank you. I'm good."

"You look upset. What did Don say to you?"

"A lot of things that I need to think about."

"I warned you about him. He's slick. He's a liar, Klock."

"He told me about your little brother. How your mother booked the investigation of the Overlook on the anniversary of his death. The details are where a case is solved. How can you be so sure your mother didn't kill herself out of grief?"

"There was no way she killed herself. The entire reason why she formed the Ghost Chasers was because of what happened to him. We conducted investigations every year on the anniversary of Joey's death and why didn't she kill herself before?" replied Julia with a distressed voice that told Klock not to push it.

"Okay, I hear what you're saying. Listen, I'd like to talk with the rest of the Ghost Chasers and especially Velvet Blue. Any chance you can help me put that together?"

"You can come to the next meeting of the Ghost Chasers and talk with John and Steve but Velvet never comes to the meetings. She never leaves her home so we would have to go out to her place. She lives way out in the boondocks where no buses go so I'd have to drive you. She only comes out of her house when she comes to our investigations and that's rarely. She only does select places. My mother would always take the long drive out to see her. It's about forty five minutes north of the city. Out towards Boonville but off on route 28 on White Lake."

"That's fine," said Klock. "I have an appointment tomorrow but after that my schedule is wide open. I didn't realize the group was still operating after your mother's death."

"We took a short sabbatical but I decided to step into my mother's place as the lead investigator. She would've wanted it this way. I'll continue her work."

"Talk to Velvet and find out when we can get out to see her. I better get going or I'll miss the last bus back downtown."

Julia walked away and Klock wanted to reserve judgment until she spoke with the other members of the Ghost Chasers and the psychic. She smirked and chuckled to herself at the name Velvet Blue. It had to be a psychic non-de-plume for nobody named their child Velvet. She shook her head at the charlatans and wondered what kind of mumbo jumbo she'd be in for when she went out to this woman's shack in the woods. She could almost picture it with a stone fireplace, nestled in the midst of Adirondack pines, smoke rolling out, a cauldron over the fire simmering with a homemade brew of something Velvet had dug out of the earth in the woods and of course the mandatory black cat. A modern witch performing her abracadabra. As with everything Klock decided she'd do research into psychics, their techniques and skeptics. Nobody ever accused her of not doing her homework when it came to any topic she focused on. The devil of detective work was in the details.

* * *

Klock was not pleased going to the Ft. Schuyler Association for the Blind, not that they were bad people, they weren't, but the sugar coated way some of them treated her was enough to make her diabetic. She knew their job was to encourage her, provide services with a smile, and keep her upbeat, yet she preferred a more realistic treatment. She went to the association once in a while to have a therapy session with Dr. Susan Hunter, a woman more friend than mental counselor. She liked Dr. Sue because she took the word "independence" seriously for she was totally blind and had made it through medical school. Not only that, she took the train from Albany to Ft. Schuyler every day to work. Dr. Sue would get up at 4am, all for her job she loved. Dr. Sue touched everyone with her love.

Klock had barely been to the association as a visually impaired child but as her vision failed, she needed more of their services. She became legally and totally blind as a teenager. They were good to her. They taught her how to walk with a cane, how to read Braille, how to use JAWS on her laptop, as well as a litany of other things sighted people don't even think about like how to shop in a grocery store, how to cook spaghetti sauce, amongst thousands of daily living tasks the sighted easily perform. She had tried her best to come in quietly to see Dr. Sue as she didn't want to see any other of the employees since one of them speaks to her in baby talk and treats her like her mother does; like a baby bird with underdeveloped wings.

Klock was a little early to her appointment so she had to sit in the lobby with Bo and wait for Dr. Sue. The wait was making her anxious. Her fears came true when the director of blind rehabilitation services came out of her office to say hello. Klock could remember when she could see. She remembered that Sharon Grogan wore way too much makeup for an old woman. Her white hair pulled up into a bun with pencils sticking out of it, her little rectangular glasses balancing on the tip of her long crooked nose. The worse was the way Sharon talked down to people while peering with her ice blue eyes over the tip of her glasses.

"How are you, Rachel?" asked Sharon in her high pitch siren voice that politicians and arch villains tend to use on babies and kittens. "It's Sharon Grogan."

"Fine."

"Is that a new guide dog? What's his name?"

"Bo."

"He's gorgeous. Did Frederick give him to you?"

"Yup."

"Ya know, Rachel, my cousin graduated Cornell with him. They were on the rowing team with such and such. . ."

Klock basically ignored her gum flapping. She felt sorry for the people that had to work for the windbag. The woman talked so fast that Klock wondered if she ever stopped to take a breath. Sharon was oblivious to Klock's one word answers. She prayed under her breath to let somebody shove a sock in Sharon's mouth. The woman finally ran out of gas in her motor mouth and moved on.

Klock was given the OK to move through the front door. She moved down the hall since nobody would escort you in the agency. That was fine with Klock since she knew where Dr. Sue's office was located. Her only worry was how Bo would get along with Sparkle, Dr. Sue's German Sheppard guide dog. Vinny had gotten along really well with her but Bo was a different boy. He was more stubborn and headstrong than Vinny and more easily distracted. He was too smart for his own good; much like people had accused Klock of being. They were the ultimate blind person guide dog match all right. She walked into Dr. Sue's office and the dogs didn't bark or growl at each other which was great. Their hiney and pee pee canine sniffing were the most difficult instinct to break. It was the canine version of a handshake.

"Morning, Klock," said Dr. Sue.

"Dr. Sue!" Klock reached out and touched Dr. Sue's arm. It was a few seconds until they both connected hands that culminated with a hug and pat on the back.

"I haven't seen you in a while. So many changes for you. You have a new guide dog?"

"This here is Bodacious but you can call him Bo," said Klock with a big smile on her face. Dr. Sue made her happy.

"Very good. It looks like Sparkle approves of him. Come on in my office so we can talk."

It was the one place where Klock could let her emotional shield down, for everything they talked about was kept confidential. Klock said, "forward" to Bo as they went straight into the office. She had Bo lay down on the floor but not before giving him a small dog biscuit as a reward for fantastic behavior.

"I was stuck in the lobby and Sharon came out to see me," said Klock. "Why does she talk to me in that high voice like I'm a toddler, Dr. Sue? It's demeaning."

"She can't help it, Klock. She thinks she's being helpful."

"By putting me on a pedestal and clapping because I'm blind and I can walk? I'm not a trained seal begging for fish."

"The sighted will never understand what we have to go through and most really could care less about our situation. It is what it is."

"There's your favorite saying."

"So what honor do I have in your visit?"

"Oh, I got a doozy for you, Dr. Sue."

"Is that right? What is it?"

"I have a partner."

Chapter 8

"Are you in love?" asked Dr. Sue. With whom?"

"Gosh, no," replied Klock feeling a little flush. "He's really sweet and nice but I meant working on a case together. He's a cop. A criminal investigator to be exact. He's a little older than me but he's been so helpful to getting my career going. He sent me my first case which I'm working on right now. He's giving me help as I need it but I'm working on my own. I'm the lead anyway."

"Well, you're not a little girl anymore, Klock. What are you twenty now?"

"Eighteen."

"I'm pleased to hear things are going well for you. Other than the case, Bo and this cop, anything else new for you?"

"I haven't seen you since I moved into my own apartment."

"I'm sure your mother took it well," said Dr. Sue.

"Well, you know how she is. At least she doesn't try to sit in on our meetings anymore so we have progress."

"The sighted want to protect us. They're afraid to let us try and fail. How would we ever succeed if they didn't learn to let us go?"

"I know, Dr. Sue. She was really mad because I moved into Castlewood Courts. It's a dreary place but it's all I could afford. It's not too bad. I'm not dead yet."

"So, you have a case? I know you studied and worked really hard to get your private investigator license."

"That's going great so far but I'm not sure it is what it is. I can't really talk about it. Client privilege don't you know."

"Good for you, Klock. I can tell your confidence is growing. Just keep forging ahead."

"Thanks. Sometimes I have nobody to talk to about other issues."

"Depression?"

"Of course," said Klock. "I'm now taking public assistance to live which I can't stand but it was the only way to break the chains of my mother. She means well but she's mad about the subsidized housing that I live in. I'm bringing nothing but shame and embarrassment to her and my father."

"That sounds like your mother talking," said Dr. Sue. "And there's nothing wrong with taking disability payments. It's not like its enough to get rich off of it."

"That's for sure. I have nothing but peanut butter, crackers and cereal. I spend more on Bo's dog food than my food. But I wouldn't have it any other way. My goal is to get off the monthly checks and make it on my own. Thinking of everything does make me depressed. I guess it comes with our affliction."

"You need me to write you a script for some pills?"

"You know I don't like those pills. The last ones you had me take, I couldn't think properly. It was like my brain was scrambled. I don't want to be happy drooling in a chair. I'd rather deal with the depression and have clarity."

"I know. You can come see me as much as you like. If you think our sessions are making you feel better," said Dr. Sue. "Is there anything specific?"

"Well, I really like working with Dom and I hope he likes working with me as well. I get the feeling he's assisting me out of pity and a need to protect more than out of mutual respect. On top of that, I still have issues with the things people say to me. I feel like God punished me and made me blind. How else can I explain why this happened to me?"

"You can't eat yourself up worrying about why this happened to you. I know how you feel, Klock. It's always better to think of those that are worse off than us. You have a sharp mind. You have your beauty, your career, and your entire life ahead of you. You've done so much and you're still a teenager. Your life will inspire others like us to go forward."

"You're totally blind like me, Dr. Sue. How would you know that I'm beautiful?"

"I've heard staff comment on your appearance but it's also your heart, your soul, your chutzpah. The entire package," said Dr. Sue.

"Well, I can have a temper, as you well know. I can't tolerate when others say and do things against me or the blind in general. I wouldn't call that part of me beautiful, Dr. Sue."

"You bet it is. Being headstrong, fighting for what you believe in, charging ahead against obstacles is why you're so unique. I see a lot of myself in you. The comments I got in medical school from peers was atrocious, especially when I was beating them in grades. As if the professors were giving me good grades out of pity. I wish. We rise above it. You want to be a successful detective?"

"Of course. You know that," said Klock.

"I know you will be."

Klock hit her talking watch and decided she'd had enough talking with Dr. Sue and wanted to be on her way to conduct research on psychics. She reached out and hugged Dr. Sue again and said, "Thank you for seeing me. Bo and I have to be off."

"Listen, Klock. I want you to do me a favor."

"Sure. Anything."

"I want you to stop in and see Mitchell Taylor before you leave."

"The workshop manager? No way."

"He knew you were coming in. He has openings in the factory. It could be a way of supplementing your income."

"Sheltered workshop is more like it."

"Its real work with real benefits, Klock. They don't call it a sheltered workshop anymore."

"Did Kathleen Statler put you up to this?"

"I don't meet with her. She's a New York State Commission for the Blind employee and not affiliated with our agency, Klock."

"Every time she stops to see me she asks me if I want to work here."

"I know. That's her job to find employment for her clients. Mitchell has openings and he sees a healthy young woman. Would you go over there and just meet with him? For me?"

"Fine, but I'm not happy about it. You're lucky I like you, Dr. Sue, or we'd have words."

"I have no doubt about that, Klock. Please stop and see me whenever you'd like."

"No problem."

"I'll call Mitchell and he'll meet you in the hall."

Klock wasn't happy as everyone since the time she had become legally blind had told her a job waited for her in the blind factory. She hated the fact that people had to settle for a job in a protected environment rather than go out into the sighted world and compete. She figured she might as well meet with Mitchell and tell him once and for all to stop telling her mother, her therapist, and anybody else to stop asking her if she wants to be employed in the workshop. She got out in the hall and he was already there to greet her.

"Good morning, Rachel. I'm Mitchell. I run the Industries program here at the Ft. Schuyler Association for the Blind. If you follow me, I'll give you a quick tour and we can talk about possible employment."

"Ok," said Klock.

She followed Mitchell to the other side of the building she had always avoided and never had been. She could always hear the hum of sewing operators and clanking of machines when she'd walk down the hall for her services. It was much louder out on the factory floor. Mitchell had them come to a stop.

"We have about forty people who sew full time on some New York State and Federal projects. Mainly sheets, towels, pillowcases. We also sew t-shirts for the coast guard. We also have around thirty people who package envelopes."

"You make those here?"

"Nope. We have to count them out to their precise amount and package them in the customer required configuration. Come in my office and have a seat."

She sat in a chair and Mitchell shut the door that allowed her to hear better.

"We have openings right now, Rachel," said Mitchell.

"Paying sub-minimum wage?" asked Klock.

"No, we don't operate under a 14C."

"What's a 14C?"

"That's a certificate that allows the blind or disabled agencies to pay sub-minimum wage to their employees. But we don't do that here. We pay prevailing wage rates and fully loaded benefits. If you work here, you'd have the same benefits that I have, that the CEO has. We're not a sheltered workshop paying piece rates of one dollar an hour."

"I don't know about that, Mitchell. You have blind people segregated out here."

"I have sighted working along the blind, I assure you. We're fully integrated here. This is not the 1950's anymore where people were paid ten cents an hour with no benefits caning furniture or selling pencils out of cups. If you gave it a try, you might like it."

"How about your job?"

"Excuse me?" asked Mitchell.

"How many blind people have the necktie jobs? Or are they all sitting at sewing machines and packaging?"

"I don't understand where you're coming from."

"It's called upward mobility and other than Dr. Sue, it doesn't exist at this company. I might only be a teenager, Mitchell, but I'm no fool. When you're ready to promote some of the blind employees into positions of significance, you let me know and I might consider your offer. I have a career outside of here I'm trying to build on. I appreciate what you do but it's not for me."

"I appreciate your honesty, Rachel. If you ever change your mind, you know where we are."

Rachel nodded, shook hands and got off the floor of the factory as quickly as she could. She knew she was being unfair to Mitchell and to the hard working people who were blind. She had fear. Fear of being locked into the workshop for life. Fear of being around her peers that settled for their station in life, happy to exploit the soft soul rehabilitation sighted employees for personal gain. One thing she knew, people who were blind were just like regular people, including unbelievable acts of selfishness. Not like the saintly people who are blind portrayed in the media. They were just like the sighted but with a license to break balls and she wouldn't have any of it. She knew they were doing great things and making strides in wages and employment but fear of failure was her motivation. She couldn't even think of having a guaranteed job. She needed to plow ahead on this case and her law enforcement career. Some of the blind were happy to sit at a sewing machine but not Rachel Esther Klockowski.

* * *

Klock couldn't believe all the stuff on the Internet about psychics. She was particularly fascinated and enthralled with the Encyclopedia of Claims, Frauds & Hoaxes of the Occult & Supernatural by James Randi. She liked the parts about the Eysenck Personality Scale that determined if someone had extrasensory perception (ESP), Dr. Albert Abrams, the dean of the 20th century charlatans, who used his "Dynamizer" to bilk naive believers, as well as Albert Magnus and his philosopher's stone that could make gold, along with dozens of other tidbits that made her squeal with delight. Her take on psychics were they were damaged people that wanted attention or had the desire to think they were somehow separate from the rest of the herd, that they were special, and bestowed with gifts mere mortals couldn't comprehend. Klock had never experienced anything psychic in her life but could understand how someone like Cora Masters could be tricked and plied into believing everything, especially when they're mentally fragile from the loss of a loved one, especially a child. She wondered if

Joey's death had made Cora ripe for the picking, to the point of having to conduct paranormal investigations every year on the anniversary of his death. There was something pathetic, sad, and creepy about doing such a practice. The sheer number of psychic blogs were mind-numbing with many believers and non-believers plastering the message boards with their viewpoints, evidence, and counteractions. She noticed Bo was deeply snoozing so it must've been getting late. She pressed the button on her talking wristwatch. It was close to three in the morning so she got off her computer and got ready for bed. She pulled the covers up tight and smiled for she felt she was armed and ready for Velvet Blue or whatever her name was.

Chapter 9

Klock sat in the front seat of Julia's car as they drove out of Ft. Schuyler and north towards the Adirondack Mountains, where she had not been since everything went squid ink black. Julia grilled her about what Don had told her, and kept reiterating the theme of him being an insurance scammer, so Klock asked her for specifics.

"Well," said Julia. "He got in a car accident. He drove in front of someone and slammed on the breaks. His fake neck injury netted him a good twenty thousand dollars that he threw away with his gambling addiction. Then he said his tools were stolen and he got another monetary settlement but the one he got busted on was when he put clothes under a pipe in the basement of his house, cut it with a hacksaw then tried to put in a claim that the winter cold burst the pipe and ruined his clothes. He's such a genius that he didn't realize that clothes get wet when you wash them. The insurance adjuster denied the claim and he was charged with insurance fraud. My mother paid for a lawyer, as she always did, and got him off."

"Has he ever done time in jail?" asked Klock.

"Here and there. He went down south to try to make his fortune and was jailed for scamming people for their cash and he did a good solid month in an Alabama slammer. He's a pathological liar. Know how you can tell he's lying?"

"I have no idea," said Klock.

"His mouth is moving."

Klock shook her head and smiled. "Good one."

Bo shifted on her feet and she had wished she had put him in the back seat for the ride as she didn't realize how cramped Julia's car would be. She asked some more questions about Cora Masters.

"So, how was your mother when you were growing up?"

"Tough and demanding. Everything had to be perfect or she'd get really upset. She was such an organized person it was insane. She'd alphabetize her pantry and categorize them by fruit, vegetable, grains and pasta. All the labels had to be forward and everything blocked to the front."

"That sounds like fun."

"Report card time wasn't great either. She'd sit down and figure out our grade point averages then grill us on how we could've done better. Don always had higher grades than I did so it was always, "Can't you be smart like your brother." That was not a fun experience."

"Was she like that way with you and the ghost hunting?"

"Well, that's why I was in and out all the time with the group. If I displeased her she'd leave me off an investigation, however, she darn well made sure I was there on her annual one for my dead brother."

"I guess you know Don told me all about it. That would've been helpful if you had told me that when we first met, Julia."

"I didn't think it was relevant."

"The anniversary of the death of a child, I'm sure, has to be one of emotional stress. You don't think this would cause your mother to jump to her death?"

"Not at all. You'll see why I know she didn't kill herself when you meet Velvet."

"Okay. Does she live in a shack in the woods?" asked Klock.

"Hardly. She lives in one of the largest houses in the Adirondack Park. It's on White Lake and it's HUGE," said Julia putting extra emphasis on the end of her sentence.

"Is being a psychic that lucrative? I predict you will be soon separated from your wallet, Julia."

"Not really. What helps is being married to the owner of all the Dipster Donuts in New York State."

"I love their half moon cookies, chocolate frosting on one side and vanilla on the other," said Klock. "I wonder if her husband likes his wife running around doing this stuff?"

"Oh he's very supportive of her gifts. That's why she never charges a penny for any of her work. She feels her abilities should be a gift to the world," said Julia.

"This should be fun," said Klock.

They pulled up to the house and Klock couldn't tell anything fancy in regards of one house from another but when she got out of the vehicle she certainly liked the fresh crisp mountain winter air that filled her lungs.

"I wish you could see the view of the frozen lake and the décor of Velvet's house," said Julia. "It's spectacular."

"It has a toilet right?" asked Klock.

"Of course, Klock," replied Julia in a confused tone.

"Well, no matter what fancy walls you put around it, a toilet is still a toilet," replied Klock with a smile on her face as she held tight onto Bo's harness. "Bahwhooshhh!"

"Okay," replied Julia. "No need to knock. Velvet sensed our presence and is already standing in her doorway waiting for us."

"Forward, Bo," said Julia. "Don't worry, boy. There's nothing to fear here. She only sacrifices chickens not yellow labs."

Klock could only imagine how upset Julia was getting for it was quite clear that she was dedicated to the sincerity and authenticity of Velvet Blue, psychic. Klock's little jabs were not soliciting a response. They got up to the door and before she could introduce herself, the psychic said in a sweet and pleasant voice, "You're Rachel Klockowski. Nice to meet you. I'm Velvet."

Klock reached out assuming the psychic wanted to shake hands but she didn't take her gloves off for they were still outside.

Velvet gripped Klock's hand tight and shook. "Please come in and we can chat."

Klock picked up on the flowery scent inside of the home that reminded her of the fresh flowered fields of her youth when her parents would take her out of the city to nature hikes. It was more pleasant than some of the odors in Castlewood Courts. Burnt bacon, Lysol and no deodorant armpit were some of the highlighted scents of her apartment building.

"Let's go to my atrium," said Velvet. "You like honey in your tea, Klock?"

"Sure. Thank you," said Klock knowing that Julia must've told everything about her so this was no cold reading, it was hot all right and Velvet knowing what tea she drank and what name she preferred was nothing more than someone doing their basic homework. Klock felt that nobody worked harder on their research than she did and she knew all the tricks of the trade with mental exploitation humbugs. She found a chair with her hand and took off her hat, gloves, and jacket before sitting down. She led Bo to her side and she could feel a sunbeam coming into the room that was easy to detect for the streak of light had more warmth then the rest of the room. Bo was happy to lie right in the middle of it and soak it up.

"Velvet will be right back. She went to get our beverages, Klock," said Julia.

Klock nodded while she took out her handheld digital recorder.

"I don't think Velvet wants you to record this interview, Klock," said Julia.

"Nonsense, Julia," said Velvet. Klock could hear her walking back into the atrium with what must be their beverages on a metal tray for she could hear the clanking. The drinks jostled and clinked while Velvet set them on the table. "I don't mind one bit if you record this conversation. I don't want you to sell it. As long as we can agree on that."

"I only use this because I cannot see a sheet of paper to take notes. I only use this for my investigations and it's never posted or given to anyone else," said Klock.

"Do you believe in psychics?" asked Velvet.

"Do I?" asked Klock looking towards the psychic and cocking her eyebrow. Doing that in class used to drive her teachers nuts. They'd call it out as a sign of disrespect and they were right. "Where's your familiar?"

"I don't have a black cat and I'm not a witch. I see you need verification of my abilities," replied Velvet, really slow with a light breezy tone. "I need to prove myself to you. Might I have your hand, Klock?"

"Sure," she said all smug as she held out her right hand. It was hard to describe the jolt Klock felt when Velvet took her hand as if the psychic's hand were the aftershock of a baby electric eel. Klock couldn't think of any other way to describe it. She felt a little sick to her stomach and nervous.

"It's ok. Just relax," said Velvet. "You're on this journey, this investigation but I don't think you'll see what's coming. I sense a scared little girl disguised as a confident woman."

"Blind," said Klock pointing to her eyes with her one free hand.

"I'm looking into your soul, Klock and your darkened eyes are not the window, it's your aura. It's a bright white which I find very curious for your mannerisms are that of a red aura."

"Okay," replied Klock, all smug, yet she was churning butter with her stomach. Something weird was happening and she was going to do her best to remain calm, cool, and collected.

"You are a complicated person all right. You crave to be solo yet you want this man in your life to take care of you, to protect you, to guide you," said Velvet.

Julia wasn't saying anything but humming affirmative while Velvet was doing her thing.

"Impressive, Velvet. Did you get that from your blue book?" asked Klock.

"Looks like somebody's been doing their research. I'm not a part of the psychic mafia and I don't have a blue book with your information in it, Klock," said Velvet.

"Fair enough, but I'm not here for a palm reading, Velvet. I'm conducting an investigation into the death of Cora Masters and I need to question you on what you saw that night. To find out what happened."

"Let's get to that in a minute. Before I give you what you want you need to give me what I require," said Velvet.

"Sure, Velvet Blue, or whatever your name is. It couldn't be an ordinary name like Mary or Alice could it?" said Klock trying to throw the psychic.

"You're a tricky one," said Velvet. "You're a very complex young woman. You're strong, no doubt, but not ready for the fight," said Velvet as she let go of Klock's hand.

"Is that it?" asked Klock pulling back her hand that felt on fire yet the rest of her body was chilled and covered with Goosebumps.

"You rely on your technology, your devices, and one will be the reveal, the solver, the solution you're looking for," said Velvet. "Mark my words, Klock, and heed my warning."

"What warning?" asked Klock.

"Don't meddle with that which you don't believe or mock," said Velvet.

"I mess with what I want to mess with, Velvet. Don't think I'm feeble because I'm blind. I'll outwork any sighted person any day of the week and don't try to throw me with your fortune telling lounge act." Klock was getting worked up.

"Please have some tea," said Velvet. "No need to get upset. I'll gladly answer your questions."

Klock was a little thrown by the sweet arrogance and confidence of the psychic and wondered if the lady put something on her shaking hand that would cause Klock to react physically the way she did. She knew that Velvet would throw a bunch of vague statements at her and try to gauge her reactions then counterattack based on them. She's read all about the way psychics would try to trick customers with lights, sounds, puppetry, whatever would work then they would gently ply their money away from them but she got the feeling Velvet's purpose was insidious. There was something off-putting about the woman that Klock couldn't put a finger on. She took her time and sipped the tea before gaining composure for the Q&A on Cora Masters.

She set the cup down and went into the questions. "You were there the night of the investigation at the Overlook Mansion?"

"She was there all right," answered Julia.

"No offense, Julia, but I need her to answer my questions. Unless I ask you something specifically, please remain quiet."

"Yes, I was," said Velvet.

"Describe to me why you chose that place as Cora's next place to investigate," said Klock.

"I told Cora that the Overlook had a portal in the turret of the mansion."

"What's a portal?"

"It's a doorway to another dimension or spiritual plane where spirits, entities, and ghosts travel back and forth into our realm from theirs.

"You mean like limbo?"

"There are many names in many cultures for their place," replied Velvet. "Limbo, purgatory, the Twilight Zone, many names. To answer your question, yes, like limbo. It's a waiting station for spirits that have yet to move on. Most are there as they've left this world with unfinished business or they're so longing for the pleasures of the flesh that they can't let go and move on."

"Move on to where?" asked Klock. "Heaven?"

"The next state of consciousness, whatever humankind calls it. Many cultures have many names for the next level."

"So why would having a portal intrigue Cora Masters?" asked Klock.

"After years of searching for the right conduit to her son's spirit, this was the one. I felt his presence would be there, coming through the portal, especially on the anniversary of him leaving this material world."

"Really?" asked Klock with her eyebrow raised to its maximum height.

"Of course. I see these things, Klock. I know you don't believe me but its okay. I understand those who have to feel to believe. And, please don't correct me and say "Blind" in your ways. I mean seeing with your spirit, your soul, your blinding white aura."

"And the owners of the Overlook Mansion conveniently let you in there? I heard no ghost hunters had ever been allowed into the place yet you get a vision and suddenly the Ghost Chasers are in there. How did that happen exactly?"

"The new owners were very cooperative," said Julia interrupting. "My mother, and all the paranormal groups throughout the United States, have had the Overlook Mansion on their wish list. A new family moved in and my mother got there first."

"Is that how it happened, Velvet?"

"Not quite," replied the psychic.

"I knew it. I knew there was something that gave Cora Masters and the Ghost Chasers the competitive edge. Let me guess, you paid money to the owners to let you get in there and dazzle them with your psychic mumbo jumbo. Right?" asked Klock nodding her head.

"You are not a very good investigator, Klock. Your questioning is not up to par; however, I think you have a little psychic twinge," replied Velvet. "That's going to serve you well as you proceed in your career as an investigator. Speaking of that, might I see your qualifications?"

"Sure," replied Klock as she took out her badge and held it towards Velvet.

"Might I hold it?" asked Velvet. "I promise to return it. I wish to glean from it."

"Glean away," said Klock as she held it out to Velvet who took her badge. Klock imagined the psychic holding it while she rocked back and forth rolling her eyes as she tried to read something from an inanimate object. She heard Velvet set what she assumed was her badge back on the table in front of her. She felt around and picked it back up.

"You are in danger, Klock. Don't go to the Overlook. It's going to lead you down an evil path," said Velvet.

"I know that cliché, be careful what I look for, I might find it," said Klock as she put the badge away. "Can we get back to the events of the death of Cora Masters and enough of the hocus pocus?"

"As you wish," replied Velvet.

"Were you with Cora Masters when she fell?"

"No."

"You left her alone by the portal?"

"She was channeling the spirits and was waiting for her son to answer. It was a private moment so I left."

"How long after you left did she fall to her death?"

"Within a few minutes I would say."

"Were there any witnesses to state you were not up there?"

"I don't know."

"You do realize that Julia here has hired me to investigate the circumstances of her mother's death. She feels her mother was pushed. That she was murdered. How was your relationship with Cora?"

"No," said Velvet.

"Afraid to answer," said Klock trying to bait the psychic into a confession. It couldn't be that easy like it was on television. They always wrapped everything up and got the guilty party to confess right in time for the car commercials, unfortunately this was real life, not television.

"No, I didn't push her."

"Is that right? What happened then? You're the psychic. Tell me."

"I cannot," said Velvet with distress in her voice. Klock had her.

"Is that because you did it? Why did you push her?"

"Get out of my house, witch," said Velvet. "I know what you are and what you're here to do."

"I forgot my broom. This isn't colonial times, Velvet Blue. We're all adults here, tell me what happened. It's okay."

"I don't know!" yelled Velvet. "For the first time in my life my psychic abilities were blank. Something blocked my mental view. Once I went down from the turret, my second sight was cleansed, blank, dead. I was unable to see with my blind 3rd eye."

"So, that's your story. Okay, I get it. Julia, please escort Bo and me out of here," said Klock as she picked up her recorder and left it on in case Velvet blurted out a confession. She got her jacket and gear back on with the recorder now in her jacket pocket, still on. She took Bo by the harness and asked Julia to head to the door so Bo could follow. Velvet didn't say another word, even as they walked back out into the cold with Klock looking back into the house one last time to get the psychic to blurt something out. . . anything. Nothing came as Julia shut the door.

"That went well," said Klock.

"You're a fool," replied Julia.

Chapter 10

Klock downloaded her conversations from her digital recorder into her laptop and spent the entire evening drinking tea and listening to all her interviews but the highlight was her interaction with Velvet. She couldn't explain the feeling in her hand or the fact that some of Velvet's answers were blurred. She marked it down as a technical glitch and not Velvet Blue blocking the device with her mind.

She tried not to get too excited about Dom asking her to come down to the police station the next day. He said he had something for her and she could hardly wait, although professing her great fondness of Dom to Dr. Sue didn't mean she was going to ask Dom on a date or anything like that. She was thrilled that he was kind and supportive to her career. She had no clue if he was handsome but he sounded and smelled pretty darn worthy. Infatuation would have to wait until the case was concluded. She wanted to throw Velvet in the mix of possible questionable suspects although she didn't have a motive, her warning Klock to stay away from the Overlook Mansion was weird in itself. She decided that she would approach the owners and see if they'd let her in even though she hadn't a penny to pay them.

It was so quiet in her apartment that she could hear her stomach grumbling. She was glad nobody but Bo was there to hear it. She'd worry about food later. She still had a couple slices of white bread and a few scoops of the creamy peanut butter. At least she had half of bag a dog food so Bo would be fed and happy. He worked hard and deserved to eat before she did. She'd learned to go to bed hungry. She had her check but didn't cash it yet to go to the market.

* * *

Klock woke up. She was sitting at her desk with her head down and a drool trail coming out of her mouth and onto the wood. She'd passed out with her headphones on listening to her records on the case. She was still groggy when Bo started nudging her with his muzzle letting her know it must've been morning and he needed to be curbed.

"Ok, boy. Give me a second to put my jacket on and I'll take you out." She didn't place the harness on him. Just his leash that let Bo know he had a little more freedom and wasn't on the guide dog clock. She showed no fear of coming and going from her apartment and hadn't been harassed by Bookcase or anybody else although she wished some of the neighbors were a little more friendly. She figured when the spring and summer hit she'd see more people out front and get to know them.

* * *

Klock was impressed on how well Bo knew the path to the Ft. Schuyler police station. She was hoping Detective Wilson and his silent partner, Detective Hilley, were there to make their wisecracks for she'd love to give them another non-verbal response.

She walked in and Dom came out before she even asked the front desk clerk to page him.

"Morning, Klock," he said. "And, Bo."

"How did you know I was here?"

"My desk is by the window and I saw you walking down the sidewalk so I came out to greet you."

"Windows are useless to me now unless I'm opening one to get a cool summer breeze. What was it you had for me?"

"I'll tell you when you get to my office," said Dom. "Here, take my elbow and I'll bring you in."

Klock had confidence, much more than her last visit but was a little disappointed when there were no catcalls or insults hurtled from Dom's colleagues. Dom didn't say anything until they got to his desk.

"The chief wants to meet you, Klock."

"That's why you called me down here?"

"Yes. I thought you would like that. I had to tell him I was assisting you and he was happy about it."

"I'm a private investigator that's going to be looking over one of his cases. Why would he be happy about that?"

"I have no clue but I know how much you want to be a cop and how much you love police work. He's a really fair boss. Tough but nice."

"Hard to believe, Dom. All the police chiefs in the books I read and on television are usually grizzled veterans that yell at their subordinates," said Klock.

"That's such a stereotype. They love doing that in movies and on cop shows."

Klock got a serious look and spoke in a robotic voice, "take me to your leader."

"Classic," said Dom. "You supposed to be Robby the Robot from Forbidden Planet?"

"Exactly," she said with a smile.

"How about that? A female cop that's also a sci-fi geek. Don't tell me you Cosplay?"

"You bet, Dom. Supergirl is my favorite."

"I'm impressed. I love comics and costume play or cosplay but I've never been to a comic book convention. That's a secret I need you to keep. Wilson would have a field day," said Dom.

"We'll talk about going to one when I'm done with this case," replied Klock, getting back into her serious mode. The police chief was waiting to meet her and she had no clue what the man wanted or was going to say to her. She didn't care what Dom said, she was scared to meet the law enforcement boss man. He was the most powerful law officer in the city. A man who probably didn't have time to sip a root beer through a bendy straw but was going to take a moment to talk with her.

They had to take the elevator to the top floor of the police station where all the administrative offices were located. Dom brought up Klock's pistol permit as she hadn't heard on her application but it hadn't been very long. He had told her that the process speeds up when a cop or investigator is applying so it wouldn't be long. She was in no hurry to get it.

On the elevator Klock teased Dom about how many times he'd been called up to the principal's office and if he was the poster child for internal affairs. He said Darth Vader had an office up there amongst the police elite. They got off the elevator and were greeted by what Klock figured was an administrative assistant.

"Hello. You here to see the chief?" the woman asked.

"Yes," replied Dom. "He wanted to see, Klock."

"I love your dog. We have a couple German Sheppard here but they're much more serious than your pooch."

"He takes his job as serious as they take theirs, I assure you. He's my eyes."

"It's so noble what service dogs do for us humans," said the assistant. "Wait one second and I'll see if the chief is free."

It only took a few moments before the assistant called them into the office with Klock gripping tightly onto Dom's elbow but his arm was so large and solid she doubted it hurt him. He brought her over to a chair that she assumed was in front of a really large wooden desk. She had Bo lie down and could hear the chief wrapping up a phone call that seemed unimportant. He hung up.

"Hello. You must be Rachel Klockowski," said the chief.

"Yes, the one and only," she replied.

"I'm Chief Devine but you can call me Len."

"I'd rather call you Chief Devine. Anything else would be disrespectful."

"Fair enough. That's awfully nice of you. Are you any relation to Stosh Klockowski?" asked the chief.

"He's my father."

"He's a great mechanic. I've been going to that shop of his for years. How is he these days?"

"Great. He's doing really well."

"I'm pleased to hear that. Tell him I said hello. Well, Detective Mulvi here has told me all about you. You're a private investigator?"

"Yes, Chief Devine."

"You look as young as my granddaughter."

"I assure you, I'm old enough," said Klock.

"No doubt. Listen, first off I wanted to meet you when I heard that a young blind woman was showing such great interest in police work."

"I have my first case and Detective Mulvi was kind enough to talk to me a little bit about it."

"The suicide of Cora Masters I'm told," said the Chief.

"Or possible murder," said Klock. "No offense to your detectives. I was hired by Cora's daughter to investigate it."

"I know. Detective Mulvi came to me and asked if he could give you a copy of our case files. I can give you a copy as long as you promise to take it easy on us."

Klock paused a moment. She wasn't a little girl playing with Barbies, this was serious, this was someone's life and she got the strange feeling the chief thought she wasn't doing anything but pussy footing around. It made her mad so she let loose a little bit. "I'm taking this case all the way to the end, Chief Devine. I make no promises to anything easy. If I discover it's a murder and your detectives have deemed it to be a suicide, it'll be embarrassing to your department. You still want to give me a copy of the case file?"

The chief chuckled and said, "You're feisty. I like that in my officers. Why haven't you applied to the police academy?"

"Blind," she said as she pointed with both her index fingers to both her eyes.

"Well, we pride ourselves on being open to the community and special people," said the chief.

Klock didn't bother correcting the old man for saying things like special and retard were insulting to the disabled but she wasn't on a crusade. She'd heard it enough but it still baffled her how clueless people could be and this is the chief of police.

"I'm special all right," replied Klock. She raised her eyebrow. She didn't want to push her luck too much as she really wanted to go over the files.

"Here you go," said Dom as he handed Klock a large stack of paper.

It took Klock a few moments to get over the fact that it was Braille paper. She took her right fingers and brushed them over the bumps and was floored that they were the notes on the Cora Masters suicide and had Detective Wilson's name on the header.

"How?" she asked. She was floored.

"Detective Mulvi took the notes over to the Ft. Schuyler Braille transcribers and they were kind enough to do this free of charge."

"Thank you very much, Chief Devine," said Klock with great appreciation. "Don't worry I won't share this with anyone and I'll give them back to Dom when I'm through."

"You're welcome. As part of our community outreach, we are committed to assisting people like yourself. Dom can help you but not full time. He has his own case load he has to attend to."

"I won't use him unless I absolutely have too. I want to work on this case and solve it myself," she said.

"You remind me of your father all right," said the chief.

"Thank you," said Klock going from simmering anger to thrilled faster than Bo's mouth to a bowl of bacon bits. She was never so pleased than when being compared to her hard-working father. The chief was nice after all. He needed to be educated on how to talk with people who were blind and disabled, but that will come with time.

Klock shook hands with Chief Devine and held the stack of papers tight under her arm and followed with Bo. This time she didn't grab Dom's elbow. She trusted Bo would follow Dom all the way to the elevator where she didn't make a sound until the doors shut and she knew they were all alone.

"I'm so excited, Dom. I can't believe you got me the files."

"I know. I couldn't sneak around. I had to run it by the chief. I can tell he got you upset for a moment. He doesn't mean the way he says some of the things he says. The important thing is you have the files."

"What if I discover Detective Wilson is wrong? Chief Devine and the department could look bad."

"We get second guessed and questioned on things all the time. Wilson would probably be mad that you debunked his conclusions," said Dom. "Let's go to my office before you go back home and start, uh. . ."

"Finger reading, Dom. Unless you want to call it bump feeling."

* * *

Klock sat at Dom's desk and spent a good half hour giving him an update on what had happened with Velvet Blue and he didn't find it comical but warned her about interacting with the mentally ill, which did make her laugh on the inside, although he had a point. The ghost chasers and Velvet seemed to be delusional or out of touch at the least, or super craving for attention. She was excited to get home and read what Detective Wilson had to write and conclude. On the way out of the police station she heard a loud verbal blast from Detective Wilson who said, "Detective Helen Keller on the case!"

"Very clever," she said as she kept walking.

"Great comeback, Bat," said Detective Wilson.

"That's enough, Wilson," said Dom.

Klock was pushed and fell down making Bo bark as her Braille case papers flew to the floor. It took her a moment to realize what the ruckus was all about. Dom was fighting Detective Wilson right in the police station. All she could hear was grunting and the smacking of fists. She hoped Dom was winning. The commotion got louder and she could hear many voices as the fight seemed to be breaking up.

"Well, there goes my job," said Dom, as he helped Klock to her feet. "Stay right there and I'll pick up your papers."

"If you fight everybody that makes insults at me, you better carry boxing gloves everywhere we go."

"You better get out of here, Klock. I'll call you later."

Klock walked out as her knight came to the rescue of the damsel in distress, although she wasn't too happy about it. The last thing she needed was a savior of the blind swooping in and kicking ass on those who discriminate, those who mock. She was worried about him losing his job or even worse yet, in a small way, she was satisfied. She cracked a small smile and prayed that she only had her eyes back to normal for just the split second it took for Dom to smack the smartass Wilson.

Chapter 11

Klock spent the afternoon reading Detective Wilson's case files. It wasn't as exciting as she thought it would be. It was basic interviews with the ghost chasers and the Van Dreasons, who owned the Overlook Mansion yet according to the witnesses nobody saw her fall or was with her. Detective Wilson had seized the video cameras and examined the footage yet found absolutely nothing. Instead of making her feel better, reading the Braille files made her feel worse as she wondered if Detective Wilson was right. Perhaps she was wasting her time on a road to nowhere.

The Ft. Schuyler Coroner's summary was in the case file and he had determined that Cora Masters had died of blunt trauma to the skull. The cause listed was fatal damage due to the fall from the turret window. It was mentioned that the impact of her landing on the rough rocks piled next to the mansion was the death blow. The landing had smashed the digital recorder that was in her hand. Forensics was unable to retrieve any recordings on the death clutched device as Cora's body had flattened the internal hard drive of the recorder. Detective Wilson had looked over the interior of the turret and noted that the window was wide open and at knee level so she could've been pushed. However, there were no signs of a struggle and after he and his partner, Detective Hilley, had interviewed everyone present, they were deemed non-suspects. No suicide note was present. The interesting tidbit was a small note that stated that Don Masters was very upset, angry, and had the smell of booze in his breath. Klock wondered why, especially after the will came out, and Don was left everything, that he wouldn't be grilled more thoroughly when sober, or even placed on a lie detector. It made her wonder if Detective Wilson was being sloppy. It was almost Sherlock Holmes 101 that family and close friends are always the top suspects in murders, especially one that had a big financial stake. Even Julia taking over her mother's ghost hunting group could be deemed as a possible motive, or the fact her mother died on the anniversary of Joey's death, something that Cora had used as a grudge against her daughter.

Klock felt Velvet was rather odd and suspicious, especially telling her to stay away from the Overlook Mansion. The psychic was there that night yet neither Detective Wilson nor Detective Hilley had interviewed her, unless they talked to her and never put it in writing for the file. She found the entire case strange and fuzzy. Klock still needed to interview the other members of the Ghost Chasers but the big move was talking to the Van Dreason's. Could they have had something to do with it? She couldn't say yes or no until she met them and attempted to get up into the turret to feel her way around.

Klock had spent hours going over the files and hadn't thought about Dom's fight with Detective Wilson in the police station until her cell phone rang. It had snapped her out of her focus and she wondered if it were Dom.

"Hello," she said.

"Klock, how are you?" asked Dom.

"I'm fine. How are you?"

"Suspended for a couple of days."

"How about Wilson?"

"A written reprimand."

"That's not right."

"Well, I hit him first. If I didn't have the union on my side I could've lost my job. The chief was really angry with me doing this especially in front of citizens."

"I thought you ignored the taunts."

"I'd had enough of his hot air. Stupid windbag."

"Please don't do that again. I can take care of people like him myself."

"You're welcome," said Dom.

"I'm serious. It was very sweet of you but I hear comments from people all the time and if it gets beyond the pale, I step up and do something about it. I just don't want you to lose your job and career over my blindness."

"Fair enough. So you find anything interesting from Detective Wilson's notes?"

"No, it's all pretty boring and standard I'd guess. I have issues with a couple things. For instance, Don Masters was drunk on the scene, acting belligerent and he's barely questioned, yet he grills Julia and the Ghost Chasers. Don is a major suspect. He got everything from his mother," said Klock.

"Yeah, monetary gain is always a big motive."

"Exactly. Then on top of it did you know that the reason they were there that night was because it was the anniversary of the death of Joey Masters, a death that Cora Masters blamed her daughter Julia for."

"Joey Masters?"

"Cora's youngest child. He was killed by a truck when Julia was babysitting him. Detective Wilson has no mention of this in his notes and I got this information with a very simple Q&A with Don Masters."

"That's a biggie. He's not the brightest detective," said Dom. "Sometimes people are more interested in getting their paycheck and just going home. They move through their work like zombies, oblivious to everything but their own needs."

"I thought only the best were the detectives?"

"Sometimes it's political or just seniority. Some great people get into the department but we do have a few like Wilson that are related to the Mayor or stand at a backyard grill flipping burgers with a councilperson."

"Well, that certainly sucks," says Klock. "Also, as you know, I met with the psychic, Velvet Blue. She was there that night and Detective Wilson and Detective Hilley never bothered to interview her. She was in the turret mere minutes before the fall."

"Love the name," said Dom laughing.

"She could be a suspect. At the least a possible witness."

"Maybe she sent him messages with her mind."

"Very funny, Dom. I'm sure you don't believe in that nonsense."

"I'm as logical as Spock so, no, I don't follow that creed. It's a scam in my opinion. I've had psychics approach me on murder cases in the past. They love to give vague readings where upon afterwards they can point as their super clairvoyance. They never give specifics. I warned you to watch out, she sounds as loony as a straight jacketed crackpot."

"She's a strange one all right. I didn't tell you earlier but Julia Masters brought me out to her house on White Lake to meet with her."

"All the way up there?"

"It got Bo and me out of the city so I guess that was the good part of the trip. She grabbed my hand and went into some kind of trance. It was bizarre. She talked about the portal she identified at the Overlook."

"Portal?" asked Dom.

"It's a passageway for the ghosts to come back and forth from their realm to ours."

"Oh boy."

"At least the subject matter of my case is interesting. I never seem to get the straight anything in my entire life so why would my first ever case be any different?"

"This case is something else all right. You come to any conclusions yet?"

"Nothing solid. I still have to question the other Ghost Chasers and the owners of the Overlook Mansion. I did find out that Cora Masters paid her way into the place for an investigation. That alone enraged these other ghost hunting groups. The blog postings have been vicious. Many people were happy for her death."

"If Julia is a suspect, why would she hire you?"

"I thought of that one myself. Unless she thinks I can pin it on Don."

"Sure. If he goes to jail she could get all the money from her mother's estate. He had the cash motive."

"I heard Cora was a nasty person to work with on investigations. I'll know more once I chat with the other two Ghost Chasers."

"That makes sense. She could've made one of the other team members very angry. Enough so that they'd snap and push. Did Cora have a husband? And even if she did, could she have been having a love affair with one of the other members?"

"Great point. John Richards and Steve Eddy are the other Ghost Chaser members that were questioned by Detective Wilson. They had pretty bland answers so it's hard to determine exactly what kind of people they are. Cora's husband had left the family when the children were small. He took off and they never heard from him again. I have to run to the bank and store and when I get back I'll call Julia Masters and see what she can do to arrange me meeting with them. I'd do it myself but I think they'd talk if she arranged the meeting."

"The hard part of being a private investigator is they don't have to talk to you at all."

"The easy part is I don't have to obey the law."

"Nice," said Dom. "Well, it looks like you're doing a great job so far for your client unless she's the guilty party then you'll never get paid."

"Let's hope I get something out of this."

"Well, you're on the chief's radar and that's a great thing. Even when I was getting disciplined he kept talking about you. There's something about you that intrigues him."

"How many totally blind teenage certified private investigators do you know?" asked Klock.

"Just one."

"There you are."

"I hope he sees something more in you than a curiosity. You're more than a fad, I think you have great potential."

"Thanks, Dom. I've got to get going now."

"I have a few days of nothing going on so call me if you need any assistance or a ride anywhere."

"Sounds great."

Klock clicked her cell phone shut and shoved it back into her pocket. She pressed her talking watch and forgot that it was getting later in the afternoon and the bank would be closing in a half an hour. Luckily there was a downtown branch a block away for she had to go and cash her disability check. She was thrilled to get it for she was getting desperate for food more than anything. She always paid her rent first then worried about the other little things like her cell phone bill. At least her utilities were thrown in. She'd also need a couple rolls of quarters for doing her laundry. She was on her last clean outfit and her investigation had been causing her to lag on her cleaning and other duties. She was a little bit of a slob but she didn't care. It wasn't like she could see dust or things out of order. It was better than her obsessive compulsive mother running around with her rag and can of Pledge cleaner.

Klock put the harness on Bo and as always he was thrilled to be going out on an adventure. This was the second time in the same day he was going to be out and about. If the cold, snow, and wind bothered him he never showed it for he tugged her a little harder as they went to the front door of her apartment. She decided to take the stairs as she wanted to be ready in case the elevator ever broke or there was some kind of emergency, she'd be prepared and Bo would know the way. She was only on the 4th floor of Castlewood Courts so it was no big deal for her or her pooch, but the stairs smelled like a non-flushed toilet.

Klock was pleased the sidewalks were cleared, for the owners of the downtown buildings were supposed to clear them. Most didn't and the city never did it. If it snowed really bad, she would stumble and fall for she couldn't see where the ruts were. Bo was good, but not that good, since his eyes were always front and center. A few times since she had Bo she'd had to walk in the street during snowstorms which was incredibly dangerous since the drivers could care less that a blind woman and her dog were walking. They would honk and yell out at her with such foul words she wondered if they were still lingering above Ft. Schuyler.

Klock was lucky that the bank was not closed for she made it with minutes to go. The line was lengthy for everyone was there cashing their disability checks. She wished she could see what the people in line with their disability checks looked like and what was their "disability." She knew real disabled people were getting the subsidy yet others claimed their disability was from everything from fatigue to hemorrhoids. She got her cash from a friendly teller that took the time to show her the way the bills were so she could fold them at the counter right away. She'd been taken more than a few times since she went totally blind when buying things so she had to be really clear on what bills were what. She didn't get outraged by being taken advantage of or exploited; it was just the way some people were in this world. She might not believe in psychics or ghosts but she certainly believed in Karma and those that prey on people like her were sure to get theirs, if not in this life, perhaps in the next.

* * *

Klock left Bo asleep on his dog bed as she carried her laundry basket to the elevator on her way to the basement Laundromat. She didn't have her cane as she walked with one hand out in front of her since she knew the path well. The laundry room had a couple dozen washers and driers with a few that were broken. There was always somebody in there that would talk to her but this night it was empty. That was fine with her as she was kind of tired from the long day and just wanted to get the clothes done. She'd brought her digital reader that had a new mystery downloaded and ready to roll. It would take her too long to leave her clothes in the washer and come back, besides she didn't want them to get stolen, as she couldn't afford to buy new ones. She could, of course, ask her parents to buy her new stuff to wear but she needed the independence. Her mother would never respect her as long as she had to keep coming to her to bail her out. She'd rather wear an old potato sack with a neck hole and arm holes cut in it.

    Klock loaded the clothes in the large industrial washer. She never separated darks from whites since she couldn't see what was what. It didn't matter to her other than they were clean. She cracked open the roll of quarters and filled up the machine. Once it got going she put the laundry soap in, put everything on the folding table, and sat down to listen to her audio book. She was fumbling with the wiring to her earphones that had gotten jumbled when she heard a voice that made her spinal fluid chill.

    "Hey, where's your dog?" asked Bookcase.

Chapter 12

"He's upstairs sleeping," said Klock trying not to be too rude to the thug.

"You got some quarters I can borrow? I need to do my socks and underwears."

Klock took out a handful and figured if she gave the man some change he'd leave her alone. She held out her hand with the quarters in her palm and Bookcase took them out. His hands were all cold and clammy. He gave her the creeps but she knew she had to stay cool. She had been stupid and had left her cell phone upstairs. She couldn't even use her cane as a weapon as she didn't have that either. The machines were making so much noise, and being secluded in the basement, she doubted she could scream for help. It would only be pure luck that someone might hear her.

"Sorry, but that's all I can give you," said Klock trying to be pleasant. "I need what I have left for the dryer."

"You a pretty girl," says Bookcase. "You want to go out for a bite to eat?"

"No, thank you," she said trying not to be nasty. She had been a little too friendly and Bookcase was confusing that with interest. "I have too much to do."

"How about tomorrow then? I can help you out. I don't mind you blind and all. I know how to treat a girl."

"I'm sorry but I'm too busy to go on dates."

"How about I stop in your apartment and we can hang out there?"

"I'm sorry, Bookcase, but I have a boyfriend." She was trying to throw the creep off the scent although his scent of bad cologne was certainly making her nostrils burn.

"Don't lie to me, little girl. I seen you plenty of times and you don't have no boy around you other than that dog of yours."

"I'm sorry but if you think I led you on. I was just being friendly."

"You're a stuck up bitch that don't belong here. All crippled and thinkin' you're better than everyone," raged Bookcase.

"Back off!" she yelled letting her Polish temper get the best of her. She'd be damned if she was going to continue to be the polite victim. She clenched her fist getting ready to defend herself.

"You ain't worth it," said Bookcase. She could hear him walking away, causing a huge commotion with several bangs that made her surmise he'd thrown chairs and punched the washing machines on his way out.

It took Klock a good fifteen minutes for her blood pressure to drop back to normal but she still had shaking hands that she figured was from the adrenaline rush. It was at this point she wish she had her pistol permit, although it wouldn't have come to that. She wondered if she'd have the guts to pull a gun on a human being, not that Bookcase was technically human, but he was mortal. He had ruined her good mood. She sat in a chair and didn't move as she wanted to hear if he came back.

* * *

Klock got back upstairs without any more meetings with her admirer. She decided not to call Dom. She didn't want him to get into the habit of riding to her rescue every time a man tried to pick her up, a person insulted her, or anybody committed an injustice at her. She wanted to be independent and she felt this was the price to pay, besides, she did have one saying her mother always used, although she had stole it from Ann Landers, "nobody can take advantage of you without your permission." She'd try her best to not let that happen.

She was in such a hurry to get out of the laundry room she didn't bother folding the clothes, doing them on her bed instead while she played the news on the television. The enthusiastic weatherman was talking cold and snow; as if there was anything else in the Mohawk Valley during February.

She called Julia and got her voice mail so she left a message that she wanted to speak to the other two members of the Ghost Chasers and would she try to set that up. Klock hoped that she could get to them soon as they were probably the last two until she could approach the owners of the Overlook Mansion. She wanted to get from Julia a little more detail on them.

Klock spent the rest of the night on her couch listening to the television, not really paying attention too much to what was on, but rather trying to go over the case in her mind. She was trying to flush the memories of the laundry room incident. Her eyelids got heavy. She was tired. Klock was too exhausted to move so she pulled her blanket tight up to her chin and drifted off to sleep. The last thing she heard was Bo's groaning as he stretched. He lay on the floor next to the couch and not on his usual dog bed.

Something startled Klock making her sit up on the couch. She was groggy and didn't realize the television was off. She wondered if she had set the sleep timer. The scariest thing was she heard what she thought was a dog barking but it couldn't have been Bo for it was coming from a distance and had an echo to it. She was careful putting her feet on the floor for she didn't know if Bo was still asleep right below. She slowly put one foot down on the floor then the other as she said, "Bo?" and got no answer as she came more awake she thought the bark sounded like her pooch but it couldn't be. "Bo!" she yelled as she stood up and pressed her talking watch. It was three thirty in the morning. She took a step and banged her shin into the coffee table making her grab it as the pain shot up her leg. She hadn't moved any furniture so why was it right next to the couch?

Klock couldn't remember where her cane was as she was still half asleep. She walked slowly through her apartment calling out to her dog and getting more scared as she got into the kitchen and realized he wasn't there. The barking outside had to be him but how did he get out there? She got to the door and her heart skipped a beat as she felt the door was wide open. She had a sinking feeling that somebody had been in her apartment. She didn't leave the door open. She went out into the hallway and yelled, "Bo! Here, boy!" She could hear galloping of what sounded like a dog running down the apartment hallway hoping it was him. As soon as she felt the furry body and wagging tail, she knew it was Bo. She hurried him inside, shut and locked the door. It was then that she froze. She swore she heard something move in her bedroom. Someone broke into her apartment and they were still inside. Klock walked as quiet as she could into the kitchen and got the largest cutting knife she had in the drawer and held it in front of her body.

She had to remember where she left her cell phone. Klock didn't have a land line to call the police for she could only afford one phone. Her parents, like most older people, still had a phone with a cord in their home. She was more than awake now. Bo wasn't barking but was staying right next to her. It made her feel better. She was now alert enough to remember the cell phone was on her desk, in her bedroom, next to her laptop. She had to make a choice to boldly go in there or go back out of the apartment and seek help from a neighbor. She didn't have a close relationship with anyone in Castlewood Courts and she didn't want everyone talking about the vulnerable blind person, so she made the choice to go into her bedroom and get the cell phone. If the intruder was in there, she'd take them out with her knife or Bo could rip them to shreds. He wasn't a guard dog but even a loveable lab will protect their territory.

"Stay with me, Bo," she whispered. She stuck her hand out with the knife and walked slowly forward. If the person were still in there, Bo would sound the bark alarm. She was thinking it could've been a pair of intruders as Bo had chased somebody out of the apartment and down the hall.

She got into her bedroom and found the cell phone on her desk. She thought she heard a shuffle in the closet so she walked back out with Bo tagging along. She dialed 911, whispering to the Ft. Schuyler Police to get there as quick as possible as she had an intruder in the house.

The five minutes it took the police to get there was the longest in her life as she had retreated to the kitchen. Klock stood with her back to the cupboards holding the knife out. Bo didn't make a sound until, someone who she assumed was the Ft. Schuyler Police, was knocking at her door. She put down the knife as she didn't want to startle them. She opened the door.

"You call the police, Ma'am?" It was a woman's voice.

"Yes, I did. Somebody broke into my apartment and I think they're still here. I heard a sound in my bedroom. It came from the closet. It's that way," replied Klock as she pointed in the direction of her bedroom.

"Stay right here," replied the female officer. Klock heard another voice. It was of a man that she assumed was the woman officer's partner. The floor moved when he walked past her so he must've been huge. She knelt down and put her arm around Bo who had sat next to her.

"Good, dog," she said as she pat his side. He was panting so he must've spent a lot of energy chasing the person down the hall. "You're getting a treat. You're a hero, Bo." She winced as he slobbered her face with his moist sandpaper tongue.

After a few minutes the police officers returned and the female one said, "Nobody in the apartment, Ma'am. Do you have anything missing? Did you get a look at the suspect?"

Klock had her phone and had felt her laptop. She really didn't have anything else of value. Her throat got dry as she went over to the spot on her kitchen table where she had set the envelope of cash from her disability check. The envelope was there but when she picked it up she knew, it was empty. "Oh, no," she said as she reached around for a chair and sat as her knees buckled. Her entire monthly income stolen.

"This envelope contained cash. My monthly check and I just cashed it today. My dog chased somebody out my front door. They left the door wide open. I woke up and Bo was down the hall barking."

"It could be somebody that lives here. Any suspicious people live on this floor? You notice anybody following you today?" asked the female police officer. The male partner was not uttering a word. It was at this point that she thought of her interaction in the laundry room.

"There's a man that's been harassing me. He begged coins off of me in the laundry room but I don't know if he lives in Castlewood Courts. He's talked to me before and said he was following me," said Klock.

"A description would be helpful," said the female police officer.

"I don't know," said Klock holding her head in her shaking hands.

"Well, he came up to you. Basic information. Caucasian, black, height, weight, any visible scars or tattoos," said the female police officer.

"Blind," said Klock under her breath.

"Excuse me?" asked the female police officer.

"I'm not just color blind I'm totally blind."

"Okay," said the female police officer. "Is there anything you can tell us about this man?"

"He stood next to me talking and I had to look up so I'd say he's around six foot. He sounds young so I'd say between twenty and thirty years old. The only other thing is he wears really bad cologne."

"This man wouldn't have given you his name?"

"He called himself Bookcase."

"Okay," said the female police officer. "My name is Cheryl Piazza. I want to take a few moments of your time to write a police report."

"The odds of getting this guy is basically zero," said Klock. "I didn't get a look at who took my money and if he denies it, you have nothing."

"We'll do what we can. In the meantime if this Bookcase bothers you in any way, you call me and I'll personally come over here. Okay?"

"I appreciate that, Officer Piazza," said Klock doing her best to hold it together. She knew if she were to call her parents her mother would go insane with protective rage. It would be best to keep it quiet although she wondered if she'd be thrown out on the street since she hadn't paid her rent yet, let alone purchased her groceries and supplies. She had clean clothes, a jar of peanut butter, a bag of dog food, and a box of green tea. It was going to be a slim month.

Officer Piazza spent another half hour going over the details, writing everything down, and before she left, took Klock by the hand and said, "I'm serious. You call me if you need assistance."

Klock smiled and said, "I will." The exchange boosted her confidence and restored her faith in humanity. In a tough job dealing with scumbags, she'd met another Ft. Schuyler police department Angel besides Dom. She knew that Detective Wilson was the minority. It made her want to be a real cop all the more.

Chapter 13

Klock's cell phone was ringing and she scrambled to pick it up wondering if Bookcase had been arrested but it turned out to be Julia Masters.

"Good morning, Klock."

"Good morning."

"Listen, I'm having a meeting tonight for the Ghost Chasers. It would be a great place for you to come and interview John and Steve."

"Where do you guys meet and what time?"

"The Ft. Schuyler Public Library. They have a small meeting room on the second floor they let us use. Six thirty is when we start," said Julia. "I figure you could meet with each one privately as there's a room next door to where we meet. I checked and there's nothing going on in there at that time."

"Sounds great," said Klock. "I can take the bus over there but it only runs until seven so I'd need a ride home."

"That won't be a problem. Sometimes our meetings go until ten but you take as much time as you like to interview both of them."

"Sounds good, Julia. I'll see you tonight," said Klock as she snapped her cell phone shut. She still had her roll of quarters so bus fare wouldn't be an issue. She wondered if she should call Dom and let him know what happened but she decided against it since she had a great response from the Ft. Schuyler police. She wondered how the intruder thief got in there and decided to ask her father to come over and install a bolt for added protection. She knew her mother would approve the extra security but she would never tell them what happened. There was a knock at Klock's door and Bo jumped up with her shushing him as he was now a little skittish. She went to the door and opened it with no fear. She wasn't going to be a victim in her own apartment.

"Hello, Klock."

She recognized the voice as that of Kathleen Statler, her assigned counselor from the New York State Commission for the Blind.

"Did you have an appointment with me?" asked Klock.

"Yes, I did. I made it a month ago."

"Right, I forgot. Well, come in," said Klock opening the door all the way. "The kitchen table is right over there and watch out for - "

"You got a new guide dog. What's his name?"

"Bo."

Klock was not ready to deal with Kathleen or her superior attitude.

"He's a handsome, fella. You get him from Ft. Schuyler Guide Dogs?"

"The one and only," said Klock smiling as she shut the door.

"I know it was hard on you when you lost Vinny."

"Bo's doing a good job. I'm making tea. You want a cup? All I have is that or water."

"Tea would be great," said Kathleen.

Klock could hear shuffling papers that she assumed was her life story. She'd had to deal with Kathleen her entire existence except Kathleen had always worked with Kasha, her mother, until she was eighteen and an adult. Klock felt that Kathleen and her mother had formed an unholy alliance aimed at dominating her and steering her in the direction they wanted and not necessarily what her heart and mind desired. She knew they both meant well but it was her life to lead.

"A lot of changes for you since I last met with you," said Kathleen. "A new guide dog, your own apartment, and your mother told me you're working on a case?"

"Yes. I'm in the midst of it right now," said Klock as she walked over to the table with the two hot cups of tea, setting them down before she took her seat.

"Anything you can talk about?"

"You know that confidentiality is huge in what you do as well as in what I do."

"I understand. I'm glad that you're putting your private investigator license to work."

"I know you didn't want to sponsor me for that so I appreciate you backing me up now," said Klock as she picked up her cup and took a sip of her tea.

"It wasn't that I didn't support you, I just wanted you to go into an area where I thought you could get a job."

"Well, here I am, working on a case. Besides, your idea of a real job is the workshop."

"I heard you met with them the other day. They have openings if you wish to work there."

Klock looked towards Kathleen and raised her eyebrow. "You'll have to stop lobbying me on that. I'm thinking about it. I might need some additional money. I'd only agree to work part time. If I got desperate. Which I'm not. I don't want you sharing any of this with my mother. I know she calls you all the time."

"I take my confidentiality as seriously as you do, Klock. The ball is in your court if you want to go to work in the industry program at the blind association. I know they have opening and are flexible with their schedules."

"No offense but I doubt I'll call them. I still want to work as a police officer, or on the force, somehow."

"This has been a dream of yours since you were a little girl. If you want to go to school or a police academy, the commission might be willing to sponsor you."

"I got to meet the Ft. Schuyler Chief of Police," said Klock all proud.

"Is that right?"

"Yup. We talked cop stuff. Stuff you wouldn't know about."

"How exciting. Other than that, you need anything?"

"Nope. I'm good."

Klock could hear the shuffling of the papers that let her know Kathleen was moving along just the way she wanted it.

"I'll get back to you in a few months to make a future appointment. Think about what we talked about and let me know if you get serious about school or additional training. I'm pleased that we helped you get your private investigative license and it's starting to pay off."

"You bet. Don't worry, when I'm a cop, I won't bother you too much unless you do something you shouldn't then I'd be forced to tazer your ass," said Klock cracking herself up.

"I'm sure that would break your heart to have to do that to me," said Kathleen with a joking tone.

"All in the line of duty, Kathleen," said Klock. "Say goodbye to the lady, Bo."

* * *

As Klock rode the city bus to the Ft. Schuyler Public Library, she was surprised she hadn't heard from Dom all day, although, since he was suspended from work, he probably didn't hear about her robbery. She didn't want to bother him and she had nothing new to chat with him about the case. She thought about the questions she'd be asking the Ghost Chasers. She was done with the Braille files of Detective Wilson that read about as compelling as microwave instructions penned by a Chinese manufacturing corporate product guide writer.

She wondered exactly what the Ghost Chasers had to meet about? She was kind of curious about this entire ghost hunting culture that was sweeping the nation and she was certainly part of it, but she wondered how much of what was on television was real? She'd watched Cora Masters' show for years and always wondered what was left out or if things were faked or made better than they were to fool the viewers. She would find out soon enough as the bus driver announced the stop at the library. She and Bo were actually able to sit in the front seat of the bus making her guess there were no other passengers. They didn't get up and move until the bus was at a complete stop since she didn't want to fall over if there were one last vehicle jostle as it went "whump, whump."

She hadn't been to the library in many years and not since she went completely blind. Printed books no longer worked for her. Thank goodness she had audio books and Braille, otherwise she'd be cut off from her love of reading and research. She remembered the Ft. Schuyler Public Library as being a huge old brick building that had these large columns out front and concrete lions. It looked to her like it had been built at the same time George Washington was carving his wooden teeth in Ben Franklin's wood shop. Much of Ft. Schuyler was old. When in high school she'd done a report on the history of the area and had discovered settlers had come around a good hundred years before the revolutionary war.

She walked into the library and she struggled getting past the heavy front door. It was supposed to have a handicap button to press that would open it automatically yet after feeling around, and not finding it, guessed that a person who could see installed it. Probably the same goof that put Braille on the drive thru teller at the bank. She had to stop at the desk and ask the clerk how to get to the room where the meeting was taking place and had to take the stairs. The elevator was on the fritz. She didn't mind but it made her wonder how people in wheelchairs got up there.

Klock could hear the chatter of people as she walked into the room and got, "there she is," from Julia.

"Hello," said Klock to whomever was in the room.

"The room is right over here where you'll be interviewing John and Steve, Klock. Then when you're finished, you're welcome to come back in here for the remainder of our meeting," said Julia.

"Sounds good," please take my elbow and lead Bo and me in there."

It took a few minutes for Klock to get situated. She took off her winter gear, got Bo under the table, and set up her digital recorder. "Who's coming first, Julia?"

"I'll have Steve Eddy come in first. He's our do it all guy. My mother always called him her pack mule."

"Great," said Klock. She listened to Cora Masters' television show Paranormal Happenings and she would get a smidgen of the true Cora as she'd yell at them, as if Cora drank a dozen ten hour energy drinks. Klock was anxious to hear what the pack mule had to say.

"Klock, this here's Steve Eddy," said Julia as she made the introduction.

"Nice to meet you," said Klock. She held out her hand that was grabbed and shaken back. The handshake was weak and the man's hand was small. She never met somebody with two first names as their entire name. At least his parents didn't name him Eddy Eddy.

"Yup," said Steve.

"You mind if I record the interview?" asked Klock.

"Uhhh, I guess," replied Steve.

"Julia?" asked Klock.

"Yes."

"I'd like to interview both of them alone so I need you to leave this room and please shut the door. Steve can send John in when we're finished."

"Sure, fine," replied Julia as Klock could hear her footsteps on the hardwood floors and didn't say another word until she heard the door click shut.

"Is she gone?" Klock asked in a whisper.

"Yes," replied Steve. "I don't want our discussion to be recorded and I know John won't want to."

"Not a problem," said Klock as she shut off and put the recorder in the pocket of her winter jacket. She took out a pig ear and handed it to Bo so he could gnaw away while she conducted business. "Thanks for agreeing to speak to me."

"Like I had a choice."

"You were forced to meet with me?"

"Sure was. If both of us didn't, we'd be thrown out of the group," said Steve.

"Really? Is she that bad?"

"Who? Hitler Junior?"

"That's kind of harsh don't you think?"

"That's kind in my opinion. Or is this the pack mule speaking out of turn?"

"I'm guessing the stuff I read on the message boards and blogs about Cora Masters was correct?" asked Klock.

"You bet. She was a vicious, nasty person who only cared for the limelight and glory and could care less about the places we trampled on or the spirits we were interacting with."

"If she was so bad, why did you stay with the group?"

"We were considered at the top of the game. We were in books and on a television show. She was a powerful woman and I didn't want to commit career suicide so I just did what she asked. She treated me like I was a slave," said Steve as he started to tap the table with his fingers. "So why are you questioning me?"

"I was just curious about the death of Cora Masters."

"You're not a cop. I never saw a blind one before."

"I'm not a police officer. I'm a private investigator." Klock paused, took out her badge, and placed it on the table. "Did you see Cora fall from the window?"

"No, but I wish I had."

"You had that bad of feelings for her?"

"Listen, I never thought she was the type to commit suicide but maybe it was all the bad Karma and dark energy she messed with that came back to poison her mind."

"Dark energy?"

"Yeah," said Steve. "We're not demonologists but she would push the edge, challenge the spirits with her ridiculous antics. You don't ask dark spirits to come and appear then expect them to behave."

"You mean like the time on that investigation where she lay in the casket with that corpse?"

"So, you're a fan. I would never have guessed. That stunt was wrong and full of blasphemy. But it's cool; she had to film it for the stupid television show."

"You're a contradiction, Steve," said Klock. "You call Cora a demon her yet you stayed on board and reaped the benefits of fame, even after she fried you like an ant in the sun under her magnifying glass. What makes you any better than her?"

"It doesn't. I'm damned just like Cora was and now the evil seed has taken over the group and its worse than before."

"Julia seems so nice," said Klock.

"Really? You don't think she's playing you in some way? You better watch yourself. She's not up front like her mother with the viciousness but clever as a calico cat in the shadows."

"Is there anything you can tell me from that night?"

"Not really. Things were picking up as far as the paranormal activity when she died. When she her body slapped the ground, the paranormal energy went flat."

"What kind of paranormal activity did you experience?"

"We had shadow figures, sounds all over the place, our K2 meters were pegging all over the place. I'd never experienced anything that active. It was odd though that as soon as she died, so did the ghosts. It was as if the spirits knew the nasty branch had been pruned and were free or, in my opinion, glad the queen of darkness joined their evil clubhouse."

"Thank you for talking with me, Steve. I truly appreciate it."

"Please don't tell Julia what I told you. I love ghost hunting and she'll throw me out."

"Don't worry, I'll keep this conversation private." She stood up. Klock stuck out her hand. Steve grasped with a cold, limp, grip. "Please send in John."

"He's not going to talk but he's got something weird to talk about."

"I live for weird," replied Klock. Finally, she felt, the case was getting very interesting.

"Hee haw!" brayed Steve. "Time for the pack mule to get his car-

rot."
   Klock snickered under her breath.

Chapter 14

Klock just sat there for a minute since John wouldn't do anything but grunt at her questions. He was a tight lip all right but she knew that Julia had forced him into the room with her. She would have to adapt her approach or she'd get nothing. Steve's voice and grip made her guess he was not much older than her but this John seemed much more mature, strong and stubborn as a donkey's butt in a babbling summer creek.

"Listen, John. You don't want me to tell Julia that you were uncooperative with my questions. You answer me to the point and this will be over quicker than your mother pulling the band aid off your knee, otherwise, we'll be here all night long. We'll close this place and you'll lose your spot on the Ghost Chasers. Capisce?" She had stolen Dom's closing remark.

"Fine," replied John with a humph of gruff.

"Tell me what your role is in the group."

"I'm the techie."

"What does that entail? I don't recall hearing you mentioned much on the television show."

"I run all the static night vision video cameras, hand held video cameras, the K2 meters, the spirit box, handheld digital recorders and all the wiring and monitors. I follow up evidence and do all the reviews and tagging."

"I know that a K2 measures the electromagnetic spikes but do you really think that's an indicator of ghosts?"

"Sure. We normally do a sweep before we have the cameras roll and the official investigation begins. Steve and I usually go through an entire location writing down every place we get spikes. We can get them from televisions, refrigerators, electrical panels. I especially like old deserted places that have the power shut off. We mark these locations so when we get a spike on the meter during the investigation, at an untagged spot, we consider that an entity is present," said John as his voice became excited.

"I never heard of a spirit box," said Klock.

"It's a relatively new piece of equipment. It's a little box with an antenna that searches radio frequencies at a fast rate and plucks spiritual words and phrases from a different frequency we cannot hear with our mortal ears. It then takes those words and broadcasts them. We've had some great communication with the dead using the spirit box although trying to do an EVP session while this is going on is frustrating."

"I know that when you're doing an electronic voice phenomenon or EVP session you need it as quiet as possible or the evidence is considered spoiled. Then you have to debunk anything recorded," said Klock.

"I see you know your ghost hunting."

"From my reading and listening to the shows on TV, I know that no matter what new technology you come out with, the EVP recordings tend to be the best evidence of interaction with paranormal entities."

"Correct. Ghosts can be chatty, especially when they don't want you around. That old cliché of a spirit growling "get out" is really true."

"I could talk tech all night long as it fascinates me. As a blind woman I rely on a lot of technology."

"You use speech software?" asked John.

"Of course," said Klock. She had him talking all right as she talked about stuff that interested John. It was a trick she had read about from the detective for dummies book she'd listened to. "I use JAWS."

"I've heard of it. How accessible is it in the Internet?"

"It used to be horrible but it's getting much better. There are still many websites that JAWS cannot read so I don't get the full use of the Internet that others get but the playing field is getting close to level.

At least Facebook works OK. Did you see anything on the night Cora Masters died?"

"I saw things all night," said John.

"I mean suspicious or relating to her death."

"I was in the control room with my gear all night. That's why you never really see me on the television show. I'm hunkered down watching everything at home base."

"Where was the control room located?" asked Klock.

"In the kitchen on the first floor."

"That was ghost central?"

"Yes. The way we do it is we split up into two teams and one at a time goes out into the designated locations while the other half will hang out with me and watch the monitors from the cameras."

"Now, from what I heard on your television show, you usually run four cameras?"

"We actually have five video cameras. I hard wire four into the monitor and a computer hard drive so we can record the entire investigation. The fifth is a hand held one we can walk around with but the Overlook Mansion was massive. It has three floors and the turret. We heard the turret had massive activity so Cora decided to place the hand held up there but we only get two hours of footage before it goes dead where the others are plugged into a power source," explained John.

Klock was thrilled at how much the techie was talking once she used verbal force to break the seal. "Was it too far to wire up to the turret?"

"Yeah."

"Did you ever get a chance to go over the footage and the digital recordings?"

"Well, yes, once the cops got done with the stuff."

"Did you see Velvet come down before or after Cora's death?"

"Before."

"How long before?"

"A few minutes. Five maybe."

"Did you see or hear anything suspicious in regards to Cora's Death?"

"Nope. It takes long hours of sitting in a chair watching every second of every video camera and days listening to all the digital recordings. People think ghost hunting is all fun but never realize all the hard work that goes into it. You have to be focused or the split second you get lazy, you'll miss a great piece of paranormal evidence. So you can be rest assured that I spent weeks going over every second of all the recordings."

"Not even in the turret where Cora was?" asked Klock.

"No. The hand held camera had died hours before she jumped. She had a hand held digital recorder that I bet had something good on it but we'll never know."

"I know. I read the case file and it said that she had landed on one and smashed it. The police were unable to recover anything from it."

"Julia said she never got it back but at least we got the rest of the gear. That place was huge and fully loaded with paranormal activity."

"Were the owners hanging around the place?"

"Yes. The Van Dreasons stayed in the parlor all night. They promised to be quiet and they stayed out of our way. We prefer the owners vacate the premises but they insisted on staying. They live there alone so it worked out okay."

"So how did Cora's son Don behave?"

"He's a horrible person. Standing back, making fun of us, making nasty comments, constantly smoking. He was the only person that turned the Iron Lady Cora into a weak kneed girl. If it wasn't for her annual crusade, he wouldn't be there. She was convinced she was going to contact her dead son and she wanted her family there."

"So, I'm guessing Cora Masters was not very friendly with you," said Klock.

"Look at this," said John.

"Blind."

"I'm sorry. I thought you could see. You're looking right at me."

"Blackness is all I see now, John. What are you pointing at?"

"I have a small scar on my cheek. Cora slapped me across the face when one time on an investigation when a camera malfunctioned."

"She assaulted you and you didn't have her arrested?"

"She wore this gaudy ring with a big blue jewel so when she backhanded me, she cut me. Guess who is wearing the ring now?"

"Can't be Julia."

"None other. Taking her mother's nasty place as our leader. She's a chip off the old ice block. With her mother it was Iron Law of the Oligarchy and Julia has stepped into that role quite nicely."

Klock thought Julia had not received anything from her mother's estate. She'd have to remember to ask her how she came to own the ring. "So why didn't you call the police?"

"I didn't call the cops because I was afraid I'd never get the money she owed me. I could deal with the viciousness but she never paid any of us. She was getting money from the television show, the merchandise, charging for all sorts of things but she just held that over our heads."

"So how much did you find that night? Steve said there was a ton of ghost activity."

"That place is the most haunted location we've ever been in. It was an honor to be the first ever ghost hunters let in there. Now I know why it lives up to its reputation," said John.

"Anything unusual?"

"Well, yes, come to think of it. I picked up an EVP from down on the second floor that I swear was a conversation taking place when Cora was up in the turret alone. As if the spirits were communicating with her. We all think it was Joey's spirit coming back to talk with his mother."

"How do you know someone didn't go up there and speak to her? You said the camera up there had died and you don't have anything on the digital recorder she smashed in her fall. Someone could've gone up there. What about one of the team that was doing their session?"

"Impossible. I had one camera on the second floor pointed right at the door that leads up to the turret and I have Cora going up in there with Velvet but Velvet came back down before the EVP. Cora was alone. Everyone else was accounted for. It can only be pegged as interaction with the other side. Velvet was right. That turret was a portal to the kingdom of the dead."

"So you don't think Cora was pushed or accidentally fell?"

"My theory is she channeled her son and jumped to end her life to be with him in the spiritual dimension. I can't sharpen the audio of the EVP but it was another muffled distinctive voice. You can hear two voices. It's almost as if it were a heated discussion or argument. Perhaps the mother scolding her spirit son. One was Cora and the other has to be Joey."

"Would you happen to have that EVP here?"

"Sure do. I have it on my laptop in the other room along with the other evidence from the Overlook Mansion. It's just a shame we cannot reveal any of it."

"I can understand why the television show wouldn't show the footage," said Klock.

"It's not Julia. She wants to broadcast what happened and what we have but it's the Van Dreason's. The owners of the Overlook Mansion don't want us showing anything. Julia wants to do a follow up but they've shut down and won't talk to anybody. They never signed a release."

"Let's go out to the meeting. I'd love to hear that EVP," said Klock.

Klock sat with the headphones on as John kept replaying the muffled sounds of his supposed freaky EVP but all she could make out was a bunch of muffled sounds that could be interpreted as two people talking, debating or perhaps arguing but the sounds made her think of her television if she left the volume on low and was in the bathroom with the door shut. She couldn't make out words or anything specific yet the Ghost Chasers were going off the wall about what terrific evidence it was. Klock just smiled and nodded her head as if in agreement.

She took the headphones off and said to the group, "Very impressive."

She sat and listened to Julia run the meeting as they were discussing their first investigation that they would have since Cora Masters death. Julia was going to have the film crew there from Paranormal Happenings. Klock didn't understand why the other members felt she was like her mother for she didn't hear anything that would be deemed as mean and vicious coming from Julia.

The group spent the next hour discussing where they were going to conduct their next investigation, at the old abandoned Psych Center over on the west side of the city. They were going into the wing where the most insane patients had been housed and talked about everything from the Utica Crib that was utilized on the worst of the mentally insane to the chains on the walls in the rubber room.

The only member not at the meeting was Velvet Blue who would be on the investigation but never came to the meetings. Julia stated the psychic wanted to walk into the investigation cold so as not to spoil her visions. Julia said she would not have any new members come on board as they had everything they needed with the small group but did throw a curve at Klock when she asked, "Would you like to come along on the investigation, Klock?"

"Sure, I would," she replied. She was a little bit stunned about the invite but excited. She'd been a fan of spiritual investigations but never believed in ghosts. That seemed kind of odd in her mind but it was more of a curiosity in the unknown.

"That would be great. I can pick you up unless you want to take the bus. We're meeting at the psych center at 6pm this Saturday. I'd have to pick you up around 5:30 but I'll have to come meet with you one on one in the next few days," said Julia.

"Meet with me on what?" asked Klock.

"I need to go over the protocols of ghost hunting with you. You're not certified."

"Certified in what?"

"All of us are certified ghost hunters."

"There's a license you need for this?"

"We all took Dr. Herringshaw's course and are certified ghost hunters with the Worldwide Ghost Hunting Society," said Julia.

"Dr. Ghost?"

"Dr. Hans Herringshaw has been doing this for sixty years and is a pioneer in the field of paranormal investigation. His comprehensive course is respected throughout the ghost hunting world. I know we're the only ones in Ft. Schuyler certified. These other ghost groups are just winging it with no certification."

"Okay," said Klock trying not to laugh since Julia was her client. She didn't want to offend but it seemed rather silly to her. She would play along. "I have nothing planned all week. How long will this take?"

"One evening. I'll call you one night this week and come over to your place if that's okay?"

"That'll be fine, Julia," she replied knowing she'd be on the Internet when she got home looking up this Dr. Herringshaw. She was curious what this man had his doctorate in and what this certification was all about.

Klock sat in silence for the rest of the meeting wondering how this ghost hunt was going to go without Cora. Julia sparked a debate on the proper use of the equipment and threw a blunt verbal jab at Steve and John. Klock couldn't imagine any criminal investigator having any more of a bizarre case than the one she was having and this being her first case. At least she wasn't bored. She knew more exciting things were to come and perhaps she'd parlay this into a career as a ghost detective.

Chapter 15

Klock was home for a matter of minutes when her cell phone went off and she answered to Dom.

"You, okay over there?"

"I'm fine. I guess you found out about me getting robbed."

"I doubt we'll solve it, Klock. I know that you know the statistics on capture of petty theft."

"Yeah. I know. Even if you catch Bookcase I can't verify anything unless he confesses, which he won't"

"Don't worry. I'll find out who this scumbag is and we'll run him through the system. I'd bet a dollar that he has priors or might have outstanding warrants. If not, he'll stumble eventually and we'll get him."

"My father always says, "be patient and they'll deliver themselves to you,"" said Klock. "It's police business and I've studied it well."

"You need anything to get by?"

"No, I'm good," said Klock not wanting to take a handout from anybody. She'd already made the gut wrenching decision to go to the food bank in the morning and see what they could throw her way. She'd have to worry about the rent and other bills later on. She could always try to talk her way into extensions. She'd hate to do it but the last resort would be to play off on her blindness as a sympathetic move. It made her want to vomit in her mouth at the thought, but anything would be better than giving into defeat. If that were the case, she'd take the factory job working alongside other blind and disabled people and live with her mother for all eternity. Klock could picture it. They'd sit in the comfy living room chairs, eating warm chocolate chip cookies off tin metal dinner trays while watching Wheel of Fortune on the television.

"You, Okay? You're awfully quiet."

"I'm sorry, Dom. I got a lot on my mind with the case."

"By the way, I heard through my friend in the pistol permit office that you got your approval."

"How did that happen so fast?"

"He owes me a few favors. You should have it in your mail."

"I have to get somebody to read my mail for me since it doesn't come in Braille."

"You want to go shopping for a handgun?"

"I don't have the money." Klock was ashamed.

"I have over a dozen handguns. I'll have one of mine transferred over to you."

"You can do that?"

"Sure. I was thinking a revolver would be better for you. They're easier to handle and don't jam. I got a .38 special that's perfect. It's got a snub nose so you can tuck it in your belt real easy. It's not much more of a kick than the .22 you shot."

"I just don't know if this is a good idea, Dom. Should a blind girl own a handgun?"

"Sure. When I get a chance, I'll drop it off with some ammo and I'll go over the loading and operation. We'll get to the range when we have a chance. Besides, you'll need it in case Bookcase comes back."

"Ok." Klock wondered if she could indeed shoot to kill. A human being wasn't a paper target.

"Back to your case. How is that going?"

"You'll never guess where I just came from."

"I'd hate to guess knowing you," replied Dom with a chuckle.

"The meeting of the Ghost Chasers over at the library."

"Really. So the daughter took over the group?"

"Yeah. I was able to interview both of the other members that were there the night that Cora Masters died. I think both could be suspects if she was indeed murdered but I don't know, Dom. The tech guy said he has video proof that nobody went up those stairs so Masters was all alone up there."

"If that were true then your case would be either proving it was an accident or Detective Wilson concluded it correctly that it was a suicide."

"Wilson had the video evidence but I don't think he even looked at any of it, or listened to any of the digital recordings. He makes zero mention of it in his report," said Klock.

"That's not hard to believe. He's a real lazy turd with his investigations. It's not like he gets a performance bonus for extra work, Klock. Could the tech guy be lying?"

"It's a possibility because he's the one that gleans all the stuff for evidence then brings it out at the meetings. Cora Masters, Julia, or their other investigator never go through the raw evidence. They sit and debunk or accept whatever the tech guy brings to the meetings. He's the mad scientist that sits in his lab and goes over the mounds of recordings. You're talking over forty hours of video camera footage as well as that much from three separate hand held digital recorders."

"Interesting."

"Not only that, Dom, but the younger guy in the group, Cora always called him "pack mule" and his hate towards her is something else."

"So I guess these guys didn't have Stockholm syndrome."

"What's that?"

"It's common, Klock. It's where a hostage falls in love with their captor."

"Oh, I see. So everything is not completely cut and dry with this case. I still need to interview the Van Dreasons. They're the owners of the Overlook Mansion but I hear they're uncooperative so I have to think about how I'm going to approach them."

"I have a huge caseload waiting for me when I get back but I can still pitch in if you need help with anything but it looks like you got this one pretty well handled."

"I know, Dom. I don't have a firm suspect yet. Even Julia could be one with the way her mother treated her over the death of her little brother. Hey, I got another one for you."

"Here we go."

"Julia invited me to go with them on their ghost hunt this Saturday night."

"Classic. Where?"

"The old Ft. Schuyler Psych Center."

"They got permission to get in there? Number one, it's condemned. Second, the meth addicts all hang around the grounds. When I was on patrol I was constantly going over there for fights, drug busts, prostitution, along with the occasional dead body under the scraggly bushes of the grounds. I thought the state owned that place. How did they get permission?"

"Old fashioned graft," replied Klock. "Julia is now her mother. Cora Masters paid her way into a lot of things including throwing some cash to the Van Dreasons. I'm sure there's a crooked state employee somewhere with bribe money in their pocket."

"The place is dangerous but I know you're tough. You can handle it. Just watch out ghost buster."

"I don't believe in ghosts."

"No?"

"I'm fascinated by the possibility, but until something happens to me personally, I don't believe in them."

"That's you all right. You going to take Bo with you?"

"I want to. I guess I should ask Julia. Here's the next kicker."

"It gets better and better with you."

"Julia is coming over here tomorrow night to give me a course in proper ghost hunting. She's certified from Dr. Ghost and I need to be brainwashed in the proper ways."

"Can I come hang out while you do this? I would love to listen to what Julia has to say."

"Sure, I'll let you know what time but be ready to leave if she gets funny. You might be hearing stuff meant for only those that are part of the secret society."

"Sweet. I'm looking forward to that. I'll bring donuts."

"Is that part of the contract for cops?" she asked snickering.

"That joke is so old. But, yeah, cops love donuts. Listen, back to this Bookcase character."

"What about him?"

"Maybe you need that .38 right now. I can have it put on your permit tomorrow."

"I'm ok for now. Besides, I'd rather outwit than use a gun. My brain has always been my greatest weapon."

"You are sharp, but I'm thinking for personal protection as well as your career. You're going to get more cases and they could get dangerous."

"I'd rather be a Sherlock Holmes than a Dirty Harry."

"I love Sherlock Holmes but in our line of work being a Dirty Harry could be a necessity. It's what all cops dream of, carrying a hand cannon and taking down scum with no consequences."

"They're great for old movies."

"I'll stop by with the gun and I'll take care of the paperwork for you. You'll just need to sign a few things. You're taking the .38 so don't argue with me."

"Ok, ok."

"I never did ask you what your favorite male character was."

"Excuse me?"

"Cosplay. You mentioned it before and I've been wondering. What character you would want me to dress as?"

"Actually, I love Superman."

"Really? You ever go to the Comic Con in costume?"

"No. I've never gone to one. I always wanted to but my mother refused to take me. I could've taken the bus but I didn't want to go alone."

"Next time I'm taking you, Klock."

"That sounds awesome. Well, I'm tired and I have to feed Bo. I'll call you about tomorrow night."

"It's a date," says Dom as he hangs up.

Klock shuts her phone and holds it. She'd never had meaningful conversation with any man other than her father let alone a handsome investigator. She didn't go to her junior prom out of shame of her blindness and boys really didn't show anything but curiosity towards her. She knew she was in love with Dom but she knew she couldn't tell him. She didn't want to lose the only human friend and peer she had. She figured he must have a girlfriend although he never talked about anyone in his life. Come to think of it, he was as much about business as she was. They hadn't even talked about anything other than police work but somehow she felt for him in ways she'd never felt for another man. She had to keep the feelings of love relegated. She had too much to do on the case. Klock was on public assistance, lived in subsidized housing with the sorriest people in the city, was totally blind, yet she felt she was the luckiest girl on the planet. She was having fun. Life was good.

* * *

Klock was not happy about the weather in the Mohawk Valley as the February temperatures plummeted to below zero. She and Bo had to walk three blocks to the community food bank. She had nothing left to eat and her stomach was growling so bad that she was afraid somebody would hear the grumble. She had a few plastic bags in her hands and hoped they had something she could take back. Her nose felt the coldest as she was bundled everywhere else but she worried more for Bo. She had in her closet a pair of dog mittens that Vinny used to wear but Bo, being the stubborn pooch, refused to let her put them on. She'd get one mitten on one paw and while she was working on another paw, he'd rip the other one off making her give up the entire affair, but now she worried about his paws freezing from the block ice subzero sidewalks.

Klock had to ask a couple of people where the food bank was. She hated asking for directions. One nice older lady walked with her and opened the door to the place where people like Klock leave their dignity at the door. She thought there would be some goody two shoes lady overlord with her trust fund and Ivy League education in there helping the poor and downtrodden, talking all about their vacation in the Bahamas while doing volunteer work to assist the lepers of Ft. Schuyler.

She walked in and the smell was something she couldn't pinpoint. To be exact it was a combination of sewer gas, dollar store perfume, wet cardboard, and rotten tomatoes.

"Can I help you?" came a question from a woman that sounded older than Klock imagined.

"I need some food. All the money I have was stolen and I'm stuck for a month."

"How many members of your family?"

"Just Bo here and myself," said Klock looking towards the woman with a frown. Her insides were dying.

"I can help you. Do you have any food allergies?"

"No. I love peanut butter the most but I'll take whatever you have. I'm not a picky eater."

"Well, you can browse around and pick out whatever you'd like. We have boxes and bags that you can use right over there."

"Blind," said Klock waving her hand in front of her own face.

"I'm sorry, sweetie. Let me help you."

"Thank you," said Klock feeling as humbled as a person ever could be. At least the woman was nice, not like what she thought she was going to encounter. The only thing that would be worse would be running into Bookcase or Detective Wilson. She was hungry and it wasn't like she had a ton of flesh on her bones to live off of. Her mother always told her to eat more as she was too thin but Klock only ate what she could. She didn't chow down just to fill her belly. Now, she wished she had stored a little fat like a grizzly bear on the fringe of hibernation. The nice woman told her what she was putting in her bag and Klock would feel each one so she could remember what was what by its shape. Canned goods were impossible so she'd always have to open them and smell the contents. Sometimes it worked and other times she opened canned peaches when she had wanted to open a can of crushed tomatoes.

Klock was able to get a couple jars of peanut butter, bread and some Ramen noodles. She placed everything in the two plastic bags and was struggling with holding Bo's leash. The food bounced around then the plastic bags burst open and everything fell on the floor before she got out of the door of the community food bank. The lady that had helped her came running over apologizing and overflowing with sympathy. She might as well have stuck a dagger in her gut but at least the woman gave Klock an old backpack that they put all the food in. She was able to don it and still have the ability to move with Bo. The woman told Klock she could come back every week if she wanted.

Klock never cried but walking back to the apartment in the artic weather was enough to make her shed eye water but more out of pain than sadness. She didn't feel like a worthy human being, with the hand me down foodstuffs. It had to do, after all, she figured some of the clients were drug addicts and criminals that couldn't get jobs. She was appreciative for the charity that would end once she got her career going and earnings up. She swore she'd never forget the kindness of those who assist the poor and downtrodden. The desperation made her fearless. She knew she would achieve her goals, she was worthwhile, and she would succeed. She would not be afraid of failure. She was already at the bottom and surviving just fine. She smiled thinking about Julia coming over that night with her ghost diploma, teaching her the correct way to conduct paranormal research. She might have been blind but at least she was open minded and willing to learn, even if ghosts didn't exist.

When they got back to the apartment, they were both so cold, all the way down to their bones, that Klock had to brew the hottest tea. She had Bo snuggle next to her on the couch and she covered herself and him with a blanket. She was shivering, but at least she had food to eat and heat in her apartment. She pressed her talking watch and had enough time to take a power nap before Julia and Dom arrived. She leaned to the side and put her head down on the cushioned arm of the couch and drifted off to the place where her sighted memories would return in vivid colors. In her dreams she was no different than everyone else; she could see.

Chapter 16

Klock had to take a long hot shower to wake her body up and shake off the groggy fog that enveloped her post nap. She had peanut butter toast and another cup of tea. She had to reuse the same teabag for the fifth time thus making each cup a little less potent and flavorful. She'd have to make the handful of bags last the rest of the month and she was a dragon without her tea.

She brushed her hair and wondered if it were getting too long to be a private investigator. Perhaps she might ask her mother to cut it to her shoulders so she could look more like a professional woman and not so much like a eighteen year old especially since most people thought she looked twelve.

She expected Dom to arrive before Julia so she could explain the game plan and for him not to be offended if she had to ask him to leave. She also wanted to let him know this was her investigation and to let her take the lead. Not that he was anything but a gentleman but she needed to hold the reins and not relinquish them.

* * *

Dom and Klock were sitting at her kitchen table talking about everything but the case. He asked if she was going to wear her Supergirl outfit for the ghost investigation. The thought of that scenario made her chuckle. She wondered if her parents got along this well when they dated in the days before they married and had their little Rachel. She knew her parents were in love with each other and had been married a long time but the way her mother hen pecked her father seemed unfair. It wasn't what Klock thought a romantic marriage should be. Then again, she wasn't a love doctor.

The knock came on the door and Bo barked, and Klock calmed him down. Ever since the break-in he had become more sensitive and protective, which was fine with her. She rewarded his signaling with a crunchy dog biscuit. Dom offered to get it but Klock was already up and moving to the door. She opened it and said, "Hello."

"Good evening, Klock," said Julia. "Are you ready to learn?"

"Yes. Come in, Julia." Klock stepped back and let her come in then shut and locked the door. "This here is my friend Dom. Is it OK if he stays while we go over this?"

"I don't mind, Klock. It's not like you can't Google this and get it on the Internet but it's always better coming from a certified paranormal investigator rather than some anonymous hack. Nice to meet you, Dom."

"Don't worry," replied Dom. "I'll hang back and won't say a word or interrupt. I'm a big fan of this stuff and thought I could learn."

"We do public education all the time. My mother did a lot of speaking engagements at libraries, historical societies, and conventions all over the United States. I'd like to continue this practice, so the more the merrier."

"You want anything to drink before we get started?" asked Klock.

"I brought my own bottle of water so I'm good."

Klock got to her seat and could hear Bo itching himself but she didn't worry about fleas since she put the monthly flea drops on his back. They were pricey but mandatory since she didn't want her pooch to suffer with flea and tick bites. It was a sacrifice on her fixed income but she had to care for her dog. Not that there was a huge problem of that in the city but Bo could get them from migrant animals, both the four and two legged kind.

"Before you go on this investigation, Klock, I want to be sure you understand the complete standards and protocols of ghost hunting along with some of the basic terminology," said Julia.

"I did do some research on the Internet and read some of what you're talking about."

"Well, it's not the same as getting it first hand from a person who is graduated from Dr. Herringshaw's course. The first items I want to cover is how to act on an investigation. First off you want to remain professional. No screaming, shouting in fear or running for your life from the building. Even when faced with dangerous entities we act with proper ghost hunting decorum. Dark energies feed on the weak, attach themselves to the vulnerable."

"What about a blind person?" asked Klock.

"To be more specific, a mentally vulnerable person." Julia continued. "We don't want to act like the buffoons on that other television show that challenge the spirits into aggression. This is an art form not professional wrestling."

Klock heard a soft chuckle by Dom but he quickly disguised it as a cough. She missed the joy of watching facial reactions so she had to imagine what mortified or nasty look Julia might have at that point.

"I hear what you're saying," replied Klock keeping her cool, looking attentively in the direction of Julia's voice.

"What these people are doing for drama and ratings is a farce. You want gentle interactions with the spirits. My mother always said it was a spiritual ball room dance. We want natural evidence. Anyhow, you want to only talk when we are doing an EVP session and in a clear tone. Whispering is not good as it makes it hard for the tech person to glean evidence of ghost speech."

"Makes sense to me," says Klock.

"Well, most people don't have the right stuff for ghost hunting," replied Julia. "Another biggie is an over reliance on technological gadgetry. Other ghost hunting teams have all these weird devices invented by engineering wizards that overcomplicate the hunt. Hand held digital recorders, night vision video cameras, digital picture cameras and K2 meters are all you need. We've been doing this a long time, my mother had hunted the spirits for decades and had compiled more paranormal evidence than anybody on the planet and we never needed to add anything new."

"What about the spirit box?" asked Klock.

"Ok, I'll make one change to that. My mother took a lot of convincing by John to try it out and it worked marvelously. Other than that, you need nothing else. You also do not want anyone smoking, since photographs that have great ectoplasm will be dismissed because cigarette smoke can cause a similar effect. Also, orbs have to be reviewed very carefully."

"Orbs?" asked Klock. "I never heard you guys talk about that on your television show."

"That's because they're very common and show up in many pictures. Pull out old photos even from decades ago and you'll be surprised the amount of orbs you see. They're round balls of light that most of the time are from dust, water or snowflakes reflecting the flash of the camera."

"I won't be able to do that with me being blind and all."

"I'm sure Dom could look them over for you and verify what I'm telling you. Right, Dom?"

"Sure," he replied. "Be happy to."

"Anyhow. We never mention these on the television because the real ones are rare and we don't want people to think they have evidence when it's nothing."

"If they're all the same then how do you know that the fake from the real orbs?" Klock was curious about the answer.

"There's a distinctive difference and part of the certification is being instructed in this paranormal fingerprinting or entity stamping as we call it. Paranormal orbs are jagged in appearance or will be in a geometric shape. For instance, from the Overlook Mansion investigation we have a six sided orb that has a thick darker border around it. It's huge. Well over six feet across when scaled to the background. This happened in a room that was not being walked in. Even in a new, well maintained home, walking kicks up dust that produces false orbs in photographs."

Klock just nodded her head. Julia was on a roll.

"You want to ask the spirits for their permission to take their picture. You want to have a positive mental attitude to keep the dark spirits away."

"I do know that ghost hunters think dark energies can be a bad thing but you feel negative people can attract them?" asked Klock.

"Sure, they do. You want to steer clear of that as demons can lurk and leech. We once ran into this in an old abandoned insane asylum in Westchester County. One clung to my mother's back. She had to run from the building. It was a scary experience that people need to avoid so I need you positive in mind and spirit come this Saturday."

"That's not a problem at all. With my condition I have to remain upbeat," replied Klock.

"This is critically important. In respect to a proper investigation it's important to be open minded and unburdened. Friendly ghosts will tend to avoid a negative minded person much like a child or an animal will. They have otherworldly senses that bring them forth or repel. Also, we use psychics. Some ghost hunters don't believe in them but they have to be the right psychics."

"I don't understand. How do you know a good psychic from a bad psychic?" asked Klock. "And don't you answer, Dom."

"I'm just listening, Klock. I find this stuff interesting," said Dom.

"That's a great question, Klock," said Julia in a voice that told Klock she was really getting into the exchange. "First off, we don't give tests. In the past my mother has tried different psychics and they have varying degrees of abilities. Some are animal talkers, some scrye, some are only good at tarot or palm readings. We're looking for communicators and connectors of the dead. A true medium."

"Excuse me, animal talkers?" Klock had to ask. She'd never heard of such a thing.

"Yes. We had one psychic who can communicate with the souls of dead animals as well as channeling the ones around us in a live state."

"C'mon, Julia. That can't be real," said Klock smiling and shaking her head.

"I don't joke when it comes to the world we don't understand like different dimensions, the multiverse, limbo, the spiritual plane. Animal communication is real."

"I'll need the number of that person when I'm done with your case. I'd like this person to contact my dead guide dog Vinny. I figured he was in dog heaven but I would like to tell him that I miss him." Klock wasn't kidding yet Julia took offense.

"I don't wish to be mocked, Klock. I thought you were open to this."

"I am. I wasn't kidding around. I'm curious. What does scrye mean?" asked Klock.

"That's when a person uses a crystal ball, a pan of water or looks into a mirror or a small flame when they are channeling spirits or trying to tell the future. Nostradamus was the most successful at scrying and wrote all his quatrains using this methodology. That brings me to another point. Dowsing rods and Ouija boards. Ouija boards are strictly forbidden on ghost hunts. They deliver demons."

"I don't mean to interrupt, Julia," said Dom. "I know what a Ouija board is as kids we all probably tried them at one time or another and we partied hard with the demons it produced but what's a dowser rod?"

"Water witch is another term for it. These are when a person walks around with two metal rods in their hands or sometimes a branch in the shape of a Y and walks the grounds looking for water sources or other electromagnetic anomalies." Julia then cleared her throat and Klock could hear her snapping the cap off her water bottle and taking a drink. "These are not the proper ways of a ghost hunting psychic. The way we test them, for example, is a home owner will tell us what types of spirits they have in their home, the location and paranormal description."

"Paranormal description?" asked Klock.

"Yes," replied Julia. "I can't say physical description as they're not of our solid mortal realm. I'm talking about the appearance and look of a ghost. For instance we had one place where the homeowner and his daughters were seeing a young ghost girl in 19th century clothing and a long black pony tail. She was being seen by them on numerous occasions along with an elderly male ghost that seemed to be protecting her. Now Velvet comes into the investigation and the home not knowing anything about the place. She came in cold and walked to the exact location where the ghosts were being seen and described them as well as spoke to them and got their names. It turns out the grandfather was protecting his granddaughter who was scared and didn't realize she had died."

"Right," said Klock. "She must have unfinished business."

"Very good," replied Julia. "They say that spirits linger when they either long for our mortal pleasures that they sorely miss or have not moved on since they have unfinished business in our world."

"I do know that there are intelligent ghosts or residual ghosts." Klock had listened to many books and had watched all the television shows so she wasn't entirely uneducated on the world of the paranormal.

"That's correct," said Julia. "I'll tell you, Dom since you probably don't know, do you?"

"I have no clue. I didn't know there are different races of ghosts," said Dom.

"Not races," said Julia. "Types. There is no race within spirits. We all have the same chi or spirit energy within our fleshy husks. A residual ghost is one that is an energy imprint much like a record or taped conversation. It repeats the same thing over and over. It's a paranormal energy imprint left in this world but it's not a real spirit. For instance, if a ghostly entity walks through your bedroom every night at the witching hour and you try to talk to it or stand in its way, it doesn't see you or interact with you. An intelligent ghost is one that has free spiritual will and can answer questions and will acknowledge your mortal presence. It will walk through your bedroom and will look at you when you call it. It will respond to questions on our EVP sessions. There's a huge difference between the two and you have to know this when you're on an investigation."

"And you went to ghost college to learn this stuff?" asked Dom in what Klock thought was a tone that was part wiseass and part marvel.

Chapter 17

Klock spent the rest of the night just chatting with Julia, laughing and having a good time; however, in the back of her mind she still thought Julia could be a suspect in her mother's death. Klock thought Julia must've had resentment towards her mother for not only the accidental death of her little brother but that her insufferable scam artist brother got the entire estate. Klock felt in the long run Julia might be better off since the Ghost Chasers seemed to be a goldmine with appearance fees, book sales, as well as the money from the television show, unless Cora Masters left the rights to her work to Don Masters. Klock doubted it since the television show was going to be filming the ghost hunt at the Ft. Schuyler Psych Center. And Klock hadn't forgot about the blue ring.

Dom seemed to revel in the company and continued to pepper Julia with more questions on ghost hunting, what would attract someone to such a venture, as well as if she really did believe in spirits. It was this topic that Klock jumped in with, "I don't believe in ghosts."

"Really?" asked Julia. "I'd thought you'd be a believer since you watch all the shows and had such great interest in what we do."

"I have to admit I love the whole concept. It's just I need to experience things to believe them."

"Let me ask you something, Klock," said Julia. "Have you ever had or seen octopus?"

"No, I have never had one to eat or remember seeing one when I could see."

"Then how do you know they exist?" asked Julia.

"Talk your way out of that one, Klock," chimed in Dom all smug.

"I know they exist because I remember when I was little watching

National Geographic on the seas and there they were."

"You believe everything you see on television?" asked Julia.

"Well, I watched your mother on television with spirits so how do I know they exist."

"Touché." Julia seemed amused but not mad. "Well, I guess you might have me there. I will say prepare yourself to be possibly tantalized this Saturday night."

"You can't guarantee a ghost?" asked Klock.

"This isn't paranormal on demand," said Julia. "We never guarantee anything and always expect nothing. Though, I have to say the Ghost Chasers are the best at selecting haunted locations. I don't remember not having an interaction with the spirits but there's always a first. The Ft. Schuyler Psych Center is rumored to be almost as haunted as the Overlook Mansion."

"How did you guys get in there?" asked Dom. "I heard the state owns it."

Klock never told Julia that Dom was a cop and knew better not to say a word about his career, especially since Julia might slip something that could help the case, not that Klock needed him to figure it out. Still, it was a great question.

"Well, my mother was always great at getting into places and I've taken up her tactics, her techniques when it comes to getting what is best for the Ghost Chasers."

"Slept with somebody?" asked Dom.

Klock was sipping her water at the time of the question, spit it out, and started choking. It sent Bo into a tizzy with him jumping on her lap and barking. Even in rest the doggy never stopped working. The boy was dead serious about his protection of her.

"I'm okay," said Klock as she gently put Bo back on all four paws. "It went down the wrong pipe. I can't believe you asked Julia that, Dom."

"What? I was only kidding around."

"Its okay, Klock. I will say that I did not do such a thing and no, I never put such practice past my mother. Like I said, we do what we do. I don't want to reveal the secrets of how we conduct ghost hunting business. There's a reason why we're the best. Always have been and always will be," said Julia.

"Deep dark secrets, eh?" asked Dom.

"The deepest; the darkest," replied Julia.

It was in a way that made Klock jealous. Julia was flirting with Dom and suddenly Klock felt she had to end the conversation. "Dom has to go now, Julia. You and I have some personal business we need to discuss."

"Sure," replied Dom. "It's past my bedtime anyway. I need to use your bathroom before I hit the road."

Once the bathroom door shut Klock turned towards to where Julia was and said, "I want to chat with you about the case."

"Okay," replied Julia. "So is Dom your boyfriend?"

"No. But, we're very close friends. The best," replied Klock.

"I'll let myself out," said Dom. "Goodnight ladies."

Klock's heart stopped as she hadn't heard Dom coming out of the bathroom. He must've doubled back and she never heard him. If she wasn't blind she would've seen him. Her stupid eyes betrayed her and now she felt her neck get hot and her cheeks flush. She didn't say another word until she heard Dom shut her apartment door. "Is he gone?"

"Yes, he is," said Julia. "I have to say, Klock, that I enjoyed the dialogue. Don't worry about not being certified. You're a guest on the investigation and I can instruct you on what to do as the night moves along. Sorry to carry on. Do you have anything good on my mother's death?"

"I've done a lot of research and a great deal of questioning and I will tell you I have no evidence yet that anybody did anything but I will tell you everyone is a suspect."

"Really? So I might be right?"

"Anything is possible but I don't have definitive proof. I will say that I read the police case files and there's nothing there so I'm completely on my own. They feel your mother jumped to her death. Do you think there's any possibility? With Joey and all."

"I just know my mother. She was too egocentric and full of vanity to kill herself. She tried so hard to contact him through the spirit world. I just think someone killed her."

"Well, the only people there that night were you and the Ghost Chasers, your brother Don, and the Van Dreasons."

"I know. I thought you could find some proof of something. I just want the truth to be known."

"I have you listed as a suspect as well." Klock put that out there to test the reaction.

"I don't blame you. I was there. But let me ask you a question, Klock. If I did do that, why would I hire you to prove my mother was murdered? Wouldn't it be easier for me to confess and go to the cops rather than go through this entire charade?"

"True. You're the lowest on my list but I'm concerned. Your brother told me your mother blamed you for Joey's death, then she goes and leaves everything to your brother Don."

"There's no doubt she shamed me every year on the anniversary of Joey's death but not to the point where I'd want to kill her. And like I told you before I had no clue my mother was leaving all her possessions to my brother. I'll be honest, she wasn't as rich as everyone thought."

"No?"

"Nope. She spent lavishly on her purses, her clothes, manicures, pedicures, spa treatments, botox, you name it. It wasn't like she had a nest egg full of money. My brother hocked her jewelry except this ring and I had to take it off her finger at the funeral home in order to get it. He probably gambled and drank that money by now. To me, the truth is the most important. I'd take a lie detector test if the cops thought I did it. Regardless of how she treated me, she was my mother and I loved her. I know in my heart she didn't kill herself and never would."

"Do you think she fell by accident?"

"There was no way. Why would she even be by the window? It was closed when we started the investigation and it was cold outside. Why would she open it?"

"Great question. I would like to contact the Van Dreasons so I need you to give me their number."

"Good luck with that. I've tried calling them and they shut me down. The only thing I can think of is they probably think I'm going to sue them for my mother's death."

"So are you going to sue? That's the American way you know."

"I'm not but I wouldn't put it past my brother. With his scamming ways. I wouldn't be surprised if he didn't approach them for an under the table payout. So you think the Van Dreasons might have done it?"

"I have no clue. I want to interview them and feel them out. It doesn't seem to reason that they would do such a thing but weird reasons pop up in investigations. I read once about a brother that killed his older brother over a penny."

"Really?" asked Julia.

"I'm not making that up. People have fuses that light quick or burn faster with the flashpoint being anything from a word to a look, while others can have the most atrocious molestation occur and turn the other cheek. Who knows."

Klock spoke the Van Dreasons phone number into her digital recorder and decided to call them after the psych center investigation so she could have a better understanding of just how the Ghost Chasers operated. Plus she wanted to make a trip the next day to the Ft. Schuyler Historical Society to do some research on the Overlook Mansion. She knew the demon was always in the investigative exorcist details when it came to cases. She needed something and she had a hunch that she might find some little informational nugget but then again, she could pan for written diddies to Kingdom come and not get a gold molecule.

* * *

Klock and Bo had to take three bus transfers in order to get to the Ft. Schuyler Historical Society. It was over on the north side of the city. She wasn't too happy about it as every bus was packed and she had no place to sit, not that she expected any sighted person to get up from their seat just because a blind girl with her guide dog was present. Every time the bus stopped, or jostled, Bo's paws would slide and she could hear his nails clacking across the floor. There was no straight shot to the historical society so she had to do what she had to do. She could've saved all this trouble and called Dom but she wanted him to see she could work and solve a case by utilizing what the city had to offer and not rely on a Ft. Schuler Police Investigator to carry her water bucket, besides, she didn't need Detective Wilson running his mouth. She recalled the famous quote by Friedrich Nietzsche "that which does not kill you makes you stronger," although she wasn't a student of philosophy some of the tidbits from her high school class did lounge around in her gray matter.

She stepped off the bus and could feel the rays of the sun on her face. Klock was glad of a little warming trend as the snow seemed to be melting. She walked in slush. Thankfully her boots were waterproof as the sidewalk in front of the historical society wasn't shoveled, so it was a soupy slushy mess. She had to stop to curb Bo as he was making the indication he had to relieve himself. She waited and could tell by his movements that he was making a poop right in front of the building. Bo had to do what he had to do for he couldn't sit on a toilet and there was no patch of fluffy green in the winter, for him to claim and mark. While he was going she took off her gloves, put them in her left pocket then reached into her right pocket and fished out the small plastic dog poopy bag. She pulled it over her hand and up her wrist then reached down and felt around until she grabbed his warm deposit. Klock stood back up and took her free hand and pulled the bag down then knotted it sealing the feces inside. She'd have to carry it inside the Ft. Schuyler Historical Socicty and throw it in a trash can. The last thing she needed was a ticket from an overzealous police officer for Bo's public display of relief.

She walked up the steps. She'd never been there before and didn't realize there were a bunch of them. She and Bo had no problems until they got to the front and she discovered it was a revolving door that was too small. She went into it anyway worried that Bo's tail was going to get caught. Luckily, after they slowly progressed, and her heart skipped a beat, they made it through and into the building. She was greeted by what she thought might be a receptionist or guard.

"May I help you?" asked the person she assumed was a guard. He had a voice that told Klock he must be an older man. She pictured a white haired, chubby bellied man in a uniform, with thick suspenders, and a Walrus mustache.

"Yes. I need to conduct some research on an old building in Ft. Schuyler," said Klock.

"Okay. You'll want to go down that way and take the stairs to the basement. You'll see the sign on the door where the archives are located."

"Blind."

"Excuse me?" asked the guard.

"I have no sight, sir. I cannot see the sign you are referring to."

"I'm sorry, sweetheart. Let me help you down there."

Klock didn't object or mind for the man seemed to be a sweet and sincere grandfatherly guard. She followed his voice and didn't ask to take his elbow as it seemed easy since the building that housed the historical society must've been old. Walking on the floor made echoes that gave Klock the impression of wide hallways and large wooden doors. "Thank you," she said as she walked into the room where the archives were located. She froze for a quick second and realized they might not have accessibility at the historical society. She was picturing old newspapers in binders or the old microfilm, neither of which would be of use, let alone if the articles were scanned and digitized for even if they did have JAWS, the program doesn't read PDF's. "Damn fool," she said under her breath. She might have to call Dom after all. She felt down in the dumps for she knew the truth. The truth that she avoided since the day the earth went black. The truth that she did need help. She couldn't do everything alone. Rely. It was the worst word in the world and she wished Dr. Sue was there for her to vent to.

"May I help you?" said a voice of a sweet little old lady.

"Yes, Ma'am. I want to do some research on the Overlook Mansion. It's a very old building in Ft. Schuyler."

"Yes, I've heard of it. It's considered one of the top ten most distinguished homes in the history of the city."

"The issue I have is I'm totally blind so I don't know if you have a system that will work for me unless somebody can get me some basic information and tell it to me."

"We are all volunteers here. I'd be glad to help you."

"Really? That's so kind of you."

"My name is Judith."

Klock stuck her hand towards the older woman. "Nice to meet you. I'm Klock."

Chapter 18

Klock couldn't believe how nice Judith was being to her. Her new friend took her time looking up microfilm and pulling old articles about the mansion from the database. Judith explained that the historical society volunteers had been slowly scanning the city newspapers from the past two hundred and fifty years and had a searchable database. She apologized that they had never thought about how a person that was blind could delve into the information.

Klock had sat down at a large wooden table and placed Bo underneath and gave him a pig ear, not worrying if he were getting slobber on the floor. It was a reward for excellence and would keep him happy for a while, besides nobody had ever told her that her guide dogs weren't anything but cute. She wondered if anybody in the world hated dogs, if so, she couldn't imagine what soulless cretins they must be.

"This here article talks about the original builder and owner of the Overlook, Richard T. Scharf," said Judith. "He was a very rich man and one of the first settlers here to Ft. Schuyler before it blossomed into the city. It was just a small community back in the 18th century with a few hundred houses along the banks of the Mohawk River."

"Is it a Victorian style mansion? I never saw it when I had eyesight. From what I've heard, it's big and tall with a turret that goes way up."

"Oh, no. It was built way before the Victorian era. I thought I saw an article from the old Ft. Schuyler Globe newspaper from the early 20th century where it describes the style and look. Give me a minute," says Judith.

Klock reached down to pet Bo on his side as she patiently waited for Judith to give her anything useful for her case. Perhaps her instincts were not so great after all but it could help her to know everything she could for it was better than ignorance. Being a know-it-all comes with benefits, especially for a blind teenage girl private investigator.

"Here it is," says Judith. "The Scharf family mansion, which is called the Overlook by the citizens of Ft. Schuyler. It is called this due to the tall turret that has windows on all sides. The Overlook is on the highest hill on the edge of the city. Richard Scharf had built the mansion in the location to watch commerce on the Mohawk River. His textile factory would transport goods on the waterway. The grand view of the Overlook is said to be directly in line for a wonderful panorama of the eastern and western rims of the Mohawk Valley. Mr. Scharf had the Greek Revival style Overlook built in 1795 and it has been mentioned in architectural circles as a marvel in appearance and grandiose within."

"That's really a great description," said Klock.

"Well, isn't this interesting?" says Judith. "Now this is something I'd never heard of before. Hmmmm."

"What is it?"

"Listen to this, Klock. It's from an article in the late 19th century. 'The Overlook had been used on the Underground Railroad as the Scharf family had always been steadfast against slavery and never dabbled in the practice, instead hiring the newly arriving immigrants in their textile factory. Mr. Scharf had come to the United States from Germany and had a fondness for those seeking life betterment.'"

"That's interesting," replied Klock. "The underground railroad. I read once that there were a lot of homes in this area that were part of that."

"Well this article is more to do with the structure of the Overlook. Something I had never heard of in my fifty years or volunteering and researching at the historical society."

"It must be something really good."

"Sure. Listen to this. "This reporter was given a personal tour of the Overlook by Greta Scharf, great granddaughter to the family matriarch who glowingly showed me the secret rooms, hidden staircases and entrances not known to the public. These were part of the original construction and nobody knew their purpose yet the Scharf family utilized these for the slaves they protected that were on the move to Canada during the Civil War. This reporter was especially impressed with the hidden staircase that came out into the turret of the Overlook. An entrance one could not see once the door was shut."

"How interesting," replied Klock trying to be sly as overexcitement could tell Judith that there was more to her research than mere curiosity.

"It's a shame what happened to Cora Masters," said Judith.

"You mean the ghost hunter who fell to her death?"

"I'm a big fan of her show. Or was until she died. It's a shame."

"I hear you," said Klock. "That story is what inspired me to research the Overlook Mansion since that was her last investigation."

"That was sad although the newspaper called it a suicide."

"I think I have everything I need, Judith." Klock stood up, held out her hand and Judith gripped it and shook tighter and stronger than Klock thought she would.

"The pleasure is all mine, sweetie. I do love your guide dog. Did you get him from Ft. Schuyler Guide Dog?"

"I sure did. His name is Bo and he's doing a great job for me."

"They bring their dogs through here all the time when they're training. I'm sure Bo has been in here."

"That's probably why he walked me through the revolving door so well. To be honest with you that's a tough thing for a blind person to get through."

"I know. We were supposed to have an alternate entrance by now, but I bet that's why they like bringing the guide dogs through this building. We love it and everyone wants to pet them but we know they're working."

"I appreciate that. Bo is all business but parties like any dog once his harness comes off. People think I'm being rude because I won't let them pet him. They'll reach down or try to sneak him food. Just because I'm blind doesn't make me stupid. People don't realize my life is in his hands."

"He's your guardian angel all right. If there's anything you ever need help with please let me know," said Judith.

"You're so kind. Thank you so much, Judith."

* * *

Klock couldn't wait to get Dom on the phone to tell him what she discovered about the Overlook Mansion but she had to wait until she took the bus all the way back home with the transfers not being any easier or shorter. She had to feed Bo, make herself toast and tea then it was time to try to get Dom on the phone. She dialed her cell phone and was smiling before he answered. On the third ring he picked up.

"Hello."

"Dom."

"What's up, Klock?"

"Oh, I got a doozy for you."

"You must've had a break in the case by the sound of your voice."

"You think so, eh?"

"You're practically giddy over there."

"I went to the historical society and did some research on the Overlook Mansion and guess what?"

"I don't know. It's haunted?"

"Everyone says that. No. The place was a part of the Underground Railroad and has secret rooms, tunnels and staircases all over the place."

"Really?"

"You bet. A nice lady at the historical society helped me do the research. She was kind enough to go through the old records. They have a catalog system that helps you get specific articles through a search engine. Anyhow, she found this obscure article in the newspaper from over a hundred years ago and it mentioned this."

"I've lived here my whole life and I never heard of that, Klock."
"Well, here's the real kicker."
"There's more?"
"Does a bear poop in the woods?"
"You're killin' me over there."
"Okay, okay. The article mentions a secret passageway that goes right up into the turret. The reporter at the time says it was impossible to detect until they were shown where it was."
"Wow, that's huge."
"Right. That means that a person could've gone through that passage, come out in the turret and pushed Cora Masters out the window. This is why the techie from the Ghost Chasers never caught anybody on his video camera. He had it on the only known entrance but nothing was on the secret entrance."
"That's incredible."
"And just think, Detective Wilson missed that."
"What did you expect, Klock, from a slug with a badge." said Dom cracking himself up.
"On top of that I listened to what the Ghost Chasers thought was an EVP of Cora having a disagreement with an entity. There wasn't a ghost up there, I bet it was a person up there arguing with her and then pushed her out the window."
"That's major. What do you do now?"
"I'm going to keep this information just between us. I still need to go on the investigation of the psych center. I'll need to hook up with the Van Dreasons to interview them. If Cora Masters was murdered it has to be either her son, Julia, the Ghost Chasers or the Van Dreasons. Julia is the only one I don't think did it but I can't completely dismiss her. She's probably the least likely suspect."
"Who would be the strongest suspect?"
"I'm thinking the son Don since he inherited her estate although Julia seems to have the better end of the deal. She gets the future earnings from the Ghost Chasers and she told me her mother didn't really

have a lot of liquid assets."

"That could be the smokescreen right there," said Dom. "Julia could be a suspect since she has gained financially with her mother's death. What about the others?"

"After my interview with the other members of the Ghost Chasers, they both had motive as she treated them badly. The wildcards are the Van Dreasons."

"Devil's advocate, Klock. Why would the Van Dreasons invite Cora Masters into their home just to kill her? It doesn't make sense."

"Who knows, Dom. Cora had the flaming temper of a Roman candle. She could've snapped on them during the investigation and it could've been spur of the moment kind of killing. I can't dismiss them yet."

"I didn't think you had much of a case but you certainly have one now don't you."

"Is it wrong for me to be so pumped?"

"No way, Jose. I always get that tingle when I think I'm getting my suspect. I think that's why some cops are better suited for this kind of work unlike Wilson and Hilley who are just punching their time clocks until they can cash that fat pension check."

"I prove this is a murder and he's going to hate me even more."

"Yup. Not only that, the chief might be disappointed at his sloppiness. Then again, I think he expects mediocrity out of that guy."

"Careful, you don't want to punch him again, Mr. Anger Management."

"Good one. It's a great idea to keep a lid on this, even to Julia."

"I know. She hired me and if she did it, I won't get paid."

"You'll get paid in the satisfaction of knowing you did a job well done."

"That's why I got my private investigator license. Solve cases and make a living," said Klock. "I'll call you after the investigation unless I need you for anything before Saturday."

"You know you can count on me, Klock."

Klock / Dennis Webster

"I'm counting on it."

Chapter 19

Julia picked up Klock and seemed to be in a great mood to investigate. Klock wondered why anyone would say Julia was a dragon lady like her mother. She had been nothing but kind and professional towards her. Now she'd see how Julia acted under the glare of the television cameras.

She'd never been in the part of the city where the psych center was, which seemed rather odd since she lived her entire life in the city. Whenever her parents could, they'd escape the city for the northern woods so they never went south. She'd almost forgotten her parents were coming to see her the next day to take her out to lunch. Sunday was usually the only day her father never worked at the garage. Her mother had been pestering a lot to eat out together. Although, they never went to any of the fancy places since her parents didn't have much spending money and she had none. She was fine with that. She had to get her mind ready for the investigation.

Klock took in what Julia had told her about the proper ghost hunting protocols and decorum practices. She was excited to see if something paranormal was going to happen to turn her from skeptic into a believer. She was sure it was nothing like the television shows. She was about to find out. She had left Bo home for they were going to be in the unheated psych center all night and she was told to wear her winter gear. They would be warm in what Julia referred to as "ghost central."

"This should be a great investigation, Klock," said Julia as she drove up and stopped the car. "We're there but I wanted to go over a few things with you one-on-one before we go in."

"Sure."

"With Velvet we have four so we will break up into two teams and each goes in so you can go along on all of them or some of them. This should be great. Just act natural around the cameras."

"I don't know if I want to be on television, Julia."

"You kidding me? You can't be serious?" Julia's voice got harsh in a snap. "Why didn't you tell me this before? What the hell. They're going to ask you to sign a release form. This could jeopardize the entire operation. You might have to stay in ghost central all night."

"It's just; I don't want people to see me on television."

"Why? Because you're blind?"

"Actually, yes," said Klock. She didn't want to flip out on Julia as she knew it would inflame her even more. She was confident but not when it came to the public seeing her on a television show. The poor blind girl with the cane.

"I think you're scared, Klock. Honestly, I think you are going to be proven wrong. C'mon, you can do it," said Julia in a much nicer tone.

"OK. I'll do it," whispered Klock between her gritted teeth. She didn't like going against her stubborn Polish personality but she wanted to be in the investigation not sitting on the sidelines watching.

Julia patted her on the leg and said, "Fantastic! OK, let's get going. This is going to be the night you become a believer."

"I'm not afraid."

"You should be, Klock. This place was brutal and there could be all kinds of negative energy. Just do exactly as I say and you'll be fine."

Klock nodded her head and stepped out into the cold wind that kicked up mere hours before the investigation. As she walked holding Julia's elbow the lead investigator made a comment how the lunar cycle was in the proper position for the paranormal to be at its spiritual peak. They came to something that Klock figured was a tent and she could feel the warmth when they stepped in. It must've been a high ceiling tent with a heater in it.

"Welcome to ghost central, Klock," said Julia. "This is where we stay when we're not inside the building. We have monitors in here to watch the action inside. You'll have to be careful walking in here as we have five cords going across the ground. They go inside and power the night vision cameras."

"Where are the television cameras?" asked Klock.

"The television crews have their own cameras and will be following us around not saying a word. They stay in their van until we're ready to roll. The boys are inside hooking all the equipment up. Velvet just sent me a text. She will be here soon, then we will gather around and I'll go through everything. Sound ok to you?"

"Yes."

"I didn't mean to bark at you, Klock. I'm under a lot of stress here following my mother, the legend. I just want you to experience what a ghost hunt is like."

"Its okay, Julia. I've never been on television before."

Within a few minutes John and Steve came into the tent talking about the power that ran from their van. Klock wondered why she could hear a vehicle nearby running. It must've had a generator. She knew the abandoned psych center had no power. She didn't have to worry about carrying a flashlight for she had the advantage in complete blackness.

The guys were talking technobabble that Klock didn't understand but they seemed to be happy with the pictures from the video cameras that were wired into a monitor. Klock was glad she didn't bring Bo for she didn't want him exposed to the cold. It was chilly in ghost central even with the portable heater. Bo needed a vacation and Julia had told her they would escort her to and from the internal locations where they would be conducting their electronic voice phenomenon (EVP) sessions. For once Klock didn't have her hand held digital recorder on her. Julia had explained that they had their own and she wouldn't allow John to take her recorder away from her as she needed it for her investigation. She still had interviews and personal notes on it that she didn't want him to hear.

Klock was a little shocked when Julia started yelling at John and Steve about the locations of the cameras. That the direction they were pointing was not the precise place she had told them. Klock could hear nothing but groveling apologies from them as she heard them scramble from the tent to fix them with Steve grumbling about being the pack mule.

"People called my mother a nasty beast and now I'm her," said Julia. "The Ghost Chasers are the best because we don't settle for mediocrity and sloppiness. These guys have been with the team for years and they continue to do the same mistakes. You think people would learn after being told so many times."

"So how is this going to work?" Klock was trying to get Julia off the topic.

"Once Velvet gets here, and the boys return, we go over the logistics. We then do an opening prayer. None of this is filmed as its private. We don't want other ghost teams to mock or copy. Then we break up. Team number one goes in with one of the cameramen from the television show. The second cameraman takes turns filming for their gear is larger and heavier than ours."

"So do you have say over what they air?"

"For the most part. I signed a new agreement with them since my mother died but it's the same contract. I get to be part of the editing process but they have final say of what airs. They've been great to work with since we make them money. They get terrific ratings and charge more to advertisers and we get a flat fee for each airing. It's not just the money though, we feel the Ghost Chasers are providing a valuable community awareness."

"Good evening," said Velvet who must've just walked into the tent. "Cold one tonight."

"Yes it is," said Julia. "John and Steve will be back any minute and we'll get going. I have to step out for a second to talk to the television crew about the inside of this place. It's very dangerous and I'm sure it has asbestos. They might want to don a mask."

Klock heard Julia leave and she took the opportunity to speak to Velvet. "You know Julia feels her mother was killed. That she didn't commit suicide."

"I know."

"Well, what do you think?"

"Julia has a psychic twinkle. She has the feeling her mother is trying to communicate with her. That's why she wants to get back into the Overlook. She's desperate but the owners refuse."

"You can't channel Cora remotely?"

"No. She's probably hanging around the mansion and using the portal to come and go. Some spirits can attach themselves to us grounded beings while others cannot."

John and Steve walked in so Klock stopped talking but they were too busy crabbing back and forth at one another. They stopped when Julia came back in and started calling everyone together. Klock just turned in the direction of Julia's voice.

"Ok, the cameras look perfect now," said Julia. "We have the cameras in the locations that ex-employees had told me where the greatest frequency of ghost sightings. The hot spot seems to be room number 103 that still has an old patient bed in there. I'm assuming this room used to be where they employed the Utica Crib. We're going to go with a single digital recorder that each team will pass back and forth. Each team will spend an hour then come back and switch off. This will be an hour spent at each camera location. Klock will be going on all of them so we need to be mindful that she's disabled."

Klock didn't say anything but she did fold up her cane and shove it in her pocket. She'd have to be led around much like the old days of the blind where a person would tie a couple of feet of rope around their waist. The blind person would hold as a tether and be led around. She would be as helpless as the three blind mice.

"As in the past, remember not to look at the television cameraman, don't speak to them. Just ignore their presence. This place has been called one of the most haunted locations in Ft. Schuyler. It's not the Overlook but we'll see," said Julia. "Remember to sit still while talking so we don't get anything other than pure paranormal evidence and remember to tag everything."

Klock raised her hand and asked, "Tag?"

"That's a term in the field," said John. "If you bang into something, shuffle or make any noise, you have to speak clear and aloud that it was you so I don't mark it on my review as evidence."

Klock nodded her head as she understood clearly. She felt her private investigator badge that was in her back pocket in case the cops showed up and got them for trespassing. She could try to talk her way out of trouble.

"Thank you, John," said Julia. "The first group will be Klock, Velvet and I. I'll have a walkie talkie so you boys can let me know if I go over the hour. I told the cameraman to wait for us just inside the building. You carry the digital recorder, Velvet. We're ready to go. Gather in a circle everybody for our opening prayer."

Klock felt someone grab both of her hands. All she knew is it wasn't Julia as she was speaking directly across from her in the circle. She closed her eyes and bowed her head.

"Let us pray," said Julia. "St. Peter, St. Michael and St. John, protect us from any negative energy or dark spirits. To all the positive spirits, please come forward, talk with us, we will not harm you, we respect you and ask your permission to film you. Protect us Lord and keep all of us safe in our investigation, Amen."

They all said Amen with Klock whispering "Oy Vay" under her breath, wondering if an ordained minister had written that prayer but probably not. It sounded like something Julia just cobbled together. She wondered if Julia even knew what the particular protections were available by the saints. Klock waited until Julia took her by the hand. "Give me your elbow," said Klock. "Then I can walk behind you as you move."

"Sure," said Julia as she did what Klock instructed and they went forward in a herky jerky fashion.

"Just walk natural," said Klock. "You don't have to move like Frankenstein; all stiff. Just go natural. It's much easier for me."

"Sounds good. Take this flashlight Velvet and shine it out front as I have my hands full here," said Julia. "I have the K2 in my pocket so we have everything we need."

The tent flap smacked Klock in the face as she couldn't see to get out of the way. At least she wasn't victim of the beach ball test. When Klock was in her senior year of high school and completely blind, the captain of the Ft. Schuyler football team had bet the other players that Klock was faking her blindness so he brought a beach ball into the cafeteria. He blew it up, walked by her and threw it at her face. She'd not seen it coming and it smacked her straight on the nose. The entire cafeteria erupted in laughter. She laughed along to mask the pain. She was not going to give those bastards the satisfaction of being superior and she wouldn't do it this time. She had to live with material objects regardless of the injuries they caused. Her shins were sore from bumping into random below knee items the sighted took for granted.

"We have steps here, Klock," said Julia.

Klock stopped and felt forward with her foot. They were a handful of steps and were wide so it wasn't a big deal going up them and the entrance door was plenty wide that they were able to go though side by side. Julia was doing great with her escort skills and obviously felt comfortable for she started talking to Velvet.

"You getting anything in here, Velvet?" asked Julia.

"Oh, yes. I saw entities walking the grounds before I got out of the car. This place is loaded with ghosts," replied Velvet.

"Great," said Julia. "We're going to room 103. That's the supposed hot spot, Velvet. At least according to several employees who used to work here that I spoke to."

Klock listened intently as she might get something that might help her with her investigation. She felt a sneeze coming on as the air inside the psych center was extremely dusty and musty. They walked down what she thought was a hallway and she could hear papers crunching under their feet. It made her wonder if the place closed and staff scrambled like rats, scattering their work as they fled. She didn't worry about breathing the air yet the cameraman from the television show must've been wearing one for his speech was muffled as he walked behind them.

"Here we are," said Julia. "He'll start filming us in a few seconds, Klock. As soon as we're set and ready to begin. Now remember to act naturally."

"They never had me sign the release form, Julia," said Klock. "Are we cool?"

"I have it. I'll have you sign it before the night is over. Let's not worry about that right now. I'd like you to sit on the bed. It's old and kind of gross but it's either that or sit on the floor, or stand up the entire hour."

"Ok," said Klock as she felt the mattress before she sat down she was a little skeeved for it didn't have a sheet on it and she couldn't see if she were sitting on a stain. The springs underneath squeaked as she settled into a comfortable position. She felt sad for the mentally disabled patient who must've been caged to the bed with the medieval restraining devices they had used in the old days.

"I'm going to be in this corner, Klock. Velvet is over there. It's best to spread out when doing an EVP. We don't sit all together. We're also in front of our digital video camera and the cameraman is in the hall shooting us but he won't take part in the discussion. The K2 meter I'm placing on the bed near you, Klock. Ok?"

"Sounds good," said Klock as she started to get excited. She'd always wanted to be on a ghost hunt and here she was. She was ready for the paranormal experiences to start happening.

"It's ten pm," said Julia as the EVP session began. "We're in room 103 of the Ft. Schuyler Psychiatric Center. This is Julia and we have Klock and Velvet here."

Klock didn't say a word as nobody spoke for at least five minutes. She had an impulse to press her talking watch but decided not to do it. At least she'd been smart enough to put her cell phone on vibrate. She was surprised at how quiet it was inside the room with every shuffle amplified. She tried not to move a muscle as she expected a spirit to speak at any moment.

"You sensing anybody, Velvet?" asked Julia.

"We have an entity in the room. I can see a shadow figure in that corner but it's hard for me to make it out," replied velvet.

"What is your name?" asked Julia who paused for ten seconds between each question. "Are you a man or a woman? Were you a patient here? Was this your room?"

"I see it more clearly now," said Velvet. "I see a man in a uniform. He's wearing nursing scrubs."

"Were you an employee here?" asked Julia. "Did your favorite patient stay in this room? Were you a resident here? Are those your pajamas that you're wearing?"

"We mean you no harm," said Velvet.

"It's fine if you don't want to speak," said Julia. "Can you make a noise? If you can understand me, make a noise."

"Thank you," said Velvet.

"We appreciate your letting us know you're here," said Julia.

Klock was confused for she was listening as best as she could and she heard nothing yet they were acting like this ghost had just made some kind of noise. She couldn't verify anything. She felt the room was old and smelly and that was about it. They sat for another half hour with nothing happening before they spoke again.

"You can ask the spirits a question if you want, Klock," said Julia.

"How are you tonight?" asked Klock trying not to ask the same old EVP questions she'd heard dozens of times on the television show. There was no answer. "My name is Klock, what's yours?" There was no response that Klock could hear.

"The spirits like you," said Velvet to Klock.

"Klock is blind," said Julia. "She's like you when you were a patient in here."

Klock couldn't believe what she had just heard and it made her blood boil. She couldn't restrain herself and was going to release her

Klock / Dennis Webster

Polish thunder.

Chapter 20

Klock was furious. "What do you mean by that?"

"Not so loud," said Julia. "You'll disturb the entities. We'll talk when we get back to ghost central."

Klock didn't say another word while Velvet and Julia continued their attempt to communicate with the ghosts yet nothing seemed to be happening. They were raving about the interaction and that the K2 was pegging to red, whatever that meant. Klock was getting mad as her feet were frozen numb in the unheated room. She was trying her best not to yawn so it wouldn't get caught on television. At least she didn't have her cane out.

The hour sitting in the room asking questions of the undead was the longest and most boring of her life. She was very disappointed in the paranormal investigation. It made her wonder if the ghost hunting was exaggerated or wishful thinking.

"If you are there, please make a sound," said Julia with no response. "We wait for your signal from the other side."

All Klock heard was a wisp of a shuffle out in the hall and Julia and Velvet gushed at the response.

"Thank you," said Julia. "We appreciate you letting us know you're here."

"I see a malignant shadow figure in the doorway," said Velvet. "What is your name?"

There was a pause as Klock couldn't verify anything.

"James," said Velvet. "What are you doing in this realm?"

"I can see him," said Julia. "Are you trapped here?"

"He's talking to me," said Velvet. "He's looking for his sister that was in this place. Her name was Bernice."

After a few minutes Julia and Velvet determined the shadow figure had moved on, perhaps to other rooms looking for his institutionalized spirit sister.

The longer Klock sat, the more absurd the entire affair had become and the less she was upset at Julia's comment. She realized that most people like her are ignorant. They have no clue how insulting they can be to a blind person and sometimes forget they're dealing with a flesh and blood person, especially Julia who seemed to like mute ghosts more than walking talking human beings. She couldn't help it that her mind began to wander. She thought of the case. The information on the Overlook Mansion was way better than sitting on a crusty soiled psych center mattress with frozen toes.

The last thing Julia did before they left was the flashlight test. She took out her flashlight and explained to Klock that she was unscrewing the cap so the spirits would have to power it on.

"Their paranormal energy will make the flashlight illuminate," said Julia. "Ghosts will try to use the energy around them to appear as an apparition or shadow person. They also give off electromagnetic energy. That's why the K2 will light up."

"Ok." Klock said trying to keep from freezing to death.

"If you are there, James, please put your energy into the flashlight. The light is on. We thank you for talking to us tonight," said Julia.

"We appreciate you showing yourself, James," said Velvet.

"Let's head back to ghost central," said Julia. "How are things looking back there?" asked Julia into the walkie talkie that Klock had heard her turn on.

"Great," came the static reply from the other end. "Lots of orb activity in that room, especially around Klock."

"Ok," our time is up. "We're coming back," said Julia.

Not much was said on the way back. Klock was happy for she needed to warm up. The inside of the psych center was a frosty depressing tomb. She felt Julia and Velvet were making things up for she couldn't verify anything they said with the noise reaction being the worse. She wondered if a mouse had scattered or if the cameraman had thrown a pebble to make the noise. She was savvy enough to know shooting a television show was expensive and they had to have something to show the audience so fakery could easily come into play. She remembered the one time where the other ghost hunters on television had been on an investigation of a haunted restaurant and found gaffs – dummies behind mirrors, speakers in ceilings, all to produce a fake haunt.

When they got back to ghost central Klock asked Julia to take her by the heater.

"Cold spots are a sign that the spirits are present," said Julia.

"They are curious and sympathetic to Klock," said Velvet. "Almost like a special kinship. Perhaps it's the young lady's blindness they find attractive. Or, perhaps, sympathy. Fascinating."

Klock was embarrassed at the attention as she has told people she has no special gifts and no enhanced superpowers. She's blind and nothing more. She didn't want to be treated different. She wasn't "special".

"The orbs were swarming around her," said John the techie. "We have a lot of great stuff and it's only the first session."

"Wasn't that exciting, Klock?" asked Julia in a tone that told Klock that they weren't faking any of this. They truly believe something paranormal was happening yet Klock felt nothing.

"Sure." Klock tried to mask her indifference but she never did have much of a poker face. She decided to let Julia's comment go unchallenged unless she gave a heartfelt apology.

Klock stayed back with Julia. She was too cold and bored to venture back in. John, Velvet and Steve went inside the psych center for round two of the investigation. She signed a form she could only hope was the release for her image to be used on the television show. It wasn't like she could sign away anything of value. She had the priceless Bo and nothing else except the private investigator badge in her pocket and the optimism in her heart. She'd had people in her life tell her they couldn't believe that she could be so upbeat when she had such rotten luck with her eyes. She didn't know what they expected, her to be dour and sour? Nobody wanted to hang with a blind wet dour bar towel. She thought of Bo laying on his bed, all toasty and chillin' out while she was sitting in a tent with an icicle on the tip of her nose.

"I wish you could see the monitors," said Julia. "There's a little bit of paranormal activity with a random orb here and there but not anywhere near what we experienced."

Klock just nodded and wished she could hit her talking watch yet that would just tell her how much longer she'd suffer. She rubbed her biceps with her gloved hands in the hopes of warming up. If only someone would show up and toss them from the property.

"What if someone shows up and throws us out of here?" asked Klock. "I'm sure they have a state employee that's supposed to be watching this place. Not only that, I heard a lot of really bad people hang around the area."

"No worries. The criminals don't come out much in the cold weather. As far as security showing up, I took care of it," said Julia. "We're in great shape."

Klock knew they had at least two to three more hours of this so she had to try to make the best of it, and who knows, she still might have a paranormal experience. At the point she thought nothing fun or interesting was happening, in came Don Masters.

"What do you think you're doing?" he said in a voice that seethed anger.

"Don't worry about it, Don. How did you know we were here?"

"You don't think I know what the hell you're up to, Julia," said Don. "This is wrong!"

"Mom would be happy that I'm doing this. You're drunk. Do you mind," is all Klock heard before a loud crash. She jumped back a step and fell down into the side of the tent. All she heard for the next few moments was yelling, screaming, and things smashing all around. She heard threats of calling the cops and charges to be filed for property damage. She could hear Don fleeing and Julia chasing him out of the tent. She could hear them yelling outside in the cold midnight still air. Their shouts were echoing in the chilly night. She was shocked and felt around. She checked her body and was happy she was uninjured. She stood up. She took out her cane, unfolded it, and swung it to and fro, smacking it into items that must've been tossed.

Klock could hear a siren and swore under her breath. She'd run for it but she'd have no idea where to go and how to get back home. It was the middle of the night in a bad area. There was no way any buses were running. She didn't know if her private investigator badge would save her from being arrested but she'd soon find out.

John and Steve came running into the tent yelling to Klock to stay out of the way as she could hear them scrambling and picking up equipment at a frantic pace. She could hear the television crew van start up and pull away. The yelling of Julia and Don was still going on but seemed further away.

Julia came back into the tent spewing venom. "I can't believe he did this. He ruined the investigation. Hurry up you two. The cops are going to be here any second. Where's Velvet?"

"She took off," said Steve. "Along with the camera crew."

"We're never going to get everything picked up in time," said John.

"Keep going," said Julia. "I need to get Klock out of here."

"You're going to leave us?" asked Steve.

"Move as fast as you can," said Julia. Klock felt Julia grab her elbow. She had to take the time to fold her cane up and place it in her jacket pocket. "This way, Klock. Hurry."

Klock almost fell a few times as Julia was yanking her by the elbow but she couldn't run. She hadn't sprinted since she lost her vision. Running full speed with the wind in your face was too dangerous for a person who is blind. Julia was grumbling under her breath and kept saying, "C'mon, let's go" and "move, move, move," like a chanting monk. "I can't believe my brother. If any of our equipment is broken, he's replacing it."

Klock got in the car and the sirens sounded like they were right on top of them. She knew they were not going anywhere as Julia got in the car and didn't even start it.

"What's wrong?" asked Klock.

"A cop car has blocked me in."

"What's Don's problem?"

"He drinks and gets unpredictable. He's in a rage. Just the fact I'm continuing my mother's paranormal investigations is pissing him off. He really doesn't need a reason to be what he is."

Klock could hear the door open.

"Step out of the car," said only what she assumed was a police officer.

Klock had already taken the badge out of her pants pocket and palmed it for she knew if she reached for anything, she could be tazed or beaten. Cops hated sudden movements and many times on her favorite shows they would Swiss cheese your torso for itching your eyebrows. She came out of the car holding the badge out.

"You a police officer?" came the question from the man that asked her to come out.

"No, sir. I'm a private investigator. My name is Rachel Klockowski."

"So you're not a real cop. Your group is trespassing here. This is state property. On top of that someone called us about a disturbance on the grounds."

"I have permission to be here, officer," said Julia. "I was the one that called you. My name is Julia Masters and I'm the lead investigator with the Ghost Chasers. My brother, Don Masters, showed up drunk, throwing my equipment around. He assaulted me as you can see from my face."

"Did he hit you?" asked the cop.

"No. He threw a monitor and it smacked me in the face when I tried to catch it. My equipment is very valuable and he smashed it."

"Ok," said the cop. "Hey, you two over there! Put that stuff down and get over here!"

"I assure you officer, we meant no harm," said Klock.

"Are you here investigating a crime, Rachel?" asked the cop.

"No, sir. I was here on the ghost hunt."

"All of you stay right here and don't move," said the cop.

Klock could hear the officer's steps crunch across the snow as he must've headed back to his patrol car. She could hear him talking on his police radio and mentioned Julia's name but also hers. He had held onto her badge. She didn't think this would be good and hoped breaking the law wouldn't result in her losing her private investigator license. The regulations on having it were that she couldn't break the law in any capacity or it could be revoked if the Ft. Schuyler District Attorney felt it justified.

"What was your brother doing, Julia?" asked John. "He damaged a lot of stuff."

"He's a mental case," replied Julia. "Don't say anything to the police. Let me do the talking and follow my lead."

Klock could hear another car pulling up and knew that it was going to be difficult to talk their way out of it now that a second police officer had arrived. She could hear the two officers talking but she couldn't make out what they were saying and Julia was chattering to them so fast that it was hard for Klock to hear what the police officers were saying to each other. She thought she recognized the voice of the one that had arrived but Julia's chattering made it impossible. The cops stopped talking and she could hear the crunching snow of the two as the footsteps were getting closer. Julia stopped talking as the police officers got next to them and halted.

"Well, well, well," said the other cop with a thick combination of sarcasm and joy.

"Hello, Detective Wilson," said Klock.

Chapter 21

Klock felt a cold chill go down her spine and it had nothing to do with the winter weather or scary spirits, it was something far more scary and dangerous, a goof with a badge. A man with license to break your chops off the pork.

"Having fun out here, kiddies?" asked Detective Wilson.

"This one handed me her badge," said the one cop to Detective Wilson.

"I'll hang onto that," replied Detective Wilson. "We might have to take them all down to the station and book them with trespassing on state property. We'll fingerprint you, take your mug shot, and place you in your own private cell for the rest of the night unless we have some criminals in there."

"Why are you even here?" asked Klock. "This isn't your job is it?"

"I don't answer your questions, you answer mine," said Detective Wilson. "You don't have Detective Mulvi here to fight your battles."

Klock decided to just stand there and not say a word for she knew that Detective Wilson could let them go or bust them for trespassing and disturbing the peace.

"The rest of you, I want your identifications," said the other cop. "Also, registration and insurance from both of these vehicles."

"Don't you remember us from the Overlook?" asked Julia. "You were the cop that talked to us the night my mother died."

"Do what's asked," said Detective Wilson.

While they were all scrambling Klock just stood there alone with Detective Wilson as the other cop had walked with the group back to the tent.

"Where's your dog?" asked Detective Wilson.

"Home resting."

"Listen. I know we got off on the wrong foot but I'm not such a bad guy."

"Okay." Klock didn't want to be rude but she wasn't going to flirt with him either.

"I'm not joking about you and your friends out here doing your ghost busting. The police department is always chasing vagrants from here and I've had to investigate many deaths out here."

"So I hear."

"I also heard that you're investigating my closed case on Cora Masters."

"Julia Masters hired me to look into it. She thinks her mother was killed."

"That's ridiculous. You're going to look like a fool when you find out you've wasted your time. The broad did a suicide swan dive off of there and that's that."

"You might be right but Julia is paying me to look into it."

"Might be right?" Detective Wilson chuckled. "I don't need some teenage gimp greenhorn with a junior detective kit looking over my shoulder."

Klock just folded her arms and looked to the ground. She wasn't going to take the bait.

"No smarmy retort? Ain't you gonna' give me the middle finger like you did in Moe's?"

"I've got nothing to say to you, Detective Wilson."

"That's what I thought. You ain't nuttin' but a scared kid trying to play grown up. Why would they give a badge to a blind girl? This isn't a game for cripples. They have jobs for people like you and it ain't solving crimes."

"I'd like to think I can do anything a person with sight can do."

"Keep telling yourself that, little girl. Do us professionals a favor and stay out of our way before you get someone or yourself killed. You and that dope Mulvi."

Klock didn't respond as she could hear Detective Wilson walk away towards his car, open and shut the door. She couldn't see if he was coming back with a knight stick to crack her across the shin. She'd never see it coming so she picked her head up and raised her chin. If she was going to get it, she was going to be a trooper about it; however, all she heard was Detective Wilson drive past and stop to mumble to the other cop who must've come back ahead of the Ghost Chasers. The car took off without Detective Wilson saying another word to her but she did hear the other cop coming her way and was ready to have the cuffs snapped on.

"Here's your badge," said the other cop.

"Blind." Klock had a frown when she said it while waving her hand in front of her open useless eyes.

"I'm sorry, Ma'am. I had no clue you can't see."

Klock held her hand out towards the cop who gently placed it in her palm. She wondered if her tin badge really mattered as she shoved it into her back pocket.

"So what happens to us now?"

"The others are picking up the rest of their gear and getting out of here as fast as they can."

"You mean we're free to go?"

"Yes."

"What about Don?"

"The woman decided not to press charges."

"Okay. I'm really cold so can I get back in Julia's car now?"

"Sure."

"Can you please guide me to the passenger door? All I need is your elbow, officer."

"Not a problem, Ma'am."

Klock took his elbow and was walking with the cop who was kind enough to open the door for her.

"So you're a private investigator and you can't see?"

"I know, It's crazy. Blind teen girl playing cop."

"Not at all. I think it's admirable."

"I appreciate that. Listen, I'm friends with Detective Mulvi. Do you know if he's on duty tonight?"

"I haven't seen him tonight so I don't know. He's your friend, eh?"

"Yes."

"He's a great investigator. Stick with him and you'll learn something I'm sure. I miss having him on patrol."

"Unlike Detective Wilson."

"No comment."

"Got it." Klock smiled and said, "I have to shut the door now, I'm really cold."

"I'm taking off so let your friends know to get out of here ASAP and don't give me a reason to come back here or you'll all go to the station. Believe me, you don't want to be there."

"Thank you, officer. I appreciate it."

"Have a nice evening."

Julia's car wasn't running but at least Klock had her feet off the frigid turf. She turned her cell phone back on and tried to call Dom but got his voice mail. Her hands shook from anger, fear, and adrenaline. She didn't leave a message and would try him in the morning. She just wanted to get away from the psych center and under her comforter in the warmth of her apartment. She needed the warmth and safety of her bed.

In a little while she heard the driver door open and assumed it was Julia who didn't say anything until she was inside and started the vehicle.

"That no good brother of mine."

"At least we didn't get arrested." Klock wished Julia would crank the heat as her teeth had started to chatter.

"We were never in danger of that," said Julia. "Many times the Ghost Chasers have been caught in cemeteries, old abandoned asylums and we've always talked our way out of it. As long as we weren't vandals, kids partying, or thieves ripping out the copper pipe, we were fine. Most people, especially cops, are fascinated by what we do."

"Alright," said Klock.

"At least we had a successful ghost hunt. I'm sure the television show will have enough footage to air the first show with me at the helm."

"Don't you have to wait until John goes through the digital evidence then meet to go over it before you can determine it was a success?"

"You were there, Klock. We had a boatload of paranormal events. Take away the Overlook Mansion and this was the most haunted location we have ever investigated."

"You mean there's worse?"

"Of course. Not all locations are as active as this place. Velvet was on a roll. We had EVP's, intelligent entities, shadow figures along with partial and full body apparitions along with boatloads of orb activity."

Klock just nodded as the heat was finally warming up her up. A little bit. She was hoping Julia wouldn't press her more as she would have to let loose and tell her the truth.

"I get the feeling you weren't impressed with the investigation."

"To be honest with you, I wasn't."

"You don't have to have sight to experience a paranormal hot spot, Klock. You can have cold stalks, sounds, ghosts having physical interaction."

"I didn't experience any of it, Julia. I appreciate you bringing me along and I'm thankful I didn't get arrested but this is nothing like on television."

"Of course," said Julia. "They take footage from ten hours of an investigation and cut it down to the half hour show which is really twenty minutes when you take out commercial time."

"I just didn't feel anything or hear anything."

"I'm flabbergasted. That can't be true."

"Sorry."

"You still don't believe in ghosts?"

"You're paying me to investigate your mother's death not give you my opinion on the paranormal."

"I want to know."

"OK. As I said before, I don't believe ghosts are real. I don't think Velvet or whatever her real name happens to be is anything other than a drama queen who wishes she had special powers."

"I'm not angry with you, Klock, just disappointed. I don't understand how you can have happen to us in room 103 and you still don't believe."

"I love listening to the shows on television and audio books. I love a good ghost story as much as anybody."

"This is real life not a book. We take what we do very seriously. Do you believe in angels? The afterlife?"

"Sure I do," said Klock thinking of her dead grandparents looking down on her from a better plane of existence.

"Then how can you not believe in ghosts? And Velvet is correct on everything. She's a brilliant psychic and identified that portal at the Overlook Mansion. She's channeled the dead over and over."

"I'm just skeptical, Julia. I need to experience things in order to believe."

"That's messed up logic but I can't convert. I can only preach the truth to people. I can't help the closed minded. Mark my words, someday something will happen and you will be convinced."

"I agree with you." Klock didn't want to argue anymore on the topic. She found the entire ghost hunt a joke. All she got was probably a cold. It was the most unfulfilling evening she'd had in a long time.

"Have you any idea who killed my mother?"

"I still have to interview the Van Dreasons. I still don't have proof to debunk the Ft. Schuyler police report. I can write up my case notes and print out a determination for you and the case will be wrapped up."

"You can type?"

"Sure. I do everything on my laptop that you can do. I have JAWS. It's talking software and tells me what I'm typing. I can e-mail, surf the Internet. I just have trouble if online pictures aren't tagged or some websites that don't have accessibility."

"You really think you can get the Van Dreasons to talk?"

"Of course I can. It's what I do."

"I never considered them a suspect but I get they'd have to be. They were there."

"I have a bunch of ideas, Julia, but nothing I can share with you. Not yet."

"If you get in there to talk to them, you have to ask them if I can get back in there with Velvet. I need to contact my mother's spirit. I know it's hanging around that portal."

"Why is this so important to you?"

"I need closure. She never forgave me for the death of Joey."

"Can a ghost grant such a thing?"

"You bet. She could be hanging around wanting to send me that message. She probably has unfinished business. Perhaps if you help me identify her killer she will finally forgive me. I need this."

"I understand." Klock was a little shocked at Julia's emotion and for the first time was afraid she might not prove anything in the death of Cora Masters. She didn't say another word until Julia pulled up to Castlewood Courts. "Thank you for inviting me on the ghost hunt, Julia. Good night."

* * *

Klock was nervous to have her mother Kasha and her father Stosh, over to her apartment for dinner. She had tried to make it a going out to a restaurant dinner but her mother insisted on having it at Klock's apartment, to the point of non-argument. She wished Julia had given her an advance for her work on the case for she knew her mother was going to make her usual nit picky comments about her apartment, the criminals in the area, and for certain, the lack of food in her cupboards. She didn't mind using the food bank and had made a trip that morning to get what she could but the pickings were slim. They told her that the recent economy, and lack of supportive funds, had ravaged their foodstuffs. She only took what she needed. She had another three weeks until her next disability check would arrive and she still hadn't paid that month's rent or other bills. Her cell phone was the must have. She needed to be connected to the world in order to continue her investigation and get new cases. At least her new Facebook and Twitter accounts were free. She hadn't yet thought what to post on there. She had yet to add friends or new possible investigative clients.

Klock tried her best to clean the apartment. She had purchased a second hand vacuum cleaner at the thrift store for two dollars. She vacuumed over the entire carpet of her apartment. Dusting was the toughest for she couldn't see it and couldn't feel it unless it was really thick.

She had tomato sauce in her crock pot but tasted it and it was bland. She didn't have any garlic or many spices to flavor it up. She was able to get a couple dented cans of crushed tomatoes from the food bank. She dreaded it but she knew her mother loved her and wanted the best for her but would have to understand she was working towards her dream, even if Detective Wilson felt it was futile. She was going to be an investigator and solve crimes.

Klock heard the distinctive three knocks her father always used and almost got knocked over from Bo's excitement. The smart boy knew it was her parents and adored them for they always had a few treats in their pockets. "Watch it there, Bo. I know you're excited. Grandma and grandpa are here."

She opened the door and got the hug and kiss from both Stosh and Kasha. Her mother started in before she got her coat off.

"Honestly, Rachel. I saw a bum peeing on the side of the complex when we were walking in," said Kasha.

"Do I need to have a DNA test run on that?" asked Klock smiling.

"I'm not going to win with you," said Kasha.

"Take off your jackets and stay awhile. I got sauce cooking and I'm going to boil some spaghetti."

"You mother made beef stew," said Stosh.

"That's great."

Klock loved the chunks of carrots, potatoes and other fixings thrown in with hunks of beef. She could smell the stew and it made her mouth water. It was her mother's specialty and she hadn't had it in a while. She was in the kitchen with her mother and she could hear her father playing with Bo out in the living room. She didn't say anything as her mother went through her cupboards and fridge.

"You have a brick of government cheese in here, Rachel and your cupboards are bare. What have you been eating?"

"I'm fine, Mom. Don't worry."

"You have more dog food and dog treats than human food. I'm concerned. You are too thin."

"I'm eating plenty."

"Isn't that disability check enough for you to buy food? I can't imagine the rent in this place can be very much. I though with subsidized housing they base your rent on what income you have."

"I'm good. I had a few things come up. I have plenty of food." Klock didn't dare tell her about the break in and the theft. Her mother would go insane if she knew about Bookcase in the laundry room. She'd start World War ten.

"Come in here, Stosh," said Kasha.

"What is it?" asked Stosh as he came into Klock's kitchen.

"Our daughter is starving. We're going to go shopping after we leave here and get her some food."

"Sounds good." Stosh went back into the living room to hang out with the man of the apartment.

"Not going to lecture me about coming home?" Klock was a little set back by her mother's response.

"I can tell you're becoming a strong young woman, Rachel. You're walking with your shoulders back and your chin up. Being on your own is good."

Chapter 22

Klock was shocked at her mother's statement. It was so unexpected that it threw her for a loop. "Wow. I don't know what to say." Klock was stunned for her mother was a tough Polish woman that threw compliments around like manhole covers.

"Don't get too excited. I'm not happy about you not having any food in this house. I still hate where you live. It's so dangerous here but I understand you need to be out on your own."

"Just so you know I'm still going to see Dr. Sue at the blind association."

"That's great."

"I did talk to the workshop manager but I turned down their job offer. It's there if I don't make out in my private investigation career."

"I don't doubt you'll make it. You're too much like me."

Klock looked towards her mother and smiled. It had been a long time since they had a special moment. They spent the next hour getting the dinner ready with her mother finishing up while she curbed Bo by taking him outside Castlewood Courts to perform his daily constitution. When she walked back into the apartment, Klock was overwhelmed by the mouth watering scent. Spaghetti and beef stew didn't really go together but she didn't care. Bread and butter was the bridge between the two. Her mouth watered and she was ready to feast.

Klock and her parents held hands and were thankful for their meal. They dug in and the stew was so good Klock couldn't stop eating it. She ignored her father who must've been sneaking bits of beef to Bo under the table. She was sure that her dog was loving a little something different than his dry nugget food. Spoiled dog.

"So how is your case coming along?" asked Stosh.

"Great." Klock wiped her mouth with a napkin. "I've been to the public library, the police station, and the historical society. I've been doing a lot of research, interviewing suspects."

"Are you in danger?" asked Kasha.

"I may get into some sticky situations but it's not like I'm dealing with violent criminals in a prison yard or going undercover busting a drug deal. But I did get to shoot a pistol."

"You can't be serious, Rachel," said Kasha.

"Dom took me to the gun range where all the cops practice and showed me how to load and fire a pistol."

"Did you hit the bulls eye?" asked Stosh.

"Stosh, please," snapped Kasha. "That is incredibly dangerous. You're blind and you're shooting a gun? Detective Mulvi must be out of his mind having you do that."

Klock snickered as she took a sip of her water. Her mother had snapped back to reality. The pod person that had taken over her had vacated the premises. Thank goodness she didn't know about the .38 handgun in the shoebox under her bed. "It's no big deal, Mom. It was only one time and I won't be packing heat but don't lecture me about safety since I don't carry a pistol."

"So how is Dom, Klock?" asked Stosh. Her father was too sweet for his own good.

"He's great. I forgot to tell you, Pop, that I met the chief of police."

"Chief Devine is a good customer of the garage."

"He spoke very highly of you, Pop."

"Of course. Everyone loves your father," said Kasha. "He undercharges for his work and does too much for everyone."

"I enjoy what I do," said Stosh with a voice of pride that Klock enjoyed. She understood her father completely and was very proud at what he did. She didn't need him to be a doctor or lawyer. He had joy in his work just like she did in her detective career.

The rest of the meal went without any more drama. The joy and laughter warmed Klock's heart as much as her stomach was full. Her mother put the leftovers in the fridge so she could be able to eat great meals for a couple of days. Her parents left then returned with a couple bags of groceries and Klock didn't reject it. She knew she couldn't live without assistance, besides, her mother had finally backed off about her living at home. She had the entire evening free so she thought she would finally call the Van Dreasons and see if she could get to them for an interview, preferably at the Overlook Mansion, but first she wanted to see what else she could find on the Internet.

Klock spent time going over the Blogs, the message boards, and Ft. Schuyler Topix reading what she could about the Overlook and the death of Cora Masters and nowhere did anybody mention she was murdered. There was nothing about the secret passageways of the building. She did find that the Van Dreasons had only moved into the mansion a year earlier. They were the first people that were not direct descendants of Richard T. Scharf to reside there. That was probably the reason why no ghost team had ever gone into the Overlook. By the time Klock decided to call them it was too late. Her talking wristwatch told her it was much too long into the night to cold call. She didn't want to wake them if they went to bed early. She'd have to try the next day but it didn't look promising for the weather forecast was calling for a massive winter storm.

* * *

Klock's cell phone was ringing and she picked it up knowing who it was since she had programmed the ring tone to the theme from Baretta for whenever Detective Mulvi called.

"Hello, Dom."

"I'm not going to ask you what's new, Klock."

"I guess you heard about the investigation at the psych center."

"Detective Wilson won't shut up about it. I've never seen Detective Hilley laugh so hard and I thought the man was mute."

"He acted the same way he always does towards me. What is it about me that makes him so angry?"

"He's just a bitter old jerk and that's putting it kindly. I'm trying to be a kinder and gentler detective."

"Yoga classes working out well for you?"

"You bet. So anything else new with the case?"

"I didn't pick anything new up from the investigation except Don Masters is a drunken goof. The only reason the cops came was because Julia called them herself when her brother showed up drunk, yelling at her, throwing the equipment."

"Classic."

"I know. Something is wrong with these people, Dom. I was on the ghost hunt and it was bizarre."

"You get spooked over there?"

"It's nothing like you'd think. All I did was get frost bitten toes. There was nothing going on and they were calling it 'paranormal emission'."

"That's funny, Klock."

"It was strange. Like the other members of the Ghost Chasers were afraid to say a word against her. They fed her ego and delusions. I felt nothing, heard nothing, and experienced nothing. I was so excited to go on a ghost hunt and it was as thrilling as watching paint dry and I can't even see it to watch it dry."

"So what's your next step?"

"I'm going to try to call the Van Dreasons and see if I can get over there to interview them and maybe they'll let me go through the mansion."

"Good luck with that. When were you planning on going over?"

"Today, I hope."

"It's starting to snow like crazy out there. They're talking about declaring a snow emergency by tonight. I would wait if I were you."

"Can you give me a ride?"

"I can't today, Klock. Not only is the snow bad but I have paperwork on my desk that would choke a goat. I'm on my way to work now and will probably be there until late into the night. I'm playing catch up from my recent suspension."

"I'll see if I can get them for another day but we'll see. I think I have enough for cab fare to get out there. I don't think the bus runs over to that side of the city."

"Why would it? The rich people over there don't need to take a bus and they don't want any of the class of bus riders getting let off in their area. No offense."

"I don't blame them. Have you seen the people that ride the city bus?"

"Let me know if you need me for anything else."

"You know I will."

* * *

Klock dialed the number of the Van Dreasons and was surprised when it was picked up on the first ring.

"Hello," said a man on the other end.

"I'd like to speak to Milton Van Dreason."

"This is. How many I help you?"

"This is Investigator Rachel Klockowski. I was wondering if I could interview you and your wife about Cora Masters."

"Isn't the case closed?"

"I'm doing a follow up investigation. I assure you I won't take up too much time of you or your wife."

"Well, we have a major snowstorm right now and my wife and I don't want to leave our home."

"I can come to you."

"I guess today would be fine if you can make it up here. It looks like the roads are slick."

"It won't be a problem at all, Mr. Van Dreason. I should be up there in an hour or so. I can't give you an exact time for my travel schedule is based on this snow."

"That would be fine, Inspector Klockowski."

"Very good. I will see you this afternoon."

Klock snapped her cell phone shut and went onto her laptop to Google a Ft. Schuyler cab company. She spent the next half hour calling all of them until one finally agreed to bring her over to the other side of the city where the Overlook Mansion sat atop the rim of Ft. Schuyler. She had nothing but a roll of quarters so she'd have to break out the credit card that she had for emergencies. She'd pay the balance off when she got her next disability check. At least she was smart enough to keep a small limit on the card in case it was ever stolen.

She bundled herself up for the snow and put the harness on Bo for he was coming along this time. She had her hand held digital recorder in case she would be able to tape the Van Dreasons but she wasn't confident that they would fully cooperate, especially if they asked if she were an official police officer.

Klock understood why it was difficult to find any driver that would come to the east side of the city for they were always getting robbed and stiffed fares. On top of all that there was the blizzard hitting and nobody liked sliding all over the unplowed streets, especially since the taxes had been slashed. The mayor of Ft. Schuyler suspended all snow plowing unless Mother nature herself farted a dump truck of snow on his majesty the mayor's front lawn. She knew the politics and the east side of the city was always the last to be plowed since most of the mandated government funded money suckers resided there, herself included.

Klock stood by the front door of Castlewood Courts with her coat, hat, and gloves on as she had instructed the cab driver to honk when he got to the apartment complex. Bo was standing at attention as she had his leash for she figured the cab driver would not wait very long.

She heard the horn honk and came out to a wave of snow blowing around. It was ankle high as she stepped and could feel some snow spilling over the top edge of her shoes. At least the snow was keeping all the rowdy neighbors from screaming and yelling. All she could hear was the grumbling of the taxi engine and the loud muffler. She assumed she wasn't getting a five star cab or even one that's clean. As long as the paid traveling jalopy could get her to the Overlook Mansion she would be happy.

She walked towards the noise until she heard the cab driver yell out, "Hurry up, lady! Roads are gonna close!"

She could only go as quick as Bo and her could go and no mad cab driver was going to make her go any faster. She got to the side of the cab and felt for the back door handle and opened the door and Bo jumped in and she followed. She shut the door and was relieved the snow wasn't hitting her in the face anymore.

"Where you heading?" he asked.

"To the north side. Do you know where the Overlook Mansion is? It's on Rocky Hill Road."

"In this weather, it's going to be tough. They ain't plowin' the roads right now," replied the cab driver with the worst iguana breath that Klock ever experienced. It was as if the man chewed on a week old grilled limburger cheese sandwich smothered in onions.

"Get me there and I'll give you a good tip."

"It better be," he replied as he took off. Klock could feel the back end of the cab slide back and forth.

Klock held on for her life as the reckless driver was bouncing, sliding and fish tailing all over the place and cursing a purple streak that hung in the cab clung to his noxious breath. This was the one time she was glad she had no sight as she didn't want to see how many traffic infractions the cab driver was committing. She grumbled under her breath at Dom for not being available to give her a ride.

Within a half hour she could tell they were getting close for the steep hills had leveled off until the car stopped. "Here you are," said the cab driver. "The driveway is far too steep for me so you'll have to get off here."

She handed over the credit card and hoped the cab driver didn't rip her off for she wouldn't see the receipt and not know what he charged until the statement came in. "Put an extra twenty bucks on there. And give me your card for when I need a ride back."

The driver grumbled under his breath and her heart paused as she wondered if she had activated the card or if it was still good after sitting unused for over a year.

"Hear ya' go," said the driver.

Klock held out her hand until he placed the credit card, his business card and the receipt inside. She shoved everything in her pocket, put on her gloves, and felt around for the handle, opening the door and getting out into a wicked western wind that blew the thick snowflakes sideways into her mouth and into her eyes. She blinked. They still had that function. She couldn't see but that didn't mean she couldn't sense or feel pain with them and the snow with a little sleet made her close them.

The cab rumbled away making her gag on the thick exhaust fumes that were an actual relief from the cab drivers nasty breath.

"Ahead, Bo," she said as he led her up the driveway until he halted making her know there must be some kind of fence or gate. She felt around and indeed it was a wrought iron gate at the bottom of the driveway. She went to her left until she felt a box. She took off her gloves and felt around until she found a doorbell button that she pressed. Her hand got really cold but she couldn't operate the button with her gloves on.

"Hello?" came a woman's voice from the intercom.

"I hope this is Mrs. Van Dreason. This is Investigator Klockowski. Your husband said I could speak to the two of you."

"Of course. I'll buzz you in," replied Mrs. Van Dreason. A loud buzz and click of the gate let Klock know she could go up to the mansion.

She opened the gate and proceeded up the steep driveway that was rather slippery with fallen snow. "Here we go, Bo. No turning back now, boy," she said with joy in her voice as she felt rather excited. She followed the driveway all the way to the top and slipped and fell a few times onto her knees. Her boots were not great of tread, then again, nothing would work well in this blizzard except metal spikes tied to the soles of her boots.

She got up the bottom step of the Overlook Mansion and was greeted with a harsh voice that startled her.

"You're not a cop! Who are you?" asked Mrs. Van Dreason.

Chapter 23

Klock stopped short and knew she had to come clean. Obviously she didn't look like a cop with her guide dog. "I'm a private investigator. My name is Rachel Klockowski," she replied as she tried to brush snow off her pants. Her right knee ached where it had smacked on the ground.

"I have no comment. Now leave before I call the real police."

"Might I please borrow a band aid? I think my knee is bleeding," said Klock.

"Does your dog bite?"

"Only if I ask him really nice," she replied smiling towards Mrs. Van Dreason.

"You can come in but after you fix your knee, you must leave immediately."

"Thank you very much. I appreciate that," replied Klock. She stepped up the porch not reaching out for a hand rail and hoped she didn't slip as the snow was getting thicker and the air colder. When she walked into the Overlook Mansion Klock smelled cinnamon. It made her remember when she was a little girl and her mother would sprinkle it on her pumpkin pie.

"Please come this way," replied Mrs. Van Dreason.

"Forward," said Klock to Bo who tugged her straight and kept her from obstacles. The footsteps echoed which told Klock they were in a cavernous entranceway or room.

"Here's a chair. Please sit and I'll get you something to clean your knee up."

Klock sat there and had Bo lie on the floor next to her feet so he could relax for a minute. She took off her hat and gloves and set them on the floor next to the chair. She rubbed her eyes and exhaled slowly from the ache that had recently popped up. She heard a step come from the other direction than Mrs. Van Dreason had moved.

"Hello?" she asked and got no answer. She hated when people did that as if her being blind couldn't tell when someone was nearby. She didn't have bat radar to detect objects both in motion and static. She did crack up at people who were under the false impression that just because she was blind her other senses had become heightened. She only had the gifts that God had bestowed on her and she wasn't bitten by a radiated arachnid and given special powers; however, she did have to rely on the other senses she still had, as limited as they were, to get her through the world of the sighted. She heard the step, knew somebody was there and thought she would up the ante a little bit. "I know you're there. Who is it?"

"It's Milton Van Dreason. I thought you were a cop?"

"I'm a certified private investigator for the State of New York," answered Klock as she was cut off by the return of the upset wife.

"Don't talk to her, Milt. She's not the police," said Mrs. Van Dreason in a curt tone that wasn't as harsh as before.

"I didn't mean to deceive you two. I'm blind and I'm a private investigator. I only needed a moment of your time." Klock felt she was winning them over, if not she knew Bo could get the job done. Nobody on Earth could resist the gentle nature of a yellow lab with a wagging tail. "I was hired by Julia Masters."

"Hired to do what?" asked Mrs. Van Dreason.

Klock knew it was time to flour the baker. Time to put it out there and this would be the make or break moment for she needed the Van Dreason's to cooperate if she were to prove murder or confirm accidental death. "She doesn't think her mother's death was an accident. She thinks her mother was murdered."

"We didn't kill anybody," replied Mrs. Van Dreason. "The police were here and declared it an accident. Haven't we been through enough?"

"I apologize for the inconvenience. I would like to interview you both and get your recollections of what happened. I won't be too intrusive. Please. I came a long way in a bad snowstorm."

"I guess we can talk to you," said Mrs. Van Dreason. "First, let me help you with that knee."

"Great. Thank you," replied Klock trying not to smirk. She pulled up her pant leg over her knee and she winced at the pain. It throbbed. She felt the cold wet swab of something followed by the application of a band aid.

"There you go," said Mrs. Van Dreason. "It was just a scrape. Do you mind if I ask how old are you?"

"I'm eighteen. Thank you." Klock pulled her pant leg back over and rubbed the side of her knee. "Is there someplace we can sit or do you want to do the interview here, Mrs. Van Dreason?"

"Call me Noreen."

"Appreciate it, Noreen. This here is, Bo. I'd let you pet him but he's working right now."

"Ok," said Mrs. Van Dreason. "Let's go into the dining room and we can sit at the table. Milt and I would be glad to give you a recap. Heaven knows we've done this already for the Ft. Schuyler police department."

Klock followed the Van Dreasons and wondered how large this place must be as the footsteps were echoing off the floor. She sat at the table, made Bo lie down next to her, took out her digital recorder, and set it on the table. "Do you mind?"

"I don't know if I like being recorded," replied Milton.

"I'm totally blind so this is the only way I can remember things. I'm no genius," said Klock looking towards Milton's voice.

"It's perfectly acceptable," said Noreen. "What do we call you if you're not a cop?"

"Klock is what everyone calls me." She took out her badge and held it up. "This proves to you that I am what I told you."

"What would you like to know, Klock?" asked Noreen."

Klock clicked on the digital recorder and started. "I have no clue if it was murder but I know at least one person involved that had a financial motive. And just because the police detective didn't find anything doesn't mean much. They're not me."

"Well," said Milton. "We moved here when my company relocated me from Vermont. I work at CompuTech. Their Ft. Schuyler operation needed a boost so they sent me in. My wife and I bought this place not knowing its history."

"Yes," said Noreen interjecting, which made Milton stop talking, and defer to his wife. "The architecture of this mansion is unparalleled. It needed a little loving care but nobody told us it was supposedly haunted. We were still unpacking boxes when the vulture weirdoes started circling. They were knocking on our door at all hours, acting as if it was a right to do their silly ghost thing on our property."

"But you eventually let the Ghost Chasers in here. What changed your mind?"

"Uhhhh," stammered Noreen.

"I heard you got paid by Cora Masters."

"She didn't pay us much but it was not just that. We had an event," replied Milton.

"What kind of event?" asked Klock.

"Well, we didn't believe in ghosts or any of that nonsense," said Noreen. "We traveled the world and stayed in draconian castles and Colonial New England estates yet we never experienced anything like what has happened in this place."

Klock interrupted with, "Well, I'm a skeptic myself. When I had sight, I'd never seen anything to make me believe in ghosts. I was recently on a ghost hunt and nothing happened. From what I've read and experienced it's rather played up by these groups. They pray on the fears and mental instability of their intended victims."

"We are anything but victims," snapped Noreen.

"So you're saying you seen ghosts in here?" asked Klock.

"You've never experienced anything so frightening," said Milt in a trembling voice.

"An imaginary Casper floating through the air doesn't frighten me."

"Then you better prepare yourself to be frightened, Investigator Klockowski," said Noreen. "For the spirits in this house are anything but a friendly cartoon ghost.

"Tell me your ghost story, Noreen," said Klock.

"I never believed in any of this paranormal stuff," said Noreen. "Until we moved in here. At first it was a creek here and a slight clack there and it slowly progressed into cabinet doors opening, waking up and hearing something walking down the hall, yet when Milt or I went to investigate, there was nothing there."

"And it only got worse," chimed in Milton. "I saw a black mass in the shape of a man coming down the grand staircase. It froze me in fear. Another time I got shoved from behind as I was walking down the stairs. The ice cold hands of this malicious entity felt like they went right through me. Only a quick grab of the handrail as I fell saved me from disaster."

"So you both were experiencing these supposed ghosts? And now you both believe in this stuff?" asked Klock.

"If we didn't have everything invested in this house, we would've moved by now," said Noreen. "And on top of it Milt can't get transferred back to his old job so we can sell this place and get out of this city."

"Do you believe?"

"Yes, we do, Klock," replied Noreen. "It's gotten worse since the death of Cora Masters. I really don't want to get into any more of the details of what's happening here."

Klock could care less for she thought this stuff was nonsense. "So you decided to have Cora Masters in to help you out?"

"Well, I picked Cora Masters because she was on television being interviewed and I liked her style. That plus she had come here and pleaded with me in a professional manner. I felt the Ghost Chasers were the best group I could find," said Noreen. "Why don't you go get me a cup of coffee, Milt. You want a cup, Klock?"

"I drink tea if you have it. I heard Cora's son Don was here and acted very bad."

"Her entire team was rude and disrespectful. How wrong Milt and I were about them. . . especially Cora."

The conversation stopped when Milt came in with the coffee and tea. He set the cup down in front of Klock. Her hands were still cold from the cab that had no back seat heat and the stroll through the blizzard up the driveway. She held her hands on the ceramic mug that was wonderful to warm her hands on.

"Right on my front lawn is where Don stood drunk. He was crying. It was rather ugly. The members of the Ghost Chasers were not well behaved and Cora's son was the worst. He's an odd man."

"Did you two know that the night of the ghost hunt was the anniversary of the death of Cora Masters child?"

"We did not know that," said Milt.

"And that the psychic Velvet felt his spirit would be here up in your turret. She claimed that it's an interdimensional portal. One that ghosts use for going from their world into ours."

"I had no clue about Cora's child," said Noreen. "No wonder they were all acting so odd. They were mad that we wanted to stay but we had our reasons for staying here. Cora had with her this really wacko psychic. Velvet is what you just called her. I mean, I had my palm read once when we were in New Orleans so I don't frown on this stuff but this lady was bizarre."

"In what way?" asked Klock.

"Tell her, honey," said Noreen.

"Well, she zeroed in on me. This is really embarrassing. This woman said she knew me from a past life and that we had been lovers."

Klock could tell that Milt was ashamed by the tone of his voice and said, "That was pretty direct, Milt."

Noreen took back the conversation from her husband. "Then when we were doing the walkthrough, showing the Ghost Chasers where the ghost hot spots were, Velvet continued her inappropriate behavior."

"You did the walkthrough that night?" asked Klock as she set the mug down.

"Yes. The ghost group had Milt and I take them through the mansion to point out anyplace we had experienced anything paranormal. Cora was asking us questions but then this psychic was saying the mansion was a woman and was pleased my husband was within its bosom. She was dressed like a hippy and was walking around with a bundle of burning sage. She claimed the evil spirits were allergic to the smoke of the sage. It was all so strange."

"After the walkthrough, what happened?"

"Well, we retired to our study where we stayed for the rest of the evening."

"Up until Cora fell from the window?" And the police questioned you?"

"Yes," said Noreen. "We told them pretty much what we told you but not the complete ghost thing. Next thing you know we'd had television cameras filming the Overlook and teenagers driving by. I'll never forget the look of horror on Cora's face."

"They let you see her?" asked Klock with a twinkle of surprise and astonishment. From what Klock had read, police would never let somebody see a dead body on the ground, only fellow investigators, the coroner or EMT's.

"Well," replied Noreen. "I walked by and looked as they were covering her body with a sheet. It was awful."

"Not only that," said Milt. "When that woman landed, she crushed one of my flower boxes."

"Milt!" scolded Noreen.

The statement didn't bother Klock. She just plugged ahead with the interview. "I read they found her body on rip rap." She had read it in Detective Wilson's report.

"Rip rap?" asked Noreen.

"Stones," answered Klock.

"Yes," replied Milt. "Her body did hit the stones but her feet hit my flower box. They were homemade. I was rather sad at that."

"Is that it?"

"Yes," replied Noreen. "I almost forgot. Cora's son seemed to be the only one in a good mood. After the death. I mean it was unsettling how he was smoking and smiling, pointing to the turret while the others were in shock. The only other thing I noticed was one of the equipment guys was throwing a mini hissy fit that the police were taking all the gear."

"Really?"

"Yes," said Noreen. "He was upset at their handling of the gear. They weren't exactly gentle with the stuff."

Bo let out a little snore making Klock stop to reach down and pat his back a little bit. Silly dog. "Any chance you can take me up to the turret where Masters fell?"

"Sure we could," said Noreen.

Klock picked up the digital recorder then reached down and took Bo by the leash and the dog sprung to life from his nap. "Just lead the way and Bo will take me right behind you."

Klock couldn't believe the Van Dreasons were being so darn cooperative. She was amazed at how vast the Overlook was. She had always heard of the place but never bothered seeing it. When she could see. They came to a staircase and she had counted three floors when they finally came to a stop.

"This is the door that takes us up to the turret. The Ghost Chasers wanted to go up there although we were told by the real estate agent it was in a fragile state," said Noreen. "The stairs are very narrow so I don't know if you can get Bo up there."

"I'll leave him here with Milt. I can hold the back of your jacket and follow you up there."

"Ok."

Klock instructed Bo to lie down so he obeyed as a great guide dog always does. "Lead the way," said Klock as she grabbed the back of

Noreen's clothing and held the digital recorder in her other hand. She found the stairwell very narrow and now understood why Bo wouldn't make it as he travels by her side and not out in front or back. This would throw him off. Her orientation and mobility wasn't half bad without Bo but she wasn't as confident on her own. The dust started tickling her nostrils that culminated with a powerful sneeze that Klock blew right into Noreen's back.

"Bless you," said Noreen.

"I'm sorry about that. I didn't have time to stop that."

"It's OK. It's rather dusty and old up here. We haven't been up here since Cora fell."

Klock found the stairs to be steep and rather rickety and they groaned and creaked with every step. She could hear the wind whipping all around the turret as they climbed higher and higher. She felt the walls, wondering where the secret entrance could be. They stopped on the stairs.

"I have to open the trap door so we'll hold here," said Noreen. Klock listened to the door groaning on its hinges and thumping to the floor above. She only wished she could see, just for a minute, to get a glimpse of Ft. Schuyler from the highest window, of the tallest mansion, on the tallest hill, overlooking the city.

Noreen led her into the turret and Klock was amazed at how cramped it was as she could feel the walls around her. It was circular and could only hold a handful of people. She couldn't find the secret entrance. "Show me the window Masters fell out of." Noreen led her to the window and Klock felt around the jamb. She couldn't believe the breeze that was coming through the cracks. It was frigid. She could feel a slight sway in the tall thin structure as the Mohawk Valley winds slammed against it, making old man winter whistling sounds. She felt the lock on the top and found it difficult to turn. "Was this open the night Masters fell?"

"Yes." We were trying to air this room out as it was musty in here.

Klock felt the size of the window and it was rather large with a low sill that was below her knees. She was only five feet tall and she could easily fall if this were wide open and she tripped. She went back to feeling the edge that felt rough and some of the caulk crumbled in her hands as she felt around. "Was there a screen or anything keeping someone from falling out?"

"No. It is rather large. I was told the original owners had this built so the woman of the house could see her husband returning on the Erie Canal from his overseas trips. But then the real estate agent said they used this to watch the Mohawk River and their factory."

Klock followed Noreen back down the steep steps and took her time as she was a little unsteady. They got all the way back to the ground floor before Klock spoke. "I wanted to ask you both one more thing."

"Yes," said Noreen.

"Do you know about the Underground Railroad history of the Overlook as well as the secret passageways?"

Chapter 24

Klock went for it and wondered if they knew about the secrets of their mansion.

"Well," said Milton. "Yes."

"Do you know where all the secret tunnels and staircases are located in this mansion?"

"We do now but we didn't when we moved in," said Noreen. "The real estate agent never mentioned it. Milt discovered them by accident. He's very curious and was inspecting all the moldings when he discovered an abnormality that was a release button. What do these have to do with Cora Masters suicide?"

"Nothing." Klock didn't want to give anything away. "Listen, I wanted to ask you both one more thing. Did Cora Masters do anything that night to upset you two?"

"Besides being rude?" asked Milt.

"We didn't kill her if that's what you're asking," said Noreen. "We'd have nothing to gain from such a thing. Yes, she was a horrible person but it would take something beyond the pale of scumbaggery for my husband or me to do anything of the sort, Klock."

"I'm not accusing you or anybody of anything. I'm trying to get to the truth of that night."

"Well, you asked about the secret passages. None of the Ghost Chasers or their psychic knew anything about them. They didn't ask and we didn't show them."

"I best be on my way. Thank you very much for taking the time to see Bo and me." Klock stuck out her hand towards Noreen who promptly took it and shook.

"You're very much welcome," replied Noreen.

Klock let go of Noreen's hand. "I still think the Ghost Chasers or Cora's son might have been up to no good that night but I'm no miracle worker, just Anne Sullivan without the charm. Now, I better call that cab company to get Bo and I back home."

Klock took out her phone and dialed the number back to the cab company and it rang several times before a grumpy dispatcher got on the line and told her all cabs were called back to the station due to the massive snowstorm hitting Ft. Schuyler. She slowly clicked the phone shut without saying a word, put it in her pocket and reached down to pet Bo. The few seconds of getting the courage to ask for a ride was mortifying. People who could see and had the freedom to get up and drive themselves anywhere at anytime, never respected, nor understood the privilege and independence. Having to rely on others was difficult and scary.

"The cab company won't come and get me. Any chance you or your husband could bring me home?"

"Where do you live?"

"On the west side," said Klock. The pause was enough that it made her heart sink. She felt so low she wondered why she decided to use her private investigator license. She didn't need a quick response to know they didn't want to drive in the crime-riddled area, even if the weather were clear. Klock was worried she'd be walking across the city in a blizzard.

"My husband and I loath driving in the snow so we cannot give you a ride," said Noreen in a tone that made Klock's heart sink. Her stubborn Polish muse took over.

"That's OK. Don't worry about it. Bo and I can walk back no problem. I need my hat and gloves. I left them by the chair but I can't see where that is." She was mad at herself for having to mooch a ride, then to be rejected was almost too much to take.

Klock heard the chair slide that Noreen was sitting in and slight steps as the woman left the room. She could hear her and Milton talking in the other room but she couldn't make out what they were saying.

She figured they were fighting over her soul. She was playing tough but she knew there was no way she could walk with Bo across the entire landscape of Ft. Schuyler to get back home. She knew she'd never make it alive. She could care less if she froze to death but she couldn't let that happen to Bo. He was so loyal and dedicated a yellow lab that he would easily lay his life down for her but that still didn't make it right. Besides, she knew she was going to a warm room in the afterlife for her sins and she didn't want the pitchfork man to think they were a package deal. Bo deserved doggy heaven where he could run in a field with his brothers and sisters, gnaw on bones, and nap in the sun, beside blossomed wildflowers. She knew she was done for. She could always try the police but she doubted they would come and get her. Dom might if she could get him on her cell phone. She was tired of waiting for her hat and gloves.

"Forget this," she whispered under her breath as she felt around on the floor and only got Bo. She put on her coat that was draped over the back of the chair, zipped it up, took Bo by the leash, and said a stern, "forward." Bo took her right to the front door so she grabbed the door knob, turned it, and was taken aback by the blast of cold air and snow. She remembered the time she listened to her favorite forensics show on television that featured the death of a homeless person who had died in a city alley in the middle of winter, how he was frozen solid to the ground and they had to use flat metal shovels to scrape him free and his body stayed flattened on the one side until he thaw out later in the morgue. The fate of that frozen bum would soon be hers. The Van Dreasons didn't come for her so she went out onto the porch and shut the door behind her. Her ears and hands were instantly cold. "Dupa." Klock cursed herself for her stupidity, her Polish stubbornness, her being Rachel Klockowski, pretend toughie and crack newbie investigator. Now reduced to being the gimp she never asked to be. She took a step and slipped to the ground.

"Klock!" yelled Noreen. "Please come back inside. We want you to stay the night."

Klock didn't argue, she just got up and came back inside the Overlook Mansion. For the first time in her life Klock didn't argue, posture, or stand stubborn, but submitted. It was a humiliating experience. A shameful move. "Thank you," she replied with barely a whisper as she crossed back into the warmth of the mansion feeling like a walking piece of garbage.

"We have plenty of room up on the second floor. If it's okay with you," said Noreen as she shut the door and locked it. "Milt and I sleep on the first floor. The only reason we're afraid to have you here is because of the ghosts."

"What? You're more afraid of what ghosts would do to me in comparison of freezing to death."

"We're sorry," said Milton. "It's not good what's happening here."

"First off. Thank you both from the bottom of my heart. It's difficult for me mooching off people; however, let me get something through to you both, ghosts are poppycock."

"We're not making this stuff up, Klock," said Noreen. "This place is highly haunted and my husband is especially being tormented. I did research online and it's a succubus."

"I think I've heard of that before. What exactly is that?" asked Klock.

"It's umm. . ." stammered Noreen.

Milton chimed in with the shocking statement, "It's a female spirit that comes for me at night."

"Now I've heard everything," replied Klock. "You're being stalked by a female ghost? It has a crush on you?"

"Yes," said Noreen. "Please don't mock us."

"I have to see things to believe them, Noreen. Well, not see them. Experience them is more like it. Based upon my recent experiences, I put ghosts up there with the Easter bunny, leprechauns and Santa Clause."

"Well then don't come screaming to us in the middle of the night," said Milton. "We're concerned."

"You both don't have to worry about me. I live in an apartment all by myself in the worst part of Ft. Schuyler with all the bums, prostitutes, drug dealers, you know, my friends. I'm not afraid of anything."

"Ok then," said Noreen. "Do you want to come in and have another cup of tea? I have chocolate chip cupcakes."

"That sounds awesome. Seriously, I'm a little hardened so forgive my outbursts. My counselor tells me depression, bi-polar, and fits of rage tend to come with us blind folk. But I'm a sweet mental case. I would love to have another cup of that awesome tea and chocolate chips in a cupcake can't go wrong."

"That's great," replied Noreen. "And I'm sure we have something we can give Bo."

"I'm looking forward to meeting some spirits face to face but first I want that cupcake in my face."

Milton said in all seriousness, "You'll get your wish."

Klock spent the next few hours talking with the Van Dreasons and liking them more each minute. Dom was about all she had for human interaction beyond her parents, social workers, and therapists. She thought most people were soulless shells. She wasn't worried in the least about staying up on the second floor alone. She secretly wished something would come and haunt her but she knew better. She was as logical as a physicist and pragmatic as a sports writer. She did her research. She knew everything that had been said about the Overlook Mansion had been rumors and legends, nothing factual to back anything up, except that vague EVP that the Ghost Chasers had captured. She knew the EVP had to be someone arguing with Cora up in the turret. She knew when she pinpointed that person, she'd have a strong suspect.

Before she went upstairs to sleep, she had to curb Bo, so she brought him out into the snow. It was still coming down thick but that didn't stop her boy from doing his duty with his dog doody. She took out the small plastic baggie and took care so as not to leave a deposit on the Van Dreasons front lawn. She came back in and asked Noreen to show her to the trash receptacle where she threw it out. She never wanted anyone saying her dog laid one out on their yard.

She pressed her talking watch and it said it was ten thirty p.m. so she asked to go to bed. She knew she should be tired yet her body clock has never been adjusted. Especially since she lived in a 24/7 365 pitch black world. When she was sighted she could tell by the sun fall that it was time to go to bed but she was now an infinite vampire that thrived in the squid ink blackness of her messed up body clock. Anybody that thought blindness was a gift was full of horse manure and she didn't even want to discuss the holy ones who would sweetly say to her, "you're so amazing" as if having dead eyes and retaining the ability to move around was some kind of merit badge moment. "Forget them" she thought to herself as she walked the grand staircase up to the second floor. She followed Noreen who also showed her where the bathroom was located. It was down the hall from her room.

"You'll find this room is rather large," said Noreen. "The bed is straight ahead. I apologize I don't have any pajamas in your size. I'm much taller than you."

"It's ok," replied Klock. I'm fine just the way I am. Don't be alarmed if I go outside early. Bo has a weak bladder."

"May I pet him?"

"Just a second," said Klock as she removed the harness. Bo pulled away from her and she could hear his nails clacking across the hardwood floor as he went quickly towards Noreen who was praising him with love and affection. Bo deserved it. All he cared for in life was pleasing others.

"I pray you have a pleasant night," said Noreen with a tone of caution.

"Don't worry about me, Noreen. I'll be fine," replied Klock. She tried not to laugh at the warning. All she could think of was the old black and white movies she watched as a sighted kid. The ones with people walking haunted castles, in floor length nightgowns, carrying lit candles nestled in an elaborate candlestick, with the spirit nothing more than a solid human in a sheet with two eye holes cut into it.

"I'm going to shut the door behind me. Do you want me to leave the hall light on?"

Klock raised her eyebrow and said, "Blind."

"Oh, I'm so sorry."

"Not a problem at all. Good night."

All Klock heard was the footsteps of her hostess and the door clicking shut, then her and Bo were now alone in the room and on the second floor of the massive mansion. She took off her pants and socks having no problem sleeping in her underwear and t shirt. At least she didn't have to worry if the colors matched. All that mattered was fit and comfort. The bed was rather large and plush. She only wished she could have Bo up in it but she didn't want to take the chance. The Van Dreasons might not want him on there. She felt the floor with her feet and the hard wood gave way to a rug that surrounded the bed. Bo would have that to sleep upon and would be fine. "Good, boy," she said as she pat him on his side. She was low enough that he licked her cheek making her wince. She'd never gotten used to his slobber. "Now you can sleep right here, Bo. Any ghosts come in here and you have my permission to bite their night stalking dupa."

Klock got into the bed and pulled the covers up to her chin. She lay there for at least an hour listening to the wind whip outside and whistle slightly through the window near her bed. She was tired, yet she didn't want to admit she was a little afraid to fall asleep in a strange house and bed. Growing up an only child, she'd gotten used to being alone from the time she could walk, except when her mother helicopter parent hovered.

Klock was to the point where she was drifting off, the time she had once heard someone refer to as twilight time, though she thought that was a goofy phrase. She was right on the edge of being completely out when she heard the creak of wood, then another and then another as if someone were walking across the floor of the room and coming right towards her. She didn't hear the door open. The old hinges groaned as

Noreen had opened the door. Klock could've missed whoever was coming in the room. She balled her fists and was prepared to punch whoever was playing this practical joke. She didn't understand why Bo wasn't up and barking, unless he was so far out himself, yet she didn't hear his distinctive snoring. She heard the floorboard croak right next to the bed but on the side opposite of where Bo was sleeping. She quickly sat up, swung in the direction of the ball breaker and hit nothing but air. "What the. . . ?" she whispered.

Chapter 25

Klock spent the entire night clinging to her bedding as she listened to floors creaking, doors opening, and she could've sworn she heard talking and whispering coming from all directions, yet, she couldn't determine the gender of the voices or make out clear distinctive words. It was as if someone were talking through a wet paper bag. She could do nothing but listen. She was upset she had forgotten her digital player as putting the earplugs in and cranking a digital book or music would drown out the sounds of the night. If she had sight she could see if this was a haunting or if the Van Dreasons, or someone else, was playing tricks on her, yet this wasn't a Scooby Doo episode, this was real life; hers to be exact. She wondered if a person could be using a secret entrance to roam around the Overlook at night.

The supposed ghosts didn't seem to bother Bo who never woke up, growled, barked, or did anything. He seemed to enjoy the change in location as he normally woke her up at least once in the middle of the night so he could go outside and relieve his bladder but this didn't happen. It was as if he knew she was awake all night so he could take a shift off and dream of big meat bones and fluffy brown rabbits in a field or whatever it was that dogs dreamt about.

Klock sat up in bed and held up her speaking watch and hit the button. The electronic voice telling her it was three in the morning. The night was taking forever so she got out of bed and found her coat draped over a chair in the corner, sat in it, and rooted around until she found the small digital recorder. She felt the nudge of Bo who got up with her then lay back down next to her. She clicked the button on and started talking into the device about the experiences with the spirits, her doubts and concerns about the case. She talked about things she normally doesn't talk about aloud but she was lonely and a little scared being in the Overlook, in the midst of a snowstorm, sleeping alone on a floor above strangers. She thought she knew these people, but they still could be tricking her. She didn't know what to think but it again confirmed that she could only rely upon herself.

When she stopped talking she got a weird sensation that someone was standing right next to her. She couldn't explain the déjà vu feeling but there it was. "Who's there?" she asked, getting no response. It was at this point that she felt a sudden chill, a frigid cold spot that hit her right side. It wasn't a breeze but a stalk of ice cold air like she just stepped into a walk-in freezer. Her bare arms shivered and she felt the hair on her neck stand up. She felt something touch her cheek which caused her to scream at the top of her lungs. She got up to jump out of the way and fell over Bo, who yelped. She slammed the floor and the digital recorder fell from her hand and slid across the floor. She banged her elbow that throbbed beyond belief so she just lie there on the wooden floor holding her elbow and wincing. She could hear loud footsteps and knew it was the Van Dreasons coming to her rescue which made her mad. Bo started barking and she could hear the door open.

"Are you okay?" asked Milton.

"Fine," snapped Klock as she stood up holding her elbow. "I dropped my digital recorder."

"Its right there," said Noreen. "I'll get it for you."

Klock was ashamed and embarrassed yet she was not sure of anything that was happening. Her imagination was running wild.

"Here you are," said Noreen as she handed it to Klock.

"Thank you," said Klock as she took it. "I had a bad dream and fell out of bed."

"Are you sure you want to stay up here alone?" asked Milton.

"I'm fine. Thank you."

Klock didn't say another word while the Van Dreasons left her and shut the door. She was so mad she could feel tears well up be she refused to shed them. She wondered what she was doing on this stupid case but she was too darned stubborn to give up. She thought she may have to declare it a non-murder.

She waited a few minutes then got back out of bed, got dressed, and placed the harness back on Bo, saying very quietly, "We're going to take the fight to them." She made sure she had her digital recorder turned on and headed to the door. Klock tried to open it slow, yet it still creaked on its hinges. She stopped opening it when she could fit through. She went down the hallway past the staircase that went down to the first floor and took the one going up to the third floor. Once up there, she felt for where the door was that led up to the entrance to the turret. She didn't hear or experience the noises and sensations she had felt in the bedroom. She wondered if it had just been a dream.

She never asked or cared what was on the third floor but she did marvel that two people with no kids or pets would live in such a huge place. She got to the door that led up to the turret and opened it. "How about an adventure, Bo?" Klock let him go ahead of her as the stairwell was too narrow to go tandem. She was walking up the steep stairs, slipped and fell forward. Someone, or something, had pushed her. She had to be careful not to drop the digital recorder. "Who's there?" Nobody answered. She felt around but felt nothing but the dusty air. They went on up until they came up into the turret. She was going to ask questions even though she didn't believe in this nonsense.

"Are you there, Cora?" She paused a good twenty seconds like the Ghost Chasers. "Who pushed you out of the window?" She waited and all she heard was the whistling of the winter winds. "Is Joey with you?" She suddenly felt an icy chill that was as if she were standing in a column of freezing air. It was much colder than the surrounding air. She dismissed it as the wind whipping through the cracks of the multi century old structure. The hair on her arms rose as she got a little frightened. She shrugged it off to nerves. Klock let go of Bo's harness, set the digital recorder on the windowsill, and started to feel all around the room for any structural anomaly that could be the secret door to the hidden passageway.

She used her fingertips to go all around the window and door trim, rubbing up and down all the way to the floor and up as high as her five foot height would allow. She continued this process all around the turret for a good half hour and was about to give up when she felt a wooden pimple. A slight nub. "Hmmmm." It was a button. She pressed it and she heard a creak. Something hit her foot. She put her hand out and it was a door. She opened it all the way and took a step back. She knew as a private investigator, she had to go down into this staircase and find where it came out. She took a step back and got her digital recorder. She shut it off and put it in her pocket then took Bo by the leash and went to the door.

Klock got down on one knee and felt out with her free hand until she could feel it was a step and not just a drop off. She didn't need to step into a shaft that would cause her and Bo to plummet. She stepped down. She carefully felt with her toe the next step. She went down one more, took Bo with her, then reached up and shut the secret door until it clicked closed. If the Van Dreasons came up into the turret she didn't want them to know she was in there.

The air was thick with dust which tickled her nose. Bo sneezed. "Bless you," she said as she took each step with slow care with Bo behind her. The stairwell was much longer than the one she took up. It spiraled down. She counted each step and figured she was getting to the ground floor. She got to the bottom landing and paused for a moment. She felt a wooden door with a doorknob. She wondered where this came out. She opened the door with caution and was pleased that it didn't groan on the hinges. She knew right away that this door led outside as cold wind and snowflakes smacked her in the face. She stepped out into the winter night and brought Bo with her. She pushed the door shut and felt around where it had closed and it felt like the surrounding décor. She couldn't believe it. The secret entrance was on the outside of the mansion and may have led the person who had argued with Cora all the way up. It could've been anybody that was there that night if they found this entrance, yet the Van Dreasons did know about it. She tried to feel around for the door to get back in and her hands felt as if they were cubes of ice. She couldn't locate it.

    Klock wasn't wearing her winter jacket, hat, or gloves and was shivering within seconds. She walked along the border of the Overlook hoping to get to an exterior door then pray it was unlocked. It must've been zero outside but twenty degrees below with the wind chill. Her ears felt as if icicles were hanging from them. Her entire body began to spasm and it was getting difficult to walk.

It took what seemed an eternity until she got to the large front porch. She had trouble climbing the stairs and felt around until she felt the door knob. It was locked. She was busted but then thought. She knelt down and felt a mat on the porch. It was ridiculous to think they would do it but it was worth a try and she had mere seconds before she'd surrender to the doorbell. She picked up the mat and felt until, there it was, a metal key nestled under the mat! "Unbelievable." Her hand shook so bad she had to let go of Bo and put the key in the door with both hands. The knob felt a thousand pounds as she turned it. She opened the door and brought in Bo, put the key back under the mat, locked the door and shut it quietly.

Klock was shaking all the way back up to the second floor and was pleased that the Van Dreasons never awoke or discovered her. She was proud that Bo didn't make a noise, not even shaking the snow off of his coat, as if he knew they had to sneak. He was the smartest guide dog in the litter all right.

Klock took off Bo's harness but stayed dressed. She put the digital recorder on the nightstand, got in bed, and was still shivering. "Up, Boy," she said as she felt Bo's hundred pounds hurl on top of the covers. She shook. She smiled. Bo settled down next to her and she pulled the covers up over the both of them not caring what the Van Dreasons thought. He needed under the blankets as much as she did. It took her awhile to warm back up then drift off to sleep.

* * *

   Klock woke to Bo putting his paw on her letting her know it was time for him to go outside to relieve himself. "OK, boy," she replied. She hated to wake. In her dreams she relived what it was to see; vivid colors, but it was the faces she missed most. The faces of people with their smiles, their frowns, and the tears streaking down their faces. The disconnect of being blind was the simple burden of not seeing the looks, the expressions, the sorrows and the joys that she had to only imagine. Bo jumped off the bed thumping onto the floor. She followed out and felt much better, although her big toes were still tingling from a tinge of frostbite. She knelt down and put Bo in his harness. She paused to rub her elbow. It had an ache from her fall. She felt around and found the digital recorder and she placed it back into her pocket. She made the bed as best she could before she took Bo's harness and said, "forward."

* * *

   Klock had said "thank" you to the Van Dreasons and got out of the Overlook Mansion as fast as she could. She could hardly wait to call Dom and tell of her adventure. He'd probably think she was nuts for wandering down a strange staircase in the middle of the night, but that's what investigators did. They dug. They pulled up the rock to examine the creepy crawly things worming underneath.
   On the cab ride home she barely said a word to the driver who marveled at the amount of snow that got dumped on Ft. Schuyler and the price they pay in the Mohawk Valley for being in the path of lake effect snowstorms; the blizzards that rise from the jet stream going over the great lakes, plucking moisture from the waters, then battered the Mohawk Valley and Ft. Schuyler. It took longer than usual to get across the city as it was a work day and everyone was trying to get through streets that narrow from large snow banks. She sat back and smiled.

Chapter 26

Klock left Dom a message and was bummed that she got the voicemail. She spent a couple hours reading the Braille case files and again didn't find anything in there from Detective Wilson in regards to the secret entrances. There was nothing from the digital recorders or video that he had taken from the Ghost Chasers. Obviously, he hadn't done his homework. She set it aside.

Klock made some tea and fired up her laptop deciding to try to do some research on the Van Dreasons. She went to Google and put their names in but only got the Ft. Schuyler Daily News reports on the death of Cora Masters. It hadn't been picked up by the national media so Klock wondered how much fame Cora really had. She probably was more of a local celebrity. She did listen to the link to a news release from CompuTech announcing the hiring of Milton Van Dreason. It was a dull matter of fact article that was nothing special. Just for the heck of it she decided to go to the CompuTech home page and see what this company was all about. She was going through the news releases when she came upon a fundraising release and almost fell out of her chair. It was a silent auction that was to give away a ghost hunting excursion with the Rest in Peace (RIP) Ghost Hunters but the news that floored her was that it mentioned Tad Davis; lead investigator of RIP was standing in a photo with his uncle, Rory Davis, President & CEO of CompuTech. "No way," she whispered. So, the Van Dreasons had been paid by Cora Masters to conduct her investigation yet Milt's boss was the uncle of Cora's greatest ghost hunting rival. She needed to get a hold of Tad Davis and interview him. He wasn't there that night but she had a feeling he might shed light on Cora. Then she had an eureka moment; Tad killed Cora Masters!

Klock didn't have any evidence but just a hunch. It would've been easy for the Van Dreasons to show Tad the secret entrance to the Overlook Mansion. He had to be the person up in the turret arguing with Cora. Perhaps he came to watch the investigation and came out at the wrong time, Cora lost her temper, they argued and he pushed her out the window. Her damage had been so extensive that he could've easily knocked her over the head, made her unconscious, opened the window, threw her out, then snuck back down the entrance and he'd be gone. But if the Van Dreasons knew he had been there, why would they not turn him in? Her cell phone rang and she jumped holding her heart. She picked it up. "Hello."

"What's going on, Klock?" asked Dom.

"I think I have a break in the case, Dom."

"Really?"

"I went and interviewed the Van Dreasons and spent the night. I was trapped there because of the storm."

"I'm sorry I couldn't give you a ride."

"It's ok. It turned out for the best. I went and discovered the secret passageway up to the turret. It goes from the top all the way down to an entrance outside."

"So a person could've gone in there and up to the top and killed her."

"You got it. That's why the Ghost Chasers footage had nobody going up and down the third floor entrance."

"How many people knew about the secret entrance?"

"The Van Dreasons knew. If Cora had done her basic research on the place like I did, I'm sure she would've known but when I interviewed the members, and Don Masters; nobody mentioned it. The tech guy had what he thought was an EVP of an intelligent spirit interacting with Cora but it was too muffled to make it out. I listened to it and it sounds like two people arguing."

"Who do you think it is?"

"It could've been Don. The Van Dreasons were not pleased with

Cora's rotten behavior but my gut instinct guess is Tad Davis. He's the lead investigator of the Rest in Peace Ghost Hunters or RIP."

"A rival ghost hunter. Cm'on, really?"

"I'm serious, Dom. Go online and read the message boards on this stuff, especially Ft. Schuyler Topix. These groups are venomous towards each other and especially towards Cora Masters. She had the books, the radio appearances the television show. And she was one nasty person to deal with. She did what she could to squash the competition. Tad was a big tormentor of Cora."

"But to take the step to kill someone over a ghost hunting turf war? I don't know. It seems far fetched."

"You could be right. I could be completely wrong, Dom. Cora might've used the anniversary of her son's death to kill herself and join him in the afterlife."

"What if the Van Dreasons did it?"

"I thought of that. They could've snuck out and taken the secret stairway up there. But what's the motive? They're too nice. I have a hunch it was Tad Davis. This is just my feelings. I don't want to use the term woman's intuition but I just have an investigative inkling."

"The best detectives have that but how would he know where the entrance from the outside was located?"

"Milton Van Dreason. He works at CompuTech. I found a company news release where there's a picture of Rory Davis, President & CEO, posing next to his nephew Tad Davis of RIP."

"Smoke and fire, baby. You might have something there," said Dom. "That's where the best detectives are made, in the nose of a book."

"I might be blind but nobody outworks me."

"So what is your next move?"

"I'm going to interview Tad and see if I can get a confession."

"Alone?"

"That's when I get the most out of people."

"Not a good idea. If he has the temper you describe, and if he truly did kill Cora Masters, he's a sociopath."

"He could be innocent and really nice."

"You willing to bet your life on that? Police work is high risk, Klock. You'd be completely vulnerable."

"I won't be alone. I'll have Bo with me."

"He's a gentle guide dog. He's not like a trained German Shepard police dog. I tell you what. Give me a couple days to clear my schedule and I'll tag along with you."

"Fine."

"Good. Well, I have to get back to my job that pays the bills. Great work there, Klock. I wish I had you in my department. You'd run circles around Wilson and Hilley."

"Thanks. That means a lot. Call me tomorrow and give me a time. In the meantime I'll do some further research."

"When you're done with this investigation, maybe we can locate this Bookcase dirtbag and throw a little scare into him."

"Watch yourself. You'll get suspended again, Mr. Hot Temper."

"I forgot to ask if you saw any ghosts at the Overlook."

"Blind."

"You know what I meant."

"No, but I think the Van Dreasons were pulling some pranks on me. I had some creepy feelings but I think it had more to do with an old leaky mansion than a haunting. The turret had wind whistling through it like when you were a kid and blew air into a cracker jack box."

"So you still don't believe?

"I'd like to believe. I'd love to experience something. Some kind of proof of the paranormal but so far I got zilch."

"At least you're not bored."

"No way."

"You're not going to go meet with Tad Davis are you?"

"I already told you I wasn't."

"I know you, Klock. Don't go in like a Lone Ranger. This isn't like the stuff you read or watch on television. People get killed when they go solo."

"Oy vay! You already covered this, Dom."

"Okay. Take care, gotta' go."

Klock hung up and smiled. Dom was right, she was anything but bored and it made her wonder what kind of life she would be leading if she had listened to her mother and her state worker and had taken a job at the blind workshop. She'd have a steady paycheck with benefits but would die of boredom. She was on the hunt for a killer like all her heroes in her favorite books, television shows, and movies. She was Blind, P.I. all right.

She didn't have to research Tad's number, since it was listed on his RIP website as well as his Facebook account. Social media made it easy to locate anybody, and Klock was stunned at the stuff people placed on a public forum with no regards to privacy. At least they could block non-friends; then again, Tad Davis came across as an egotist of epic proportions.

She thought about it for all of two seconds then decided to give him a call. She disagreed with Dom and knew she could be slick. If he did it, she could get him to admit he did it. She knew she had to talk to him alone. What harm could a small teenage blind girl and her tail-wagging apprentice cause?

She dialed the number and it was picked up rather quickly.

"Hello?" It was a deep gruff voice but she could tell he wasn't very old.

"May I speak with Tad Davis, please?"

"This is."

"Hey, Tad. My name is Rachel Klockowski. I'm doing an article on ghost hunting in Ft. Schuyler and I was wondering if I could have five minutes of your time?"

"Sure. What will this be in?"

"I'm a freelance reporter with Ghost Times. You ever hear of it?"

"Sure. That would be fantastic."

"I can do it in person. I just happen to live in the city so I can meet you somewhere. I'm really interested in how you conduct your ghost hunts and perhaps we can talk about some of the most haunted places you've investigated." Klock knew she had him for his tone had changed.

"When would you like to interview me?"

"How about tonight? Unless that's too short a notice."

"Sure. I can meet you at my office in the city. Is around 8pm too late for you?"

"That's fine."

"Great because I just got up. I'm nocturnal. It works great for my line of work."

Klock thought he was a bloodsucker all right. A paranormal vampire that she was going to stake through his haunted heart.

Chapter 27

    Klock spent the next half hour reading more information about Tad on the message boards and got a lot of posts about his appearance. Apparently, he wore skin tight black t-shirts, lots of bracelets, and sported full sleeve tattoos. They made comments about his black spike Mohawk hairdo and his nose and eyebrow piercing. The majority however were slams by other ghost hunters on his investigative techniques. He had tried to put himself on public access television and he was acting like a fool, throwing his temper around, shouting at the ghosts to come and get him. Most posters thought him a pretty boy, posing as a ghost hunter, who was in love with the camera as much as the sound of his own voice. He seemed just the person to clash with the old school pedestrian ghost hunting techniques of Cora Masters and her Ghost Chasers.

    Klock would have to take another cab. They were running now since the storm had stopped. The company had told her all the streets were now cleared and downtown was merely a handful of blocks away. She didn't want to walk across the city in the cold since she still felt the chill from being outside of the Overlook. She knew that such a storm down South would've crippled the Beltway for days but not in the Mohawk Valley where it was another day in the life.

    Klock wondered if Tad was a trust fund baby and that's why he had all the time in the world to ghost hunt. She was again forced to use her credit card, which made her mad. She had no choice. At least the ride was much quicker than had been when the storm was hitting and a lot smaller fare. She had to ask the cab driver the exact location of the door to the building of where Tad's office was located. She went into the foyer, but the door to the inside was locked so she had to push the buzzer. Tad had to let her into the building, which told her it was expensive to live there, and she could tell the difference when she walked into a lobby that smelt of French vanilla. It was a stark contrast to the vomit and urine stench of Castlewood Courts. She got off the elevator at the floor where Tad's office was located and he was there to greet her and Bo.

"Hello, Rachel. I'm Tad Davis."

"Nice to meet you." Klock stuck her hand in the direction of his voice and he shook it with a firm grip that told her he was confident. "You can call me Klock."

"Sure, Klock. Come this way to my office and we can conduct the interview in there."

"Forward," she said to Bo and he did a great job of staying behind Tad until they got to the door and he halted. She stuck her hand out and it was shutting. He was smart enough to know that Tad was letting the door swing into her face thus saving her an embarrassing moment.

Klock had her badge in her jacket pocket in case she had to produce it and had her digital recorder for the interview, and perhaps a confession. The one thing that made her nervous was the .38 special tucked in the back of her pants. She didn't need a holster as it stayed firm and her jacket covered it. She had never fired a revolver before and loaded it at home before departing. She wondered if it were the right thing to do since everything was circumstantial. She had zero proof that Tad was there that night but after Dom's warning she felt she should have it on her. She felt stupid for bringing it along. She really didn't want to have a gun. The best detectives never used them and she wanted to be the same, but reality is reality, and Dom was right, she was a little teenager on her first case with her shiny new badge. She wasn't afraid. Being naïve could be a wonderful advantage yet a dangerous blessing.

"I'm sorry but are you blind?"

"Yes."

"I thought you could see. I wouldn't have shut the door on you, Klock. My apologies."

"It's okay. Everyone thinks I have some sight because my eyes look fine from the outside but it's in the guts of them where the candles have been burnt out."

"And I love your guide dog. What a smart pooch that he stopped short for you."

"Thank you for calling him smart. Don't ever use the term "dumb animal". I don't like that phrase. Animals aren't dumb, humans are. I've never met any human being as quick in the brain as Bo."

"I bet," said Tad. "I have a conference table and some chairs right here. Please sit."

"Thank you." Klock felt out with her hand and felt the top of the chair. She pulled it out sat down and reached into her pocket taking out her digital recorder. "I hope you don't mind if I use this digital recorder for the interview, Tad. I can't use a pen and paper and I want to be sure the article is perfect."

"I prefer that medium. The better it will be for me and I won't be misquoted or have anything I say misconstrued. I have bottles of water. Would you like one?"

"Sure. That would be great."

Klock sat and listened to him get up and move across the office and fumbling into what she sure was a mini fridge in the conference room. She felt a fool for having the gun for he was charming and cordial. Not only that, he smelled good. She couldn't pinpoint what cologne it was but she was sure it was a higher grade than the male body spray they sell at the grocery store.

He came back and put the bottle down on the table directly in front of where she sat. "I set it at 12 o'clock."

Klock was impressed. "You've worked with the blind."

"I volunteered with my church group back when I was a kid."

"Really? Over at the Ft. Schuyler Association for the Blind?"

"Yes. I enjoyed it as they had us work with blindfolds on the see what it was like to have a disability. Then they showed us basic things like walking with a cane, eating and other issues. It was a great program."

"It is. I wish all sighted people would go through the program just so they could feel what it's like to be blind."

"I found it rather unnerving. I was so glad to get that blindfold off at the end of the day. I though I'd go mad."

"I wish I could take mine off."

"So you work for Ghost Times?"

"Yes."

"I was interviewed a couple years ago by JC Stringer. Is he still with the magazine?"

"I honestly don't know, Tad. I'm a freelancer for this and other magazines so I don't get to meet anybody from the periodicals I write for, not even my editors. I work out of my apartment."

"I was wondering why you were based in Ft. Schuyler. I thought their offices were in another state. JC had to do our interview over the phone."

"I'm going to turn this on and we can get started." Klock picked up the digital recorder and made sure she was on a new file location as not to record over all the interviews and Overlook stuff. "Tell me about your group."

"RIP stands for the Rest in Peace Ghost Hunters. We're a small team of just myself as the lead paranormal investigator, my technician and my fellow junior paranormal investigator. We are the best ghost hunting team in the United States with plans to take our hunts to the global stage."

"What kind of equipment do you use in the field?" Klock took the bottle of water, took the cap off and sipped. She was no longer nervous.

"We use only digital recorders like the one you use and hand held video cameras. That's it. No fancy camera crews following us around on our investigations. I feel they soil what we do."

"What made you get into this?"

"When I was a small boy I was visited in my bedroom by a ghost. I was told by my religious parents that it was all in my imagination.

I've been chasing spirits ever since to prove them wrong."

"I see. What would you say to your critics who don't like your style of ghost hunting?"

"They're a blip on the radar, Klock. Sure I push the envelope a little bit but it's why we're the best. I read the blogs especially Topix and it's toxic for sure but I feel all the stronger for the criticism, the more I know I'm doing it right. I would say that anonymous bloggers are the truth tellers. They say things on a keyboard they'd never say to your face. It funny, the ones that rip me apart come to our public educational forums begging for my autograph and pleading to come along on one of our investigations."

"So you embrace the critics?"

"Embrace and ignore. Tell me, Klock, can you name me one of Shakespeare's critics?"

Klock paused and thought real hard. She had read all of his books in high school but never remembered any names of any critics. "No, I cannot."

"There you are. Critics are as insignificant as a flea on your dog's back."

"Well what if it comes from another team of ghost hunters? You know like the Ghost Chasers."

"Cora Masters felt she was the best investigator on the planet. Her methodology went the way of the dodo bird. I never paid that venomous wench no mind."

"You do realize that she died."

"Of course. It was a tragic event for sure. It was the death of her, her team, and her old fashioned ways."

"So it's almost like a handing of the paranormal investigative baton to a new generation."

"I like the way you put that. Yes, I would agree with that assessment."

"Well, the only problem with that theory is her daughter has taken over that group and is conducting investigations."

"Are you sure of that?"

"Absolutely. They conducted an investigation the other night at the Ft. Schuyler Psych Center."

"I wonder how they got in there?"

"I wouldn't know."

"Must be the daughter is doing the same payoff system that her mother employed."

"I heard that Cora Masters did that but could you say it was a wise move. It got her into the Overlook Mansion I heard."

"That one was not right. I had been after that place since I could crawl."

"In a related story, I'm writing on Cora's last investigation and I'm profiling the Overlook Mansion. I had quite the interesting meeting with Milton and Noreen Van Dreason." She picked up the bottle of water and took another slow sip looking towards Tad, trying to be sly.

"I'm sure they did. Cora Masters paid them off and that's the only reason she got in there. I had no clue that Milton owned that place until it was too late."

"Milton mentioned your uncle. He's the president and CEO of CompuTech"

"My uncle is a great man and he did what he could to help RIP but it was too late. That woman was in there."

"The Van Dreasons were very accommodating. They showed me the secret passageways that were used during the underground railroad."

"What else did they tell you?" asked Tad with a heightened distress in his voice.

"That you were there the night Cora fell to her death. Milton said he'd shown you the secret entrance from outside the mansion and you were allowed in to observe what the Ghost Chasers were doing." Klock took the chance and went for it.

"What are you accusing me of?"

"Nothing it all. Cora jumped to her death. It was determined such by the police and besides it was the anniversary of her son's death. She was distraught."

"That's a load of garbage. Cora Masters was an arrogant, no good, rotten, sub-human being."

"How would you know?"

"Because I was there. She didn't jump. An entity pushed her out the window."

"I'm sure she was upset when she saw you in the turret." Klock couldn't believe her luck but his voice was getting angrier by the minute.

"Upset doesn't describe her mood but I didn't push her. Who are you? You're no reporter. This interview is finished."

Klock knew he was going for the digital recorder so she grabbed it. That move put Tad into a rage.

"Give me that recorder. You're crazy if you think I'm letting you keep what I just said."

"I'm not going to share it with anyone."

Klock heard the movement of a chair and knew he was coming around the table so she held onto the recorder and went to stand up and Tad had grabbed her hand and was squeezing really hard. She was trying to hang on with all her might and Bo had jumped back and started to bark. Tad threw her into the table and she fell to the floor with the digital recorder still in her hand.

"What's this?!" exclaimed Tad. "You're a cop?"

Klock felt her pocket and her badge had fallen out during the struggle.

Chapter 28

"I'm not a cop. I'm a private investigator."

"Who hired you?" asked Tad. "And for what? You think I killed Cora Masters?"

Klock didn't say a word as she tried to get up but was pushed back down and Tad put his foot down on her wrist and pressed. She screamed as her arm was in intense pain. Bo was barking over and over.

"Shut up! Stupid dog," Tad yelled at Bo. "Let go of the recorder or I'll break your arm."

Klock was in pain and her Polish temper took over as she balled the fist of her free hand and swung it towards where he was talking. She felt it smack something she assumed was his face. Tad responded by clasping his hands on her throat and squeezing so tight that Klock couldn't breath. She dropped the digital recorder and he removed his foot off her wrist but clamped down on her throat making her claw at his hands. Just when she started to fade she felt Bo's body over hers, growling and biting as her guide dog was attacking her attacker. It caused him to release one hand to fend off Bo and gave Klock one breath that gave her the strength to reach underneath her body and pull out the .38. She brought it around, shoved it up against Tad's torso and pulled the trigger. The blast made her ears ring and she chocked on the gunpowder. He released her and flew off her body. She could hear chairs and the table flying as he must've been trying to flee. She got up on her knees and held the handgun out like Dom had instructed her waiting for a second attack that never came. Bo had come over and was standing his ground between her and Tad. He was barking in his distress voice.

"It's ok, Bo. Good boy," she said as she could hear faint breathing of Tad. The wounded man sounded bad. She inched towards where she could hear him and took one hand off the .38 and felt out and touched his boot then his leg. He wasn't moving. She started to wonder where her cell phone was so she could call 911.

"Ghost did it," was the last thing Tad whispered as Klock got closer to his face. She scrambled to dig out her phone and dialed it while still holding the handgun. Her hands had started to quake from the adrenaline rush as she dialed for help.

* * *

Klock sat in a chair with a blanket around her shoulders as Dom consoled her.

"You did what you had to do, Klock."

"I can't believe I killed him." She had trouble speaking as her throat was sore and throbbing. Her hands were still shaking as she tried to sip water. "My ears are still ringing from the gunshot."

"It's much louder when you don't have the earplugs in. They're going to take you to the hospital and check your throat just to be sure," said Dom. "You have nasty marks on your neck."

"Aren't you going to lecture me, Dom?"

"Now is not the time. Can you at least tell me what happened?"

"He said he was in the turret with Cora, they argued but he says an unseen entity pushed her out the window."

"Did you get that on this recorder?"

Klock shook her head yes and took another sip. "He wanted to take it from me. I wouldn't give it to him and he went out of his mind. He was trying to choke me to death. I had to shoot him. Please take the gun. I don't want it. Am I in trouble? Are you going to charge me with murder?"

"We'll talk about that later. You know I'll have to conduct an investigation. At least you and Bo are ok."

"At least Chief Devine didn't have Detective Wilson come here or I'd be in handcuffs. Bo saved my life, Dom."

"You better get him a treat for that. They're going to take you now. I'll take care of Bo. No worries." Dom put his hand on hers and her eyes got a little moist but she bit down hard on her lip as not to cry. Detectives had to be hard core.

The paramedics came and made her get on a rolling gurney as they covered her with a blanket. Her entire body was now shaking as the adrenaline pump took over her entire existence. She felt a little in shock and didn't say a word as they wheeled her out of the office.

* * *

Klock welcomed Julia Masters into her apartment and was shocked to get a hug. They sat down but Klock had nothing to offer as she had run out of tea and her food was still coming from the food bank but they were there not to break bread but discuss the closure of the case.

"I can't believe that Tad pushed my mother out the window. How did he get up into the turret?"

"I have to be careful what I talk about, Julia, as the police haven't closed the case yet. I will tell you that he did get in there by a secret passageway."

"That's amazing. That EVP that John had picked up wasn't paranormal but my mother and Tad having an argument."

"I was thinking about Velvet. She said that there was a portal to the other side up in the turret. Other than this EVP, did the Ghost Chasers find any evidence of that?"

"To be honest, not really. I'm not saying it doesn't exist but we have no proof. The Van Dreasons made a lot of claims and the Overlook Mansion is legendary but we have nothing, and after the death of Tad Davis there's no way they'll ever let us back in there. I read in the paper that Milton Van Dreason works for Tad's uncle. So Tad used that connection to get in on our investigation. I read you shot him when he was attacking you."

"Self defense. Anyhow, I guess this wraps up my first case. I hope you're happy with the outcome."

"I'm more than happy. You proved my mother didn't commit suicide. I'm happy it wasn't my brother."

"Like I said, the Ft. Schuyler Police haven't yet ruled your mother's death murder. I can't make assumptions on what they'll determine but I can't tell you anything else. I'm glad you're pleased."

"Well, here's the part that's awkward. I really don't have any money to pay you. Like I said before my mother left what she had left to my brother. I have to live with the fact she never forgave me for what happened to Joey. I have no money yet from the television show and I'm now unemployed from my day job. I promise you that I will make it up to you and pay you more money when I can."

"More money?" Klock never remembered getting anything in regards to payment from Julia.

"Well, I brought along something I want you to have. It's my mother's mason jar full of wheat pennies."

Klock heard the rattle of coin in glass that was set in front of her on the table and reached out and picked up the jar of pennies in almost disbelief. Her first case as a private investigator paid in pennies. "Thank you. I know what its like to be broke. At least I'm not penniless."

* * *

Klock was nervous as she walked into the Ft. Schuyler Police station. Although they hadn't charged her with murder she still had butterflies buzzing in her stomach. They had seized the .38 Special Dom had given her and had kept her private investigator badge. She found it strange that Dom had not come down to escort her or meet her in the lobby yet she knew the direction and the floor of Chief Devine. "Forward," she said to Bo as they moved ahead with her trying to ignore the possible stares from the cops in the station as she noticed all the talking and office accoutrement clacking had ceased.

"Hey, killer!" yelled out Detective Wilson. "Look everyone, it's the blind shooter!"

Klock ignored him and kept going towards the elevator. She wanted to yell out to him about his shoddy detective work but she knew it was futile to argue with the ignoramus. Not only had that, she heard enough from her mother about her dangerous obsession with police work. Klock couldn't help it. She felt she was born to be a cop yet she now knew she'd never get there. She got on the elevator and used the Braille above the buttons to select the floor to Chief Devine's office. She felt her heart in her throat from nervousness but at least she wasn't in pain in that area from Tad's attempt on her life.

Klock got off the elevator. The assistant to the chief was waiting for her and escorted her to the boss's office. The last time Klock was there it was fun banter but she didn't expect that this time. She sat down in a chair that she figured was in front of a large desk.

"Hello, Klock," said Chief Devine.

"Hello, Chief Devine." Klock had Bo lie down on the floor in front of her, then looked back up in the direction of the Chief's voice. "Who else is in here?"

"Well, you know Detective Mulvi. The other person in the room is Officer Danielle Sales. She handles outreach and diversity programs for the department."

"Hello," said Klock.

"I'll cut right to it," said Chief Devine. "I want you to work with the Ft. Schuyler Police Department. On future cases as a consultant."

"No offense, Chief Devine," said Klock. "But I don't want to conduct sensitivity training for your officers. Competent work is the best example. Showing the sighted that I can do it better then them."

"Of course," said Chief Devine. "Officer Sales is here to assist us in getting you involved in the department. You'd work on cases like the one you just completed. I'll be honest with you, we need the publicity and the great example you have will inspire people. Interested?"

"Of course." Klock smiled bigger than the last Jack o' lantern she carved when she could see the pumpkins.

"I want you to partner with Detective Mulvi on select cases, but not until you're ready. Knowing you that won't take long," said Chief Devine.

"You sure he wants to partner with me? I don't want him to have an inferiority complex," said Klock raising her eyebrow.

"I have no problem with that, Chief," replied Dom.

"I know you two clicked really well on Klock's private investigation of the Masters murder."

"Does this pay?" asked Klock.

"Sure does. We would pay a per diem rate. And it won't be a token position. Don't get me wrong, Klock, we want you to be an example to the community. You'll be asked to go on educational visits to the surrounding public schools and colleges. I want you two working on cases together. I want to show your successes as a beacon of hope to those who are left behind in our society," said Chief Devine.

"Not only that," said Officer Sales. "I'm legally blind so you'll have someone who understands."

"Really?" asked Klock. "Do you use a cane or guide dog?"

"Not yet. I still have enough usable vision that I can get around without them, although I fear the day will be coming as my disease is progressive. Just so you know, we're going to expect excellence. You know how some of these officers are on the force."

"Well let's get to the brass nails, Chief Devine. What about Tad Davis and Cora Masters?" Klock wanted to get right to her case and the ramifications.

"Please excuse us, Officer Sales," said Chief Devine.

"Of course, Chief. I'm looking forward to working with you, Klock."

Klock stood up and reached her hand out in the air and Officer Sales took it and shook firm. "Same here, Officer Sales."

Klock sat back down and waited for the door to snap shut then there was a few seconds of silence before Chief Devine jumped in.

"Well, you're not being charged with anything in the death of Tad Davis," said Chief Devine. "I have your handgun and private investigator badge right here. I'll give these to you on the way out. The pistol permit office declared you OK in the possession and use of the firearm. We have Davis on your recorder attacking you so you were justified in your actions."

"That doesn't make it right, Chief Devine. I took another person's life. I don't love guns."

"Consider it a marriage of convenience," said Dom.

"Take this gun, Dom, and melt it down," said Klock. "I don't revel in what I did."

"That's why you're going to be a great private detective, Klock," said Chief Devine. "Cops don't enjoy pulling their weapons, shooting or maiming or killing anyone. It's a last resort and with tazers we try to perform non violent means for taking suspects in but there's always a chance something like this will happen. Remember, Klock, what you did was a reaction based upon Tad Davis's action."

"So you are declaring the death of Cora Masters a murder?" asked Klock.

"Based upon his taped confession, yes," said Dom.

"What does Detective Wilson think of this?" asked Klock.

"He's unhappy but I made him understand. He did his best on the case," said Chief Devine. "You had the time and resources to put your focus on it. Wilson is a great investigator but all my cops have too much on their plates and sometimes if something looks neat and clean, you take the delivery, close the case and move on."

"I understand," said Klock. She didn't want to turn her happy moment into a bashing session of Detective Wilson. "Tad Davis said he didn't push her, Chief Devine."

"I know. We all listened to your taped conversations. He said a ghost did it," said Dom laughing.

"I can't put handcuffs on a ghost," said Chief Devine. "I'd thought I'd heard every excuse in my law enforcement career but that one took the cake all right."

"You don't believe that do you, Klock?" asked Dom.

"Ghosts don't exist," she replied smiling. "I've always been a big fan of the paranormal, but after experiencing a ghost hunt, going over supposed evidence, and spending the night in a legendary haunted mansion, I'd say it's all a bunch of nonsense. It's the overactive imagination of people who run around broken down places with their recorders, hoping and wishing something special is going to happen, and it just isn't there."

"We made a digital copy of the recording for the record, Klock but you can have your digital recorder back. Tad Davis is not alive to prosecute," said Chief Devine. "I want to welcome you to your partnership with the Ft. Schuyler Police department. We're looking forward to seeing the great work you two will be producing."

"Blind." Klock held out her hand.

"What?"

"Ditto, Chief Devine," said Klock. She gripped his hand tight and shook. "I take cash but you need to pay Bo here in dog biscuits."

Epilogue

Klock felt the outfit was a little tight but it was the middle of summer and the humid ninety degree weather of the Mohawk Valley was lingering over the city as they made their way in line to get into the Ft. Schuyler Comic Con. Bo got off much easier as he only had to wear a cape but that didn't stop him from fussing over the thing dragging under his paws as the massive crowd inched forward to admission in the air conditioned auditorium.

"You look fantastic, Supergirl," said Dom. "And you look great too, Bodacious."

"Do you have your outfit on, Dom?" Klock put one hand on her hip and made the pose that her hero always made in her comic book appearances.

"Sure do. I'm doing this for truth, justice, and the American way. And also because I promised you that I would do it."

"Let's get a picture of you to show everyone down at the police station."

"That ain't gonna' happen," chuckled Dom.

Klock reached out and felt the cape on Dom's costume. She reached up and touched his hair and it was gelled to perfection with the forehead cowlick that the man of steel always wore. "We're going to be the awesomest trio in cosplay."

"Is awesomest a word?" asked Dom.

"Nope. I invented it just for us."

* * *

It had been months since Klock had concluded her first private investigative case and was working on a new case with the Ft. Schuyler Police Department but the challenges were not easy. The resistance of others was a tough barrier but she carried on with strict purpose. She had come so far that failure was not ingrained. She'd still not confessed her love to Dom as she had to put her career goals ahead of her feelings. She knew she had to use her Polish common sense in the matter.

She met John Richards in Moe's for coffee and tea. She had sent him her digital recorder after the closure of the Cora Masters case wondering if he could use his technical wizardry to glean anything from her recordings at the Overlook Mansion. Klock sat in the booth and listened to John rattle on about electronic voice phenomenon (EVP's) and how the police or any human would've listened to the recordings and easily concluded that Tad was insane and had indeed confessed to murdering Cora Masters; however, the program he used to enhance digital recordings would bring forth conversations from the other side that were spoken by ghosts in a frequency not listenable to the mortal ear. John was so excited and animated about what he had found he could hardly contain himself. He jabbered nonstop about this EVP being the best evidence of all time. He continued with the verbal onslaught until he handed the headphones to Klock. She put them on and listened intently at the questions and answers she had done at the Overlook Mansion.

"Who's there?"

"Me," came the ghostly answer.

"Are you there, Cora?"

"Yes."

"Who pushed you out the window?"

"Joey."

Klock's jaw dropped. She took the headphones off slow and handed them back to John.

"That's the spirit voice of a dead Cora Masters," said John. "I'm a retired Naval Cryptologist. I've been around the world and seen and done many things. I've been on hundreds of ghost hunts and this is the best paranormal evidence and the freakiest evidence I've ever encountered."

Klock was stunned. This was no trickery by Dr. Mesmer. She was mesmerized. She believed in ghosts.

Acknowledgements: I want to thank my friends and family that gave me guidance, feedback and friendship in the creation of this book: Bill Anderson, Chris Barnes, June Campanaro, Rudy D'Amico, Mary Dougherty, Keith Haugen, Sharon Loori, Jenny Milchman, Steve Neirmeyer, Bernadette Peck, David Peck, Tamie Sins, Woody Sins, Ashley Webster, Charlene Webster, Evelyn Webster, Jakob Webster, Kelly Webster, Milton Lee Webster, Stephanie Webster, Angela Zeman, and Linda Zimmermann. Freedom Guide Dogs, the Central Association for the Blind & Visually Impaired, the Ghost Seekers of Central New York, the Oneida County Historical Society.

About the Author: Dennis Webster lives in the heart of the Mohawk Valley of Central New York. He can be reached at denniswbstr@gmail.com

Klock / Dennis Webster

CPSIA information can be obtained at www.ICGtesting.com
Printed in the USA
BVOW00s1242301013

334992BV00004B/11/P

9 780615 892269